MAGIC
AND
MUFFINS

MAGIC
AND
MUFFINS

SHADOW TRADE:
THE RUIN OF RELICS

 4

MELISSA NICOLE

Shattered Glass
— PUBLISHING —

To friendships that last more than a season.

CHAPTER ONE

EVERYTHING HAPPENS FOR A REASON, I THOUGHT AS CROSS SPOONED me on his king-size bed. Sure, it sucked that someone had vandalized the house Vena and I shared, but I didn't mind where I was now. His new room was quiet and dark, and it tempted me to go back to sleep for a little longer.

"Are you ready to wake up?" Cross asked softly.

"Is it time to wake up?"

"You can sleep as long as you'd like, but it's past ten, and Vena's called twice. She's worried about your concussion. And you have some messages from Shepard and your parents."

I sighed. "Then it's time to get up. If I don't answer Vena soon, she'll break down the door."

He quietly got out of bed and used the remote to open the window shades just enough to see without blinding me. Which was a good thing, or I would have missed an incredible view. Cross wore blue athletic shorts low on his hips, nicely showing his V-pack.

His hungry amber gaze raked over me as he returned to settle in beside me and toy with the ends of my long sunny-blonde hair.

"She would find breaking into this room incredibly difficult," Cross said. "There's a reason it's so quiet in here. The room is not only soundproofed but nearly impenetrable when locked. That's why there's a doorbell outside the room. It's the only way anyone can disturb us, excluding our phones."

The level of security didn't surprise me. He took my safety seriously.

"Did you sleep well?" he asked.

"I did. Really well, actually."

"How is your head?"

I reached up to touch the spot I'd hit on the doorframe when Vivian had yanked me from the car. The mild concussion I'd gained from the experience was much better than the bite the vampire had wanted to give me.

"A bit achy, but nothing I'd medicate."

Cross kissed my cheek and handed me my phone. I called Vena first. The last thing I needed was for her to test the impenetrable door.

"I'm alive," I said when she answered. "No headache. No need to worry."

"Pfft. I wasn't worried."

"Yes, she was," Anchor said in the background.

"What are you doing?" she asked me. "Anything that my virgin eyes can't witness."

I snorted. "Is there anything your eyes haven't witnessed?"

"Yeah, you getting dirty with Cross. It's like the book being better than the movie. I think my imagination is making it way hotter than reality."

"Unlikely," Cross said beside me, proving he could hear.

I flushed and shook my head at both of them.

"If you don't need anything else, I'm hanging up."

"Wait," she said quickly. "There was a reason I'm asking about your sex life. Can we come over?"

"Of course. But why?"

Vena never did something without a reason.

"Distraction. Anchor needs a break."

"Too much information, Vena," I said, thinking about poor Anchor's curse and Vena's subsequent attempts to wear out the curse.

She chuckled. "Be there in twenty."

I hung up and checked my messages.

My parents had sent another group of pictures from the cruise they'd "won" when the chaos in D.C. began. It looked like they were having fun and oblivious to what was happening back home.

Please let them stay safe.

While I knew I had Cross, Shepard, and the entire D.C. pack to call on, it still comforted me that my family was out of Orphia's reach.

I responded with a cheerful text, stating that I hoped they were having fun, then checked Shepard's text.

His simply said that he was still dealing with the aftermath of last night and that he would see me later. The message was abrupt for him.

"Did you talk to Shepard?" I asked Cross.

"Yes. An hour ago. He's still coordinating the cleanup at the nest locations his people raided last night. With so many vampires turned to dust, the police are struggling to identify them. They want to know how many were in the missing person's count."

I shook my head at the senseless deaths. Although I knew the pack didn't have a choice, I wondered if the people that the vampires had turned had understood their chances of surviving the change and being hunted.

Cross smoothed back my hair and kissed my forehead. "What are you thinking?"

"I'm wondering how many of the vampires who died had wanted to be a part of Orphia's army and how many were innocent victims—like the two you spared?"

"I think most of the newly turned vampires were like those two than not. If they'd truly embraced the night life, they wouldn't have run into the sun to meet their end."

"Adriel did."

Cross studied me, and I saw a glint of never-ending loneliness in his gaze.

"Adriel was tired and knew there was no hope for him. Shepard and his people would have never let him go after everything he did."

"And you? Would you have let him go?"

"No. To protect you, I would kill every vampire in existence."

Did he count himself in that number? I hoped not.

He smiled suddenly, like the loneliness had never existed, and playfully tugged my hair.

"If you want a shower before Vena gets here, you better hurry."

With a groan, I threw back the covers and got out of bed.

Cross' bathroom was a slice of heaven. Twice as big as my old bedroom, it had a fully tiled wet room type shower and soaker tub to one side and a long vanity with a lower makeup station and chair near the door. It was the stuff out of home decor magazines. He'd obviously spared no expense. While I liked to be thrifty, I couldn't complain that he had made his second-floor apartment so luxurious.

I glanced in the large mirror above the vanity and winced at my reflection. My tangled blonde hair made the dark circles under my grey eyes more noticeable. It wasn't a good look.

Cross stepped into view behind me. "You're beautiful."

I snorted. "Hardly. But thank you."

He leaned in to kiss my neck. "You'll always be beautiful to me, Everly."

The only beautiful person in this room was Cross. With his dark hair, which had a touch of auburn, and classic features, he was handsome. Add his tall, athletic physique and the expensively tailored suits he favored, and he was eye candy.

I didn't know how I got so lucky to gain his interest—or Shepard's—but I wouldn't change anything. Not even all the *unwanted* attention I'd gained after falling into the cave and waking Cross from his self-imposed hibernation.

My gaze shifted to the expensive ruby and silver necklace around my neck. A gift from Cross, the necklace held a protection spell from a powerful half-fae. It should have protected me from Vivian the night before, but it hadn't stopped him from grabbing me.

"How was Vivian able to touch me with this on?" I thought back to that moment. "Something under his veil had glowed red. Do you think he has a way to counter protective charms now?"

"I'm not sure. Shepard and I were wondering the same thing when we talked earlier. For Vivian to have a charm that overrides yours would mean a powerful fae made it. Shepard's going to speak to the liaison about it. We'll need Hugh to ask Effora."

At his mention of the fae Queen, I withheld an eye roll. Getting any information from her would be nearly impossible. The only thing she cared about was being fed sexual lust.

Cross took a brush from a side drawer and carefully began untangling my hair.

"Don't worry. We'll find out information soon. Meanwhile, you can relax and recover. I believe I've acquired your necessities." He nodded toward the makeup vanity and the toothbrush holder. "A personal shopper replaced most of your wardrobe, but let me know if you find something missing or want something else."

"You bought clothes for me?"

"As tempting as it would be to watch you go about your day dressed in nothing, I thought you might not be receptive to that level of inhibition."

I turned to hug him. "You didn't have to buy me clothes. You could have asked Vena to drop off a bag of clothes from Shepard's."

"You've lost everything, Everly. Let me take care of you. I enjoy spoiling you."

"Fine. I'll allow moderate spoiling. But just until I figure out what I'm doing with my summer now that Blur's closed."

"Of course. Would you like to see your clothes?"

Curious, I continued past the shower to check the massive closet that was nearly the size of the guest rooms. It had built-in shelves and drawers and was filled with outfits that were exactly what I would have picked out for myself.

I almost asked him when he had time to hire the shopper since the vandalism had only happened a few days ago, but I already knew the answer. The man didn't sleep and had enough money to pay people to do whatever he needed. Apparently, that meant a midnight personal shopper as well.

When I didn't respond, he said, "If you'd rather move your clothes into one of the other bedrooms, you can. While I prefer you to stay in this room, I will leave it to you to decide. I'm just happy you're here."

"I'm fine with the location—at least for now. The clothes are nice too. Thank you." I hugged him again and kissed his cheek. "I need a shower and food before Vena descends."

He followed me back into the bathroom and started the fancy shower. It didn't have the confusing user panel that Shepard's had, but it did have multiple shower heads and instant hot water.

He left the bathroom, giving me privacy as I showered quickly. When I turned off the water, though, he was there with a thick, fluffy towel. I didn't miss how his gaze swept over me or the dark veins that erupted around his eyes.

Feeling playful, I said, "I like your shower, but it would have been even better if you'd joined me."

"I was tempted but didn't think it wise before Vena's arrival."

"If you tell Vena her visit stopped you from having your way with me, she might leave fast. I wouldn't mind a second shower."

The veining around his eyes grew even darker along with the eyes themselves. He should have looked terrifying like that, but he didn't. He looked incredibly handsome and hungry. For me. But not in the usual vampire way. Yes, he craved my blood, but he craved *me* more. Just me.

"Are you teasing me, Everly?" he asked, his voice low and smooth, a seductive purr.

"What will you do if I am?"

"Spend the day thinking of everything I want to do to you once we're alone again."

"Hmm. If that's the case, I think I might be teasing you."

His mouth tilted in the corner, his signature sexy smile as he toweled my top half dry. Before he could go lower, I stole the towel from him.

"Why don't you get me something to wear while I finish up in here?"

He pretended to pout, zipped in and out of the closet, and left me alone to dry. When I stepped out of the bathroom and saw the lacy matching panty set he'd left out on the bed, I shook my head. The wrap skirt and tank top were cute, though.

I dressed quickly and toweled my hair one more time before leaving the bedroom. As I walked down the hall, the faint sound of hammering and sawing teased my ears.

When I reached the kitchen, I noticed the door to the first-floor stairs was open, as was the door to the rooftop, the origin of the noise.

Cross stood in front of the stove, making something that was smelling really good. I peeked around him at the mushroom and spinach omelette. My stomach growled loudly, and he grinned.

"Sit. This will be ready in a minute."

"Are you going to make one for Vena?"

"Not a chance."

I laughed and sat at the kitchen island.

While I ate, he told me about the swift progress the construction crews had made. The second floor was complete, except for the furnishings and decor. The first floor was mostly complete, and the third floor was less than halfway finished.

I finished the omelette before Vena's voice rang out below.

"Holy crap! This place is amazing."

Her footfalls echoed up the stairs. When she reached the second floor, she abruptly stopped and looked around. Wearing jean shorts and a tank top with her long brown hair pulled back into a ponytail, she looked relatively unscathed from the previous day's events. Just a few scratches on her upper arm from Adriel.

"Damn, Cross," she said. "Money definitely talks. This place looks even better than I imagined. Except for the old-person plastic wrap on the furniture. That's not staying, right?"

"Vena, it's new furniture," I said as I took the plate to the dishwasher that still had the plastic film to protect the stainless steel. "It hasn't been unwrapped yet."

"I love unwrapping things, especially when it's new or Anchor."

"Speaking of your giant boy toy, where is he?" Cross teased.

Anchor's voice came from the stairs. "He's right here." A moment later, the towering werewolf who'd claimed Vena's heart appeared. "The changes in this building are extraordinary. I can't believe this used to be a strip club."

I shivered at the memory of the old vampire nest, Juicy—a feeding ground the vampires had run under the guise of a strip club. Thankfully, Cross had removed any trace of the old place.

"As requested, here is the list of books." Vena dug in her shorts pocket and produced a folded piece of paper. "You might need to pad the budget. Some of those are rare."

He took the paper and glanced at what she'd written. "This won't fill the shelves."

"Not entirely. But blank space is perfect for decorations.

Like…we can memorialize Everly's favorite kitchen implements. Her first mixing bowl. Her grandma's rolling pin. Her mom's spatula." She looked at Anchor. "We were spanked with it. It didn't actually hurt. Bet I'd feel a titillating sting if you were holding the handle."

"Vena," I said in warning.

She grinned at me. "We could have a lit-up spot for your favorite whisk."

"Not my whisk," I said.

Even though I knew her reason for not wanting to fill the shelves with books had nothing to do with decorations and everything to do with her overspending, I still saw merit in it.

"I like the idea, though," I added.

"Tell me what decor you'd like in the space, and I'll get it," Cross said.

Vena nodded and hurried me toward the first-floor door. "I'll point out some spaces that would be great for decorative items."

I allowed her to usher me downstairs, where people were still working. The progress struck me again when I saw painted walls, bookshelves, and finished floors covered by protective paper. A crew assembled kitchen equipment in the main area, and another installed all the kitchen appliances and fixtures. Even the display case was already there, protected by moving blankets.

Cross' attention to detail was more than I had imagined from the blueprints he had shown us…just days ago?

"Do you see anything that needs to be changed?" Cross asked from behind me. I turned and wrapped my arms around his waist.

"It's perfect."

"It'll be perfect when we get books in here," Vena said.

Ignoring her, I glanced up at Cross. "This looks nearly finished. How long until the contractors are out of here?"

"Not long at all. The bathrooms are almost ready, and the tables and chairs will arrive in a few days. The contractors are finishing their work on the third floor, but that should be done in a few days as well. We could open next week if we have everything in place."

"Next week?"

He saw my panic and rubbed my back in response. "There is no timetable on this. I simply want it finished for when you're ready. Let me know what you need, and I'll make it happen."

"I need fluffy pancakes and lots of bacon," Vena called out from the commercial kitchen.

"Which reminds me, I need to make an order for grocery delivery for us," Cross said. "I bought a few odds and ends to get us through, but nothing you might require for baking."

"We require chocolate," Vena said, detaching me from Cross. "Focus, Everly. We need decorating ideas. You're the go-to for that unless you want shrunken heads and poisoned tribal arrows."

I cringed. "Growing up with horrible archeology gifts from your parents doesn't excuse your atrocious decorating skills."

Vena's phone and mine pinged with an incoming message, distracting her from a rebuttal.

"No, don't look," I said. "Every time we both get a message lately, it's not good news."

She laughed and pulled out her phone.

"It's from Miles. He wants to know where the book is."

"What book?" I asked, having a bad feeling it was the one we found and re-hid in Grandpa Hunter's old desk.

Her phone pinged again. "Mom says his part in what happened at the dwarf mountain is eating at him. He needs to research the importance of the rings to understand why he was used to kill Prince Hakon."

She gave me a look that confirmed my fear.

"He wants the book Grandma and Grandpa Hunter hid."

CHAPTER TWO

I watched my best friend's expression fill with fear and hurried to hug her.

"Hey, none of that," I said. "It's understandable that Miles needs answers, isn't it?"

"It is, but the book won't give him those. All that book brings is death. Look what happened to my grandparents after they started researching."

I patted her back, hating that she suspected a connection between her grandparents' disappearance and that book; the last thing they were researching before they disappeared. But I couldn't deny that since finding the thing, she and I had run into trouble again and again.

"You don't know the book's to blame for that, Vena," I said diplomatically.

She pulled out of my arms and met my gaze.

"You're right. But even if it isn't, what good will it do for Miles? We read it, Ev. There's nothing in it but weird old stories and vague warnings about otherworlder creatures that we already know about."

"The book is much more than weird stories," Cross said. "It's the first written history of otherworlder encounters back before they were as known as they are today. In terms of rare books, it's among the most rare and precious books in existence."

"Why are the first encounters so important?" she asked.

"I believe Miles will want to be a part of this conversation as well," Cross said. "Let's go upstairs and call him."

Vena didn't look happy about it but didn't argue as the four of us headed to the second floor.

Cross led us to a large study tucked away on the other side of the bookshelves that lined the living room wall. A desk sat in the middle of the space, with a sofa and two chairs positioned in front of it. Nothing had plastic on it anymore.

"Have a seat," Cross said, closing the door behind us. "Any conversations we have in here will be private."

"Soundproofed?" Anchor asked.

Cross nodded.

"Why is soundproofing needed for this conversation?" Vena asked as she sat with Anchor on the couch.

"Otherworlder origins aren't as peaceful as current human history says they were."

I went to sit in a chair, but Cross caught me around the waist, stole my seat, and settled me onto his lap. When I gave him a look, he returned a subtle, sexy smile. I rolled my eyes and snuggled in as Vena dialed Miles' number and placed the call on speaker.

"If you're going to tell me not to look into it, I don't want to hear it, Vena," Miles said instead of a greeting.

He didn't sound like himself. He sounded tired and sad—on the verge of tears.

Vena and I shared a look. No matter how she felt about the book, her brother needed some closure for his own sanity.

"Miles, it's Cross," Cross said. "You're on speaker. Vena mentioned your interest in the book, and I thought you might like to understand more about its purpose before reviewing its contents."

"I'm listening."

"The book documents some of the earliest encounters humans had with otherworlders. Its significance is not in the stories but in the locations where those stories take place."

"What do you mean?" Vena asked.

"The fae have been visiting humans for a very long time, even before humans thought of writing about them. In ancient times, the fae were often revered for their abilities. However, as humans evolved and understood more, they saw the threat in the fae. They also realized the fae weren't of their world."

What Cross was saying struck a chord in me. We called the fae, dwarves, vampires, werewolves, and every other creature an otherworlder. Why? People whispered that they were not of our world, but they'd dwelled among us for centuries, hidden in the shadows, too afraid to step forward because they were different.

"So, where are they from?" I asked.

"A world connected to this one. A world where humans lose all sense of time and self in pursuit of simple pleasures."

"And the book?" Miles said.

"The book and corresponding map are clues where to find the portals to that world."

I barely heard Miles swear under his breath.

"A page at the end of the book depicts four gems," Cross continued. "Gems found by the dwarves and enhanced by the fae. They hold the power to reopen the portals that were closed by a mutually agreed upon treaty to prevent humans from being taken to the fae realm.

"Each race had its reasons to agree. The vampires needed the humans for the food. The werewolves needed them for mates.

"Orphia, the woman I ran from centuries ago, wants the rings to reopen the portals to the fae realm. The reason for preventing access to the fae world hasn't changed. Opening the portals would cause chaos and fear during a time when relations between the races and the humans is growing into something truly harmonious."

"Except for with the vampires," I said.

"Precisely," Cross said. "I believe she wants to turn everything back to the chaotic times when all the races were equally shunned and the humans lived in fear of everything. A time when vampires could feed and kill without fear of consequence."

"Well, that doesn't sound good," Vena said.

"Not good at all," Cross agreed.

"Thank you for telling me," Miles said.

"If that's what the book is about, then how is it connected to our grandparents' disappearance?" Vena asked. "They wouldn't have been part of anything that would throw the world into chaos."

"I'm going to talk to Mom and Dad," Miles said. "If our grandparents were out in the field because of that book, it means they had help from our parents. You know Mom and Dad did all the research for Grandma and Grandpa."

I wondered how much their parents already knew and weren't saying.

"I'll need the book and map," Miles said.

"Why?" Vena asked. "Cross just told you more than what was in the book. What are you going to do with those stories? Are you going to search for the portals? We lost our grandparents because of this, Miles. I can't lose you or our parents, too."

"Vena, I owe the dwarves answers. I can't give them back their prince, but I can give them the truth about why he died and our family's involvement in everything. And that starts with figuring out what our grandparents were doing.

"I'm not going to follow in their footsteps. We already have access to more information than they had. Which is even more reason we're responsible for figuring out what happened."

Vena and I exchanged a weighted glance. I could see her worry mirrored my own. However, Miles was right. Not just about the dwarves deserving an explanation, though.

Now that we understood what was at stake, we owed it to everyone to stop Orphia since we knew what she wanted. We couldn't hide from the problem. Despite the blow Shepard and his people delivered to her army of vampires, I knew Orphia wouldn't give up. Since the book was obviously tied to the portals she wanted to open, investigating it and why Vena's grandparents were looking into it was a good starting place.

Vena must have had the same thought because she huffed an annoyed sigh. "Do you promise not to act on anything you find?"

"I promise not to go anywhere. You know me. I'm a researcher, not a hunter."

"You'll find the book and map in your grandfather's desk," Cross said.

"I already searched it," Miles said.

"Not the secret compartment. It's a clever design," Cross said. "I will text you how to open it."

Miles disconnected after a final promise not to act on anything he might uncover.

"I don't think I've ever heard him like that," Vena said. "It makes me worried."

Anchor hugged her close to his side. "He's processing his guilt and grief. Let him work through it. He gave his word, and we'll look out for him."

Vena frowned but didn't say anything.

Cross' phone pinged with a message. Since I was sitting on him, I read it with him.

Shepard: Everly's phone tracker says she's at the new place, but no one's here. Where is she?

Cross kissed my cheek and sent a reply.

Cross: Open the door off the living room.

The door opened a second later, and Shepard, the Alpha of all werewolves, walked in, closing the door behind him.

His dark blonde hair brushed the collar of the t-shirt that fit snuggly on his shoulders and chest, revealing his drool-worthy physique. While Cross was athletically muscled like a swimmer, Shepard was a solid powerhouse.

But it wasn't his muscles that I noticed just then. It was the exhaustion that gave his beautiful light grey eyes an almost haunted look.

He plucked me off Cross' lap and sat down with me in the other chair, snuggling me close.

Cross raised a brow. "Sharing is caring, I suppose."

Shepard softly growled in response. Cross chuckled.

"I suspect you're here for more than Everly, though. How are things going with Hugh and the human authorities?"

"They're relieved we killed as many vampires as we did, but they're presently informing the families of the deceased that their loved ones had been turned into vampires and are now dead. It's a mess, and people are angry."

I tipped my head to look up at Shepard.

"At you?"

"No. They're just angry they lost people they loved."

He shifted me in his lap to wrap both arms around my waist and pulled me as close as physically possible.

"I needed this," he murmured against my cheek.

I ran my fingers through his hair at the back of his neck. He sighed and dipped his head to kiss my neck.

"Has Hugh asked Effora about Vivian's charm?" I asked.

"What charm?" Vena asked as Shepard said, "He's been busy with cleanup."

"My necklace didn't stop Vivian from pulling me from the car," I said to Vena. "I think he had something to counter it because there was a red glow under his veil the whole time he was touching me."

"He has his own necklace?"

"Maybe," I said.

"I thought you bought Everly the top of the line," she said, looking at Cross.

"I did. If Vivian had anything that could negate the spell in Everly's necklace, it would have to be very powerful," Cross said.

"Which is why Hugh needs to talk to Effora," Vena said in understanding. "How long will it take Hugh to finish the cleanup?"

"A while," Shepard said. "I have my pack searching for more nests. We need to find Orphia. Until we do, Blur will be closed indefinitely."

"Will it be okay that it's closed so long?" I asked.

"I don't have a choice. It would be irresponsible of me to open again when we've been attacked twice. I won't put you or anyone else in danger. And I need to use my pack to find Orphia."

"But don't worry about your paychecks. I'll make sure the staff is taken care of."

"We're not worried," I said.

"Speak for yourself," Vena mumbled before saying, "What about the nest I found to the north? Isn't Orphia there?"

Shepard sighed and nuzzled me for a second before answering her.

"The local pack's alpha sent men to watch over the nest, but they haven't reported in. He sent more to look for them, but the place is empty now."

"Can they track the scents?" Cross asked.

"Maybe if the vampires had left on foot, but they didn't. They had cars. And one car's exhaust pretty much smells like another. The alpha's scouts lost the trail as soon as they got on the highway. The vampires from that nest could be anywhere now."

Cross leaned back in his chair, his fingers tapping his knee as he thought. "Orphia was trying to increase her numbers before, so she'll do the same again."

"Since the vampires are only active at night, excluding yourself, of course," Vena said, "I'll scry first thing every morning and update Shepard with any new nest locations.

"Any chance we can get Effora to increase the juice on this?" She held up the crystal she wore around her neck. "It was great finding those large nests, but I think they'll be onto our game and keep the sizes smaller."

"Agreed," Cross said, looking at Shepard.

Shepard growled and slouched back in the chair, pulling me with him so he wore me like a weighted blanket.

"You call Effora," he said to Cross. "I'm tired of her evasive answers and heavy innuendos."

"Innuendos?" I tipped my head to look up at Shepard in disbelief. "There was nothing hidden about her meaning, Shepard. That woman would give her left toe to sleep with you."

His gaze met mine. There was a slight twinkle in his eyes. "Are you jealous?"

I knew what answer he wanted, but he'd know if I lied.

"It's impossible for me to be jealous when I'm one hundred percent certain about your feelings for me. However, if she tries to paw you again, I'll probably lose my temper."

He grinned at me.

"But how I feel about her doesn't change anything. We still need her help. All these magical charms are becoming a pain in our backside. Vivian's was too powerful. Mine wasn't powerful enough. And neither is Vena's crystal. I'm starting to wonder who the fae really support."

"Themselves," Cross said. "Always themselves. Their truce

with the vampires was only to secure the humans they needed. Both now and back when the portals were first closed."

"Portals?" Shepard said. "Why are you talking about those?"

Cross brought him up to speed, and Shepard looked at Vena.

"I have people watching your family," he said to her. "I promise Miles won't be able to make a move without me knowing."

"Thank you," she said. "But I think Everly is right. Even though the fae are only interested in themselves, they seem to be giving all the good charms to the vampires. We need to push for upgrades, Shepard."

"What are you suggesting?" I asked.

"Whatever it takes for the end game."

I laughed. "If you think Shepard is going to whore himself out for her help, you need to talk to Anchor some more about what having a mate means. It physically won't work."

Shepard caught my chin and turned his head toward me. He was frowning. "How do you know that?"

"*The Other House*," Vena and I said simultaneously.

"And I *know* it won't work," Vena continued. "I just meant to play her game. Act like you're interested until she gives you what you want."

Shepard released me and shot Vena a look.

"I will not encourage Effora's interest."

"It's not a bad idea to play nice," Cross said, earning himself a dirty look from Shepard, too.

"Everly isn't the jealous type," Cross continued. "She knows where your heart lies and understands what's at stake. Orphia will do whatever it takes to get what she wants, and Effora isn't afraid to use people, either. Can we afford to be the only ones to hold a higher ground?"

Shepard scowled at Cross but then let out a sigh. "I'll think about it."

"Make it happen," Vena said. "I need to scry. In fact, I should start now, just in case I can find anything. Maybe I should use a different type of map. Like a topographical. Do you think that would change my results?"

I shook my head at her. "No matter the map, it still represents the same area. You know that."

"Worth a shot." She turned to Anchor. "What about a magical map? Think the Shadow Trade market will have anything?"

Before he could answer, she had already popped off the couch. "Let's head out."

Anchor dutifully followed, and I was thankful that it wasn't me she was dragging to the market. It would be a blessing if I never saw the inside of that place again.

I slipped free of Shepard's hold because he was like a furnace. Great to snuggle with, but I was already warm.

After I kissed his cheek, I opened my phone and looked at Cross. "I'll place the grocery order. Is there anything specific we need?"

"Order whatever you would like." Cross pulled out a credit card. "Use this to pay for it."

"It's my food. I can pay."

"After the bakery is running and you don't have school bills, you can argue with me. Until then, let me at least do this."

I had been independent for so long that letting others take care of me was hard, but I supposed I needed to let that go. Shepard and Cross could take care of me while I found ways to take care of them. That was what being in a relationship was... caring for one another.

Accepting the card, I added it to the payment method then returned it to him.

I'd barely finished placing a small order when Vena raced back inside with a pamphlet in her hands and Anchor only a few steps behind.

"Someone just gave me this. He's handing them out to everyone. It's not just pro-vamp propaganda this time. It's anti-werewolf. They're trying to label you as killers and 'the real threat to humanity.'"

Cross stood and took the pamphlet.

"There's a link to a video," he said.

My stomach sank as he looked at Shepard with concern in his gaze.

CHAPTER THREE

"Vampires are friends," I said, reading the headline of the pamphlet in disbelief. "Where did you get this?"

"Right outside," Vena said. "Keep reading."

"Werewolves are the killers and the real threat to humanity," I said, reading for the group. "You've been fed a lie. Don't believe it? Watch the video and decide for yourself."

I looked from the QR code to Vena. "Did you watch the video?"

"No. I scanned the rest of the pamphlet and ran back in here."

As she answered, Cross used his phone to scan the QR code. It opened a video recording that looked like it was from a security camera inside someone's well-lit house.

I watched the door to the home burst open and a group of men rush in. The people who'd been relaxing on the couch bolted to their feet.

Everyone moved so fast. But for some, not fast enough. Shouting, screaming, and growls rang out from Cross' phone as the men inside the home had their hearts ripped out within seconds.

My stomach twisted at the sight.

"They were newly turned," Cross said.

One wolf turned toward something off camera view. He disappeared from the frame only to return a second later, dragging a woman younger than me by her arm. She was sobbing and begging him not to kill her.

I squeezed my eyes shut before she screamed then went quiet.

Vena pulled me into a comforting hug as she said, "It looks like the vampires are trying to make werewolves into the bad guys. That video makes a convincing argument. Keep reading, Cross. But maybe to yourself."

"They're recruiting through Night Club meetings," Cross said after a few moments.

I opened my eyes when Vena handed me over to Cross. "I apologize for not turning off the video."

"It's okay. We need to know what they're doing." Yet I knew the image of that man dragging the young woman into the room would haunt my dreams for weeks.

Shepard was watching the video on his phone—silently this time. His visible weariness had doubled.

"Is this Orphia making good on her promise?" I asked, recalling the threats she'd made during our meeting with Hugh, Queen Effora, and King Curran.

"Likely," Cross said.

"We need to stop her before this escalates," Vena said. "Everly and I should go to a Night Club meeting. It's the best lead we have to find her."

Anchor drew Vena into the cage of his arms, hugging her as much as confining her. "It's also the most dangerous."

"She's obviously trying to replenish her numbers with this propaganda," Vena said.

"It's an effective tactic," Cross said. "She'll gain sympathy with that video. More people are likely to attend the meeting simply to learn about the aggressive side of your kind, Shepard. We need to inform Hugh."

"We need to do more than that," I said. "She's luring innocent people. How many small towns does she need to take over before the public is told what's really happening?

"While I don't always agree with Vena, she's right this time. We need to find and stop Orphia. So many people are in danger because of her." I thought of my family and how their vacation wouldn't keep them away from the danger forever.

"We're on the same page?" Vena asked excitedly.

"Maybe. I think you're right that the Night Club meetings are the best way to find Orphia and stop this quicker.

"I'm not suggesting some loose cannon escapade like we've poorly executed in the past." I shot Vena a pointed look. "I'm suggesting a coordinated effort involving all of us. Send Vena and me to the meeting since we're human while you guys tail us."

There was a chorus of "No," with one excited, "Hell yes!"

I saw the fear lurking in both Shepard and Cross' gazes and tried to get them to see reason.

"Orphia has attempted to use me several times already to force the both of you to give up your rings. Now that we know why she's doing it and what's at stake, isn't it better to find her before she finds me?"

"You're not going in there," Shepard said. "Either of you. You could get compelled or thralled and turned."

"Think of what we've already been through, Shepard," I said. "Even with you and Cross right there protecting us, I still got hurt last night. I'm not blaming you. I just don't want to extend how long I have to live with the threat of Orphia or her people doing something else to me to get to you. The faster we stop her, the sooner we can move on. I'm ready to focus on what comes next in life."

I knew I had him when his eyes flickered with gold. His sweet wolf-heart was desperate for our future together.

He glanced at Cross.

"They've had more close calls than I would care to remember,"

Cross said. "While we both know things could go wrong, Everly's right. This is our best chance to find Orphia. Even with my contacts on the inside, I've learned nothing of Orphia's whereabouts."

"We have her number," I said. "Or at least her assistant's. The other option is to call and ask for an in-person meeting like she wanted."

"No," Cross said firmly. "With forewarning, she has time to prepare, which would give her an advantage we cannot afford. There's a reason I ran from her a century ago. She's hungry for power and will kill as many people as needed to gain it. If you think the towns she converted are troubling, you are unprepared for the number she killed in the past when there were fewer people to notice."

"Seriously?" Vena asked.

"There were fewer plagues than your human history claims," he said.

"Damn," Vena said as I silently agreed.

"Okay," I said. "So the best option is the Night Club meetings. Unless someone has something else?"

Shepard didn't look happy as he shook his head.

Vena giddily cheered as she pulled out her phone. Then she shushed everyone as she dialed the number on the pamphlet and placed the call on speaker.

A chipper man answered, "Thanks for calling the Night Club hotline. Would you like to donate to the cause or attend a meeting?"

"Both, actually," Vena said. "My friend and I just watched the video. It's disgusting what the wolves are doing."

"I couldn't agree more. And you're not alone. We've had thousands of calls already this morning. Our new member onboarding is booked out for a few days, so we're placing people on a waiting list. Is this the best number at which to reach you?"

"It is," Vena said.

"Excellent. Can I have your first name?"

"Aneva," Vena said without missing a beat.

I rolled my eyes at her. It was a name she'd always referred to as her stripper name. It was also the name she'd give any guy she wasn't interested in when we went out for drinks.

"We will call you back in a few days with the meeting time and location, Aneva. Thanks for calling."

"Thanks for sending people out with the pamphlets. Without them, I would have never known."

She disconnected the call and pouted. "Days? That's bullshit."

"No," I said. "It's scary. Thousands have called. How many people are they going to convert or kill before we can stop them?"

I hoped he'd exaggerated the number, but either way, people were going to die.

"Which is why we need to get in there faster," Vena said.

"How? You heard him. He'll call in a few days."

Vena frowned. "I can't sit here and do nothing." She patted Anchor's arm. "Let's go scry. I'll let you know as soon as I hear from them."

I let out a breath as soon as she was gone.

As Shepard and Cross began talking about moving wolves from one area to another, I slipped from the study.

With nothing else to do, I checked my phone to see the status of my grocery order. It would arrive in an hour, which was perfect. That gave me plenty of time to explore the spacious kitchen and prep for some therapy baking.

I peeked into the kitchen cupboards to find new dishes and cooking accessories. However, stickers still clung to most of them, so I began pulling things out for a wash. I loved everything Cross had selected and was thankful for his understanding of my love of baking. He'd made his kitchen an oasis for me.

Cross and Shepard appeared as I was peeling off a label from a shiny sauce pot.

I saw the concerned look they shared. They knew me well enough to recognize my stress cleaning for what it was.

"If you have things you need to do, do them," I said. "I'm going to prep the kitchen for baking. The groceries should be here in an hour."

Both settled at the counter island.

"I can work from here for now," Shepard said as he pulled out his phone.

"I'm free to sit and watch you," Cross teased.

I smiled at him. "If you're so free, start brainstorming marketing ideas."

Cross frowned in contemplation. "Well, the bakery is supposed to be a place for all races. But with the vampires vilifying the wolves, I wonder if we need to change it."

"We need more inclusive places now more than ever. While I hate what is happening, I believe not all vampires are bad. Just like the wolves aren't the monsters that Orphia is painting them to be."

Shepard tensed when I said monsters. I flashed him a smile to show I didn't mean I thought of them like that.

"What about the cookie class idea we had?" I asked, finding the cutest ramekins in a drawer. "These are adorable."

"I thought you might like them," Cross said. "As for the cookie class, is that the one where women make cookies and wolves smell them to see if they can find a possible mate?"

"Yes, that one."

"Would any women show up?" Shepard asked.

"Yes. *The Other House* has been gaining fans and fueling fantasies for years. Plus, there will always be those who don't believe Orphia's propaganda. You have allies, Shepard."

His disbelieving look made me more determined to create the class.

Our phones dinged at the same time. Cross and Shepard looked at theirs.

"Is it Vena?" I asked.

"Miles," Cross said. "He verified all the locations in the book and map are in Europe and is asking if there are any known locations in the States." He glanced at Shepard. "Do you know of any? As soon as I arrived here, I went into hibernation."

Shepard shook his head. "I don't know."

Cross sent a text back to the group.

Moments later, my phone dinged with a different group message from Vena to Piper and Robyn, our college friends currently summering in Europe.

**Vena: Hey, Piper and Robyn. Haven't seen you in
forever. How's Europe so far? Where have you been?**

I rolled my eyes, seeing through the motivation behind Vena's message. Even if Piper and Robyn had been to the places mentioned in the book, would they even know what a portal looked like or how to find it? No. And even if they did, I wouldn't put them in danger by asking them to search for something Vena's grandparents had tried to find.

Annoyed, I sent Vena a private message.

**Me: Don't you dare use our friends to search for clues.
Vena: It's like you don't even know me. I would never
use my friends like that.
Me: Like when you used a friend to investigate a lead on
a fairy hoard under the ruse of a hike?
Vena: I've reformed. Did I tell you I love you and have
put our name on the waitlist for Enticed?
Me: *eye roll emoji* Why a waitlist?
Vena: They're booking out a few months. Sorry, bestie. I
know you wanted to taste-test sooner for the bakery.
But I'm honoring my promise.**

I snorted and pocketed my phone. When I looked at the guys, they were both watching me with amused expressions.

"Vena?" Cross asked.

"Yes. We have friends in Europe. She asked them where they've been, and I warned her not to use our friends to hunt for clues."

"Like she used you to search for treasure?" Cross asked.

"Exactly!"

He and Shepard chuckled.

"I remember when you showed up to work with that scratch on your cheek," Shepard said.

"Same," I said. "I thought I was in trouble."

"Never."

I smiled. "I'll remind you of that when Vena gets a call back from the Night Club."

Shepard's humor faded.

"What are your plans for the rest of the day?" I asked to distract him.

"Spend some time with you in between whatever calls I get."

"Did you want to go somewhere or do something?" I asked.

He leaned back in his chair. "Actually, it's nice here. And I enjoy watching you in the kitchen." He held up his hands quickly. "I'm not being sexist or anything. You just look really happy right now. It's nice."

I smiled at him and started wiping down the next emptied cupboard.

"I'm happy because I'm doing something I love…well, not cleaning the cabinets. And serving drinks at Blur was fun and rewarding, but it's not baking. There's something gratifying about creating confectionery that makes a person moan as soon as they put it in their mouth."

Shepard made a choked sound. I turned to see Shepard with a beet-red face. Cross had a hand covering his mouth, but I could see the humor in his gaze.

"I'm glad Vena wasn't here for that," I mumbled.

"She'll delight in the retelling of it, though," Cross said.

"Or you could keep it to yourself."

"Perhaps," he said with his sexy half-smile.

"Don't look at me," Shepard said. "I'm not repeating that. But now I know why you like baking so much."

Focusing on the cupboard I was cleaning, I kept my face hidden until my flush faded.

By the time I finished, the groceries arrived, and the pair helped me put everything away. It was nice spending time together, just the three of us, for a change. Listening to how they teased one another, they sounded like close friends or even brothers. If Shepard enjoyed watching me in the kitchen, I liked watching them as they were then. Laughing, light, and in harmony with each other.

I only managed to finish one batch of coffin scones, one of the creature-themed novelty treats for humans I'd come up with for the bakery, before Shepard got a call that killed the fun mood.

"That was Hugh. The girl in the video was identified by her parents. They want to speak to the wolf who killed their daughter. They don't believe she was a vampire since she was talking and not attacking him."

"Not all vampires are bad," Cross said to Shepard. "However, every newly turned vampire is extremely dangerous. They wake hungry and often don't care who they feed on."

"I don't think that's going to comfort them."

"She loved them enough not to go home after she was turned," Cross said. "That's what should comfort them."

Shepard nodded and left me with Cross, who wrapped his arms around my shoulders.

I rested my head back against his chest.

"I didn't know that," I said. "How many go back and kill their families?"

"Not many, but it is a concern. To keep ourselves safe and

hidden, we guard those we turn, knowing they'd go for the easiest blood source."

"Have you turned anyone?"

"Never. I would never condemn anyone to this existence."

"Not even me so we could spend an eternity together?"

He turned me around, his gaze sad. "Especially not you, Everly. Watching everyone you care about age and die is a cruel kind of torture I wouldn't wish on anyone. The cruelty of an eternal existence is exactly why the first person was cursed with vampirism."

I wrapped my arms around his waist, worried for Cross. Was he already thinking of how I would age and leave him?

"I think I've had enough kitchen time for now. I'm ready to sample something else that will make me moan."

A network of black veins bloomed around his eyes before his mouth hungrily claimed mine.

CHAPTER FOUR

BEFORE I EVEN OPENED MY EYES, I FELT HOW I WAS WRAPPED around Cross' side like a tree-hugging monkey. My head rested on his chest as he lazily ran his fingers through my hair. It felt so good, and I didn't want to move until I realized I'd drooled on him a little.

I quickly wiped my face and Cross' bare chest. "Sorry."

"Don't be sorry. You're adorable when you sleep."

"Drooling is only adorable when you're a baby, and even then, I have some issues with it."

He laughed softly and kissed the top of my head. "Still adorable."

"What time is it?"

"It's nine o'clock."

"So late?" I thought I would have woken up earlier since I'd gone to bed by eleven.

"You can sleep more if you want."

I shook my head, my lips brushing against his skin, and I grinned at his slight shiver. "Your eyes just did the black veiny thing, didn't they?"

"Maybe."

I smiled. I loved seeing his eyes turn black. It had been a little freaky at first when I hadn't known him, but now it was like seeing the subtle blush on Shepard. Those little "tells" gave me more information about their mood than words.

Cross continued stroking my hair and lulling me back to sleep. So I rolled away before succumbing and groped for the remote I knew was on the nightstand. When the curtains opened enough to see him, he pouted as if I'd taken away his favorite toy.

"I'll make breakfast," he said.

"You don't have to."

"I know. I want to." He kissed my forehead and left the bedroom, wearing only his shorts. It was a pleasant view.

Sighing, I went to the bathroom to shower. Once I was finished, I put on a cute top with a sparkly cupcake on it and matching shorts.

"I love these clothes," I said to Cross when I found him in the kitchen. "And I love seeing you cooking."

For someone who had once thought cooking was for servants, he seemed at home in the kitchen now.

"I love your clothes, too." A sexy smile played on his lips. "And I like taking them off you as well."

A memory of last night popped into my head. I tried not to blush but failed, and his eyes flashed black.

"I'll happily do an encore performance," he said.

"Focus on breakfast. What are you making?" I peeked over the island counter but couldn't make it out. "I smell sausage."

He nodded. "Eggs over easy, toast, sausage, and a special extra."

"What's the special?"

He plated the food and walked it over to me, kissing me on the lips. "That is."

"You're ridiculous," I said with a laugh.

"Only with you. Have a seat, or would you like me to feed you standing up?"

I took the plate from him and settled at the table. "I can feed myself."

While I did, I watched him check the news on his phone. He glanced at an article about a fae death before quickly scrolling past it.

"Anything new happen since last night?" I asked.

"Pro-vampire groups have been popping up and pulling people to their cause. The number of werewolf anti-fans is growing, too."

"How's Shepard doing? Have you talked to him?"

"He's fine at the moment but weary of the attention the wolves are receiving. Thankfully, his pack is relatively unknown."

I sent Shepard a quick message letting him know I was thinking of him and told him to let me know if he needed anything. Then, I read the messages on my phone while I ate.

Piper had replied to the group that they were having a great time. She included a photo of her pretending to save the Leaning Tower of Pisa from falling. However, she must have been standing in the shadow of a tree or something because the lighting was off. Still, it was a cute picture. I responded, wishing them a fun trip and asking her to send more pictures when she had time.

"I think there is a problem at Blur," Cross said. "This just posted a moment ago."

He showed me a video of protesters outside of Blur. At the bottom of the video was a banner stating, "Blur, a D.C. nightclub owned and operated by werewolves."

"So much for his pack being unknown," I said.

The people were peacefully protesting with signs that read, "Werewolves wear sheep's clothing." "Wolves kill first. No questions asked." "Leave D.C., killers." And more. All of it against werewolves.

"Do you think the protesters truly believe werewolves are bad, or are they thralled humans being controlled by Orphia or Vivian or whatever vampire to stir up trouble?"

Cross considered the question and the video.

"That is an excellent question, and one I can only answer if I go there in person."

"Is it safe?"

He kissed my forehead. "I love it when you worry about me, Everly."

"That doesn't answer my question."

"It's safe enough for me. With the ring I wear, very little can harm me."

"Okay. Then you can go."

He chuckled and called Vena on speaker.

"Hey, money-man, did you get my books yet?" she asked.

I shook my head at her as Cross answered, "I've acquired most of them. However, that's not why I'm calling. I need you and Anchor to stay with Everly."

"Where?" she asked.

"At the new place," I said.

"We really need to brainstorm a name for it besides the new place," she said.

"Agreed," Cross said. "How soon can you be here to discuss business names?"

"Anchor and I are already in the neighborhood. We can be there in five."

Five minutes later, her voice rang out from below. "Would you eat at a place called Beaver?"

She appeared at the open door. Anchor was a step behind her, frowning and flushed.

"You're adorable when you're embarrassed," Vena said when she looked back at him. "For the record, I didn't ask him if he liked eating beaver, just if he'd eat at a *place* called Beaver."

"Yeah, I'm with Anchor on this," I said. "Doesn't make it any better."

"Will you be able to watch over the pair of them on your own, or should you call someone else over for backup?" Cross asked Anchor.

"You make it sound like we're children," Vena complained.

Anchor picked Vena up, carried her to the island, and sat her on a chair. She didn't complain, though.

"I've got this," Anchor said to Cross. "She'll promise me her best behavior today."

"I will?" she asked innocently.

"You will." He leaned toward her face, and I watched my friend's anticipation visibly climb. "I'd eat at a place called Beaver."

Cross chuckled as Vena started promising to be the model of best behavior.

"You've got about ten minutes before she forgets her promise," I said to Cross as he hugged me.

"Call me if you need anything."

"I will. And you keep me updated. Shepard hasn't messaged me back yet, and I'm worried."

Cross kissed my forehead and blurred out the door.

"What's going on?" Vena asked.

I showed her the video that Cross had shown me. Anchor frowned when the video ended and stepped away to call someone.

"Orphia's actually doing what she said, isn't she?" Vena said.

"Seems like it."

"If I were Effora, I'd start worrying," Vena said, smiling. "Maybe she'll cooperate now. I overheard Shepard talking to Hugh about her yesterday. She's been ghosting both of them. According to her little underlings, it's because she's sick. Hugh seemed to buy it. I don't.

"Now, about Beaver. It's spelled out. An acronym. B.E.A.V.E.R. Get it?"

Anchor shot her a look from across the room as he spoke quietly into the phone.

It took me a second to figure it out. "We're not naming this place Brodier, Everly, and Vena's eating retreat," I said. "Ever. We need something classy yet catchy that will embody what we're trying to do: bring all the races together."

Vena nodded slowly.

"What about Bites and Delights? Vampires and werewolves bite. Fae and a few other otherworlders delight. Plus, humans will be delighted with a bite of your creations."

"I actually like it," I said.

Vena grinned. "Don't sound so surprised. I have amazing ideas all the time."

"Our opinions often differ on what's amazing," I said dryly as I pulled out my phone and quickly searched for any businesses in the area with that name. "It looks like we can actually use it. When Cross gets back, we'll see what he thinks."

"He'll go with it if you want it."

"What I want is a thriving business. The wrong name could end that dream before it becomes a reality. Cross won't set us up for failure by agreeing to an awful name."

She picked up her phone and sent a message. Hers pinged a second later, and she lifted it to show me she'd messaged the name suggestion to Cross. He'd already agreed it was fitting.

"Done. Now let's go shopping for 'Bites and Delights' decor," she said, hopping off her stool.

"Cross said he would get it."

"Cross is busy dealing with stuff we can't. So let's deal with stuff we can so he doesn't have to."

"Ugh, you're making all sorts of sense today," I said.

"Again, you shouldn't be so surprised."

Anchor hung up and hurried over to set his hands on Vena's shoulders.

"We're not going anywhere."

"Why not?" she asked.

"Cross said to stay here."

"No, he didn't. He said to watch over Everly. He also asked if you needed backup. At no point did he say the human he adored more than his immortal life was under house arrest. Also, stating facts doesn't mean I'm misbehaving."

I snorted as Anchor shook his head at her.

"Let's go," I said, grabbing my purse before she could bring up the reward she expected for her model behavior.

"Are we taking your fancy wheels?" she asked.

"You mean the company vehicle that Cross bought?"

"Yes, *your* fancy wheels." She grinned.

I rolled my eyes at her sassiness, and we headed downstairs to the company vehicle.

Anchor followed us but stopped at the door, blocking our path outside. "I need both of you together."

"Of course we'll be together," Vena said.

He shook his head. "No. I need you joined at the hip. No going down different aisles or like how you shop at the market and leapfrog to different stalls. I need eyes on both of you at the same time."

I nodded in agreement.

"Vena, I'm looking at you," he said.

"I'll stick to Ev like troll boogers. Let's go!"

Once we got in the bright red SUV, we agreed to go to a store that wasn't too far away and should have most of what we needed. The gourmet kitchen store had fun decorations that would enhance Bites and Delights.

I smiled at the name. Now that we had one picked out, the business felt more real. I couldn't wait until I flipped the open sign on the door. Or should it be a lit sign? Maybe something more sophisticated, like carved wood?

As soon as I parked and exited the SUV, Vena was at my side. She even wrapped her arm around my shoulders and steered me into the brightly lit store. Something about a well-lit kitchen store made me want to skip into it with a large basket.

I immediately wanted to veer to the cookware to admire the shiny beauties, but I didn't want to get distracted or waste time. Instead, I went to the other side, where I saw porcelain cakes and donuts, tiny menu chalkboards, and wooden signs with painted sayings.

"This place is making me hungry," Vena said.

"I'll feed you when we get home."

Vena didn't stray from my side even once as I picked out things. Thankfully, Anchor had the foresight to grab a cart and follow behind us. He looked like a large, muscular bodyguard strolling through the aisles with a dainty cart.

"Why do they have a butt plug here?" Vena asked.

I glanced at what she was holding. "It's a handheld lime juicer."

She eyed it with a little too much interest. "I need it."

"Put the innocent juicer down."

She waggled the juicer at Anchor. "Attempt number 795?"

He flushed slightly. "Put it down."

Vena snorted and put it back.

Her phone played a sinister sound, and I gave her a questioning look.

"It's an alert."

"Obviously. But what for? Are you still following that one guy who made you mad three years ago?"

"Harvey Dently will get what's coming to him, and I'm going to be ready with a haughty laugh."

Anchor raised a questioning brow.

"But no, this alert is for Orphia." She released me from her strangling arm-hold and looked at her phone. "It's another video."

My stomach roiled. "I don't think I can watch it."

"It looks fine," she said as she pressed play. "Look. It's just a bunch of people hanging out and playing cards."

Large men busted down the door and infiltrated the room. Based on the way they sprouted fur and attacked the card players, the card players weren't just people. They were vampires who hadn't had time to say anything or blur away before they died. It was just a card game, door-breaking, and almost-instant death.

It was over so quickly that I didn't even have time to close my eyes before the video cut over to a shot of Orphia. She looked different in this video. Her expression was forlorn instead of cold.

"The killing needs to stop," she said. "Werewolves are extinguishing innocent lives. As you just saw, they didn't stop to ask if the people they killed had ever harmed anyone. If they had asked, they would have learned they hadn't. Their source of nourishment —human blood—was ethically secured from volunteer donors who were well-compensated for their compassion and generosity.

"The werewolves are desperate to silence vampires, a race that has always existed alongside humans. And why? We don't kill like werewolves do. Yet, we're hated because we need blood to survive.

"We aren't new. We're simply more unjustly hated than the other races. You've been told vampires are bad and werewolves are good, so you've turned a blind eye to what's really happening.

"The werewolves need human women to survive, while we only need blood. Why is it more acceptable to humanity to surrender women to breed the next generation of killers than for a vampire to pay for a donated bag of blood?

"Our voices have been suppressed. We need you and your voice blended with ours to be heard. Speak to your local representative about how you feel vampires are being treated. It's time we all learn to coexist and stop the senseless killing of the innocent."

The video ended, and Vena snorted. "What a load of shit."

"*We* know it is, but how many people will believe it?"

"A lot," Anchor said, looking troubled.

I patted his arm, and Vena batted my hand away.

"Touch your own men."

"I did, right before you showed up."

She pretended to clutch her imaginary pearls, and I grinned.

"How many shelves need decorations?" I asked, steering us back on topic and away from the horrid video. "Do we have enough?"

"Between decorations and potted plants, I think we do. It's going to look really good. Just you wait and see."

Her phone rang as Anchor ushered us toward the checkout.

When Vena answered, I listened to her half of the conversation as Anchor placed our purchases on the counter. The cashier scanned the items and took the card Cross had given me for business purchases. Vena hung up the phone and looped her arm through mine as Anchor collected the bags.

"Miles?" I guessed as we walked toward the door.

"Yeah. He talked to Mom and Dad. Grandma and Grandpa were quiet about what they were working on before disappearing. All they told my parents was that a private broker contacted them to find a relic that could influence all creatures. My grandparents declined my parents' offer to help them research, which they thought was odd, but they were busy working on another project and were distracted.

"After Miles explained to them what Cross had told us about the book and the portals, Mom and Dad agree there's likely a connection between what Grandma and Grandpa were looking for and the vampires.

"They want to head back to the mountain to talk to Curran. He might have answers, and Miles wants to apologize again."

"King Curran? How can he help?" I asked, struggling to keep up.

"Mom and Dad saw some books in the royal library—really old books about otherworlders. Even if they can't find information about the relic my grandparents were looking for, maybe they can find more information about vampires and their curse."

"Because what's cursed can maybe be uncursed?" I guessed.

"Exactly. If we can uncurse vampires, there'd be nothing to worry about anymore."

CHAPTER FIVE

"Do you see it?" Vena asked, tugging at my arm and pointing ahead.

"See what?" I asked as Anchor put our shopping bags in the back of the SUV.

"Enticed. I wasn't kidding when I said we were put on a wait-list. Want to go in and see how many people are in front of us?"

I hadn't realized the store we'd picked was that close to the famous fae restaurant.

"If it's a lot, we can just take the next available reservation in a few months…or we could call that fae guy who gave you his number." Vena grinned at me.

"What fae guy?" Anchor asked, making me regret confiding in Vena.

"Just a customer at Blur," I said, pinching Vena's arm.

She acted like she didn't feel it.

"Let's go check," she said, pulling me forward.

Since she owed me a meal at Enticed, and we were in the area, I didn't mind checking but glanced at Anchor to see if he agreed. He shrugged.

"As long as we stick together."

Vena cheered and hurried us to the fae-owned restaurant that reflected their love of luxury and opulence. It showed in the actual silver leaves embedded in the door that the doorman opened for us and the marble tiles within.

My attention to decor drifted a bit the moment we walked through the door and I felt the subtle pull of a fae's seductive powers. The host stood near the reception desk, watching our approach with a welcoming smile. A magic current danced along my skin as my necklace protected me, proving it was charged and working. I wasn't sure how Vena's old necklace was dealing with the fae pull, but she seemed unaffected, too.

"What do you desire?" the host asked us.

"To find out where we are on the waitlist," Vena said.

"Name?"

"Vena Hunter."

He looked down at his tablet. "Two months. However, we just had a cancellation, and I can seat you if you'd like."

"Are you serious? Yes. That's perfect," Vena said. "See, Ev. I keep my promises."

"That promise feels like a lifetime ago."

"Barely. That's only because so much happened in between." She grinned at the host. "Lead on. I'm ready to have my desires fulfilled with good food."

He indicated that we should follow him. The buzz along my skin increased as the necklace continued to fend off an increasing amount of fae influence due to the dining area that had more servers stationed between the well-spaced tables than patrons.

The host had mentioned a cancellation, but it seemed more than that. With a two-month waitlist, eager diners should have occupied every seat, shouldn't they? Maybe they purposely spaced the reservations so the dining area was never crowded.

The openness drew my attention back to the decor. Cream walls with silver and blue design accents matched the crystal tables, which had a subtle blue glow. Buttery, soft blue leather chairs were positioned perfectly at the tables as if they had used a ruler. The servers wore cream standing-collar suit jackets, matching pants with silver cording, and a soft blue shirt. Even the woman softly playing the cream colored piano wore a silver gown with complementing blue embellishments.

The host stopped at a table and pulled out a chair for me, and Anchor did the same for Vena. I sat, distracted by everything until the host's fingers brushed my back as he pushed the chair in. Then he leaned over my shoulder, uncomfortably close, to hand us our menus.

"If there is anything we can do to enhance your dining pleasure, please let me know." He inhaled deeply near my ear. "The server will be with you in a moment."

"Was that weird?" I asked when he left.

"What?" Vena asked, focused on the menu.

I glanced at Anchor for confirmation, but he was studying Vena like she was on the menu.

They were right. That much attention from a fae wasn't odd. It was what they did, even at Blur. The non-stop buzz from my necklace was probably making things weird for me.

Mentally shaking my head at myself, I studied the menu. The options listed were mostly aphrodisiac foods. Not surprising really.

My necklace suddenly hummed aggressively against my skin, sending a cooling wave through me.

Something was wrong.

"Hello, beautiful," a server asked when she stopped at the table. Like all fae, she was blonde and had an elegant beauty. However, her eyes looked hungry.

She placed a bottle of carbonated water on the table. "Compliments of the house." She breathed in. "Do you see anything you desire?"

Vena nodded. "I want one of everything, and I want to eat it on him. Naked." She pointed to Anchor, who looked as if he was on board with it.

The server let out a soft moan. "Your desire will be fulfilled."

"Um, I think that's a health code violation," I said.

None of them seemed to hear me. Anchor was already stripping his shirt off.

I hopped up from my seat and yanked his shirt down.

"We need to go."

"No. Stay." The server drew closer.

I didn't feel like she was going to attack me—my necklace would have propelled her away—but she looked desperate.

In fact, more servers moved closer to us. That's when I noticed they all wore the same hungry look.

In my distraction, Anchor tugged his shirt from my hold and peeled it off. Vena stood, shoved the place settings to the floor, and climbed on top. She extended her arms to Anchor as I looked for the bottle of water on the floor, intending to douse the pair.

A hand caressed my ass. A surge of need heated my skin before my necklace glowed, and a cooling sensation swept through me. I spun around to face the aggressor. Tall with light hair and eyes, sculpted features, and a lean body, he was absolutely beautiful.

Another wave of coolness swept through me, and although he was still mesmerizing to look at, I saw him differently.

Dangerous.

The crack of my hand across the man's cheek didn't faze him. At least, not the way I'd hoped. He smiled slowly.

"You have some fire, my beauty. I like it. Give me another."

He offered his hand in the old-world way Cross sometimes did, as if inviting me to join him.

Behind me, I heard Vena whimper and knew we were in serious trouble.

"I'll pass on the slap fest," I said, grabbing the carbonated water from the floor.

I uncapped it, put my thumb over the opening, and shook it vigorously.

When I spun around, my gaze locked on Vena licking something off Anchor's chest while straddling his lap and humping him hard. I thanked every ancestor I had that they both still had their pants on.

"Why isn't it working?" Vena moaned, grinding against his flaccid firearm. "Make it work."

Anchor groaned, his hands firmly gripping her hips like he was afraid she was going to leave him.

Expertly angling my thumb on the bottle of carbonated water, I sprayed the fae surrounding the pair. I purposely got a little on Vena, too. Payback for the time she spritzed me when I'd been kissing Cross.

Dousing the fae had the effect I'd hoped for. Without their focus, Anchor regained enough sense to realize what they were doing. In one fluid motion, he stood and hoisted Vena over his shoulder.

"This directly violates the treaty," he said. "End this, or I won't use words to stop you."

"You have so much pent-up desire," a fae said. "We were trying to help."

"You were trying to feed," Anchor said angrily.

The one who'd groped my ass stepped forward.

"If that were true, we would have taken the females from you for ourselves. We were truly trying to help."

I picked up Anchor's shirt and tossed it to him.

"Where are your other customers? Why isn't this place filled?"

"We believe it's a spillover from the werewolf protests. Our numbers were lower yesterday as well, but not like this," one of the fae said. "It could also be because a fae was murdered yesterday. It didn't happen here, but people become afraid of what they don't understand. Customers might be leery of fae establishments."

"And it's early," another said. "People who eat at this hour are usually only here to experience the novelty of dining here. Our regulars typically come at the normal dining hour."

I glanced at the time on my phone. It wasn't yet five.

"We're leaving," I said.

"Stay, and we can help you," a fae said. "I can feel her desire. She's willing."

I glanced at Vena, who, in her current position, was lovingly stroking and fluffing Anchor's butt.

"She's not the problem," Anchor said. "I am. I was cursed by one of your kind. It needs to wear off."

"Only 775 more tries," Vena murmured.

"We could help lift the curse."

She lifted her head to look at the fae who said it.

"How?"

"I know someone." He reached into his suit jacket and withdrew a business card to hand her. "Call the number. Let her know a server from Enticed said she could help."

"Thanks."

I couldn't tell if Vena was seriously considering it or just playing along. Concerned it was the former, I glanced at Anchor. He nodded toward the door. With the bottle still in my grip and ready, I edged around the fae and then power-walked to the exit. Anchor was right behind me.

When I reached the sidewalk and sunshine, I stopped and waited for Anchor to set Vena down and put on his shirt.

"What the heck was that?" I asked.

"I think it might have been just what they said," Anchor said. "They're not getting the sexual feedings they need but were trying to help."

"Seriously?"

He blushed as he nodded. "If you haven't noticed from your time at Blur, we're not usually affected by them."

He wasn't wrong.

"And what about you?" I asked, looking at Vena.

She lifted her gaze from the business card she'd been staring at.

"I'm so damn horny that it barely took any nudge from them to make me want to climb Anchor like a tree. I think they might be telling the truth. They had no other guests, and he and I were willing."

I shook my head at both of them. "We're never going out to eat together again. You've scarred me for life."

Anchor looked guilty. Vena just grinned and looped her arm through mine.

"Pfft. That was nothing. Come on. Let's get you home."

WHILE I COOKED DINNER, I made Vena sit on the opposite side of the living room from Anchor. She whined that I was being unfair.

"I'm going to accidentally drop your plate of food on the floor," I said.

She pouted as she squirmed on the couch. "I just need—"

"We all know what you need, Vena. You were very vocal about it on the way home and nearly caused an accident."

She crossed her arms and sulked. "Fine."

"You can sit at the table now, but opposite Anchor."

She walked over like a petulant child but sat at the table. Anchor hesitantly took the chair across from her but kept out of reach of her feet.

"Thank you for dinner, Everly."

I nodded and served the French toast casserole I'd made. It wasn't a typical dinner, but I desperately needed comfort food. And feeding Vena a ton of carbs might slow her down.

However, instead of diving into the food, she played with the card the fae had given her.

"Put it down," I said. "Eat."

"But what if someone can break the curse on Anchor?"

She looked longingly at Anchor, who was busy frowning at his phone.

"Something wrong?" I asked.

"Shepard and Cross are still dealing with the protesters. More are joining, and it's escalating. Neither of them will be able to return soon, so I'll stay here."

"We can sleep in one of the spare rooms," Vena said with a wink.

He shook his head. "I'll need you two to stick together. Take the master room once it's bedtime. I'll stand guard. With so many contractors coming and going, I don't trust the safety of this place."

"I could sit with you," Vena said. "I'm not tired."

"Your needs will distract him," I said. "Eat dinner and take a long bath."

"With my lime juicer?"

"I knew it! You said you put it back, but I thought I saw a flash of green from the corner of your pocket."

Anchor coughed.

Vena grinned, dug into her food, and moaned when she ate it. "Best dinner ever."

"Did you at least pay for the juicer?"

"Of course. I slid them cash on the way out." She cocked her head at me. "Out of curiosity, did you happen to buy any oils? Or any other slippery edible substances?"

"Eat, Vena."

Hours later, I finally got Vena into bed. I thought I'd have to papoose her just to get her to stay still, but as soon as her head hit the pillow, she was out.

Anchor poked his head in to check on us.

"Look," I said, pointing to Vena. "She's cute when she's not crazy."

He softly chuckled. "She's cute even when she's crazy."

I shook my head at him, and he grinned before heading back out.

After sending a quick goodnight group message to Shepard and Cross, I settled into bed and hoped the protests would end soon.

SOMETHING TOUCHED MY CHEEK, waking me. "Vena, I will break bones if that's the lime juicer on my face."

"Lime juicer?" Cross asked.

I opened my eyes to see his confused expression.

"When did you get home?"

"A couple of hours ago. Anchor took Vena to one of the guest rooms so you could sleep peacefully. She seemed extra clingy with you. So, about this lime juicer."

I shook my head and wrapped my arms around his waist. "We do not speak of the juicer. Did the protesters finally leave?"

"No. They're still there, and their numbers are growing, especially after Orphia released that second video."

"Any leads on where she could be?"

He shook his head. "Not yet. But not for a lack of trying. Hugh has been a great help coordinating with the human authorities about the protests and working with Shepard to protect his people as they continue to search for nests. Vena already scried this morning and sent the new locations to Shepard."

"How many new locations were there?"

"A few."

"Did Shepard warn his people to watch for cameras?"

"He did. The girl's parents have joined the protesters and are demanding the wolf who killed their daughter be charged with murder."

My heart ached for Shepard, and Cross saw it. He hugged me close and kissed my forehead.

"He's not dealing with this alone," Cross said. "He knows we're both with him."

I tipped my head back to meet Cross' gaze. "I love you, Cross, and I want the world to know vampires aren't all evil murderers. That they can be caring and generous and protective, too."

His eyes grew darker with each word I said until the veins around his eyes spread to his cheeks. I brushed my fingers over them.

"Does it hurt when they do this?"

"No."

"Are you going to wait until after I brush my teeth to kiss me?"

"I don't want to, but I know how you feel about it." He lifted his arm. "You have thirty seconds, Everly. You better run."

With a laugh, I bolted from the bed. I had a mouthful of toothpaste foam when he suddenly appeared behind me and wrapped his arms around my waist. His eyes were just as dark.

"Wait," I said, hurrying to turn on the faucet. He gave me another few seconds to rinse and swish. Then he spun me around and set his forehead against mine.

"Say it again."

"I love you, Cross."

He groaned and cupped my face between his hands without lifting his head.

"I know I'm not the only one in your heart," he said. "And I'm okay with that. I am yours forever, Everly. However you want me in your life, you only need to say the word. But I want to be selfish just once. I want all of you. Please."

I tipped my head up to brush my lips against his.

"I'm yours. I've been yours since the first time you saved me. I just wasn't sure what I felt for you was real. Now I am."

He made a feral sound, and a second later, I was back in the bedroom and pressed into the mattress as he kissed me hungrily. When he pulled back to look at me, his eyes were pure black, and his fangs were showing.

"Say it again," he rasped.

Despite his eyes, I could see his uncertainty.

I cupped his face and leaned up to kiss the edge of the dark veining on one side and then the other.

"I see all of you, Cross, and it doesn't change how I feel about you or about us. What do you need from me right now?"

He groaned and dropped his head to my neck, where he marked me with a kiss. His teeth scraped me lightly, telling me what he needed without words.

CHAPTER SIX

THREADING MY FINGERS THROUGH CROSS' HAIR, I BASKED IN THE sensation of his mouth on my skin. His hot exhales warmed it. His teeth teased it.

I loved it but needed more, and he seemed to sense that. The gentle suction of his mouth as he left another mark on my skin fed that need, and I wrapped my legs around his waist. But it wasn't enough. I wanted what he wanted. I wanted to feel all of him…to give him everything. And I arched my neck to give him better access, openly inviting him.

He groaned and pulled back enough to look down at me. The skin around his eyes was so webbed with dark veins that very little of his paleness remained.

We were both breathing heavily. I could see his need for me but also his fear.

"When you said all of me, you didn't just mean sex, right? You're going to feed too?"

"Only if you allow it."

"Allow? I think I crave it more than you do."

"I doubt that," he said, his eyes completely black.

"Show me what it means to belong to you, Cross. Take all of me."

He made a pained sound before kissing my mouth hungrily.

"You are my everything, Everly. I didn't know I could love someone as much as I do with you."

He kissed my chin…my neck…my collarbone. Lips, tongue, and a little scrape of teeth each time. As he trailed kisses, his hands slid under my shirt, caressing the skin he revealed inch by inch until he dipped his head and kissed my stomach.

My breathing grew more ragged in anticipation of what he'd do next. When he moved farther down, slowly revealing more skin along the way, I cried out as he kissed me *there.*

I lost all sense of time, floating in a sea of passion as the pleasure he gave climbed higher. Abruptly, his mouth left me. His warmth settled over me.

"Look at me, Everly."

I did. His beautiful black gaze held mine as he kissed the back of my hands and then caged them over my head. His free hand slid down my side and hooked the back of my thigh, lifting it as he pressed against my entrance.

"I'm yours. Forever," he said, entering me slowly and watching my reaction to his sweet invasion.

My mouth opened with a silent cry when his hips snapped forward the last inch. He kissed me briefly, then set a steady rhythm, bringing me closer to the release I now needed.

The connection I had with him as he held my gaze was more than sex. He was loving me in every way he knew how, and it was unraveling me as much as his sure touch.

When I was close to breaking, he rasped, "Tell me I can still have everything."

"Taste me, Cross," I said, turning my head.

He growled, and his mouth closed over my neck. Teeth pierced the thin skin. A flash of pain and then there was more pleasure than I'd ever known in my life as he sucked at the small wounds.

I toppled over the precipice with a cry, clenching around him uncontrollably. He sucked harder. My climax felt never-ending until he withdrew suddenly with a grunt. He caged me in his arms, and I felt his release wash over my stomach.

His tongue stroked over my skin, sealing the small wounds, then he set his forehead against mine as we both caught our breaths.

"Tell me that won't be the last time we do that," I said, panting.

"It won't. There is nothing I wouldn't do for you. However, Shepard may have an opinion on the frequency at which you request I sample you."

It didn't feel wrong talking about Shepard just then. It felt right. Inclusive of his thoughts and feelings.

"You might be right." I sighed.

Cross chuckled as he lifted himself off of me and kissed the tip of my nose.

"Don't move."

He left for a cloth to clean me; then, he swept me off the bed and carried me to the shower he'd started. Rather than leaving me there, he joined me, washing my hair.

"I asked Vena and Anchor to pick up a few books I put on hold at the market," he said as I leaned on him so he could massage my scalp. "They should be here soon."

"Should we be co-ed showering then?"

"I think Vena would approve."

Snorting at how Vena would react, I took over rinsing and conditioning my hair, and we finished in record time. Cross dried and dressed at supernatural speed—the cheater—and went to open the door for their arrival while I finished getting ready at my human pace.

When I finally emerged, Vena and Anchor were already there.

Vena sat at the table, going through the books with Cross. Anchor leaned against the kitchen island, watching them.

"Cross, you amaze me sometimes," she said, sounding like she meant it.

"Just sometimes?" he asked.

"How did you find these, and I didn't?"

He smiled. "A secret."

"I know what the secret is. It's money."

"It does help," he acknowledged.

I glanced at the books and didn't recognize the languages on the covers. Rather than fawning over books I couldn't read, I headed toward the kitchen.

"What does everyone want? I'm feeling up to being a short-order cook, so whatever you want."

"An omelette with some leftover French toast casserole?" Vena asked. "Oh, and bacon."

I looked at Anchor. "What about you?"

"The same would be more than fine."

"Cross?" I asked.

"I already had a bite this morning."

I felt the flush as it heated my skin. Thankfully, the books occupied Vena too much for her to notice. Anchor did, though, and I wondered if his overly sensitive nose had already picked up my morning activities. Not that I cared when it had been so perfect.

Taking the casserole and other ingredients I needed from the refrigerator, I set to work.

As I was plating everything, my phone dinged.

"Group text from Miles," Vena said. "They are on their way to the mountain."

"Tell them to stay safe and give us lots of updates." I carried two plates over for Vena and Anchor, who had joined her at the table.

"Too bad I couldn't go," Vena said. "I still haven't seen inside the mountain yet. What's it like?"

"Lots of stairs," I answered, retrieving my plate and sitting beside Cross.

"That's all you give me? Stairs?"

"Lots of precious metals and gemstones too."

Vena sighed. "I need more. How about a road trip and meet them there?"

I shook my head. "This is Miles' apology visit. Fewer people will be better."

"But King Curran doesn't blame Miles."

"Correct. But it doesn't change the fact that he has to see his son's murderer, whether innocent or not. Let Miles do his thing. He can apologize and research without having to worry about you."

"You say it like I'd get into trouble."

I eyed her. So did the two men at the table.

Vena looked at us and sighed. "Fine. I won't go to the mountain."

We both knew she would go someday soon, though. Vena was tenacious like that.

After I cleaned up breakfast, I toyed with a few experimental recipes for Bites and Delights. Since Vena was there, we also discussed making the business' name official and what kind of signage we wanted out front.

While Vena and Anchor went downstairs to visualize the book and decor placement, Cross worked on the business management side of things, and I baked. It felt surreal but in the most amazing way. We all had our strengths and leaned into them to benefit each other.

Barely an hour later, Vena came barreling up the stairs.

"Check this out," she said, shoving her phone at me.

A video of a press conference was playing. A lady I didn't know stood at a podium.

"The Department of Otherworld Security is responsible for the peaceful coexistence between otherworlder races and humans," the lady said. "Since many races have abilities we humans cannot match, the DOS has, in the past, asked for assistance from a few of the otherworld races, such as the fae, werewolves, and dwarves. This includes the detection and removal of an increasing vampire threat.

"The DOS is aware of the misinformation being disseminated regarding the conversions of humans into vampires. The process is not simple and only has a five to ten percent survival rate. The recent discovery of failed conversion dumping grounds has necessitated DOS action. To protect our citizens, the DOS recruited assistance from our local werewolves to help find and eliminate the increasing vampire population.

"If you or a loved one were converted without permission, please contact the DOS, and the newly converted will be provided amnesty from the vampire cleanse efforts."

She looked up from her speech and added, "We're here to protect the innocent in all forms. But newly converted vampires are dangerous. If a loved one has been converted, they may not be the same person you remember. Do not engage, and call for help immediately."

The video ended as reporters started calling out questions.

"Did you see him?" Vena asked.

"See who?"

She restarted the video and pointed to Hugh and Shepard standing off to the side with several other people. Shepard looked exhausted.

I sent him a message to come home soon. His reply was almost immediate.

Shepard: I will. Tell Cross he gets the night shift tonight and I get you.

"No fair," Vena said, reading over my shoulder. "If I can't have any, you can't either."

"Too late," I said.

Her eyes went wide, and she looked from me to Cross, who flashed his lazy, sexy smile at her.

"Seriously?" she asked, her gaze still shifting between us. "I'm so jealous I'm not even sure what to do with myself. No, not true. I know what I want to do." She pivoted and made it a step toward the stairs before I grabbed her arm.

"Hold on," I said. "I'm sure Anchor doesn't want to be assaulted in broad daylight."

"It's okay," Anchor yelled from downstairs. "I'm used to it."

"Thanks for having my back, babe!" Vena shouted at the open door before looking at me. "I've been waiting for you, Ev. Now that you've finally committed, I'm ready to do the same. Please don't tell me to wait."

Her imploring expression had me pretending to pout at her.

"Does this mean I won't see you for the next ten days while you break the curse?"

"Hell no. I don't have time for that. I'm dying for some penetration. We're talking twenty-four hours tops."

"Vena."

"And commitment," she added quickly. "I want the commitment."

I snorted, knowing better.

"So what are you going to do then?"

She fished the fae's business card out of her pocket. "Anchor and I are going to get help from the same people who cursed him."

"Asherah said it couldn't be undone," I reminded her. "She should know since she was the one who cursed Anchor."

"Yeah, well, she was at the market this morning, and when I showed her the card, she looked at Anchor, shrugged, and said it would help end the curse faster."

"How?"

"Don't know. She was pretty closed-mouth about it and her connection with Adriel and Vivian when I asked if she knew where Vivian was. I got the feeling she didn't know and wasn't happy about what they did to her, though."

I thought back to the video of Adriel, Vivian, and Asherah and shuddered lightly.

"Yeah, what they were doing to Asherah didn't look consensual."

She tapped the card. "I'm going to call."

I'd prefer she didn't, but with her out-of-control hormones, I didn't think she could wait much longer, either.

"Put it on speaker," I said.

Vena dialed the number. It barely rang before a woman answered. "What do you desire?"

"To break a curse. Someone at Enticed gave me your card, and they said you could help."

"What kind of curse is it?"

"My boyfriend's happy hammer is out of commission. It's supposed to take a thousand attempts to get it working again. We've made over two hundred attempts so far, and I'm about to break him."

"Dreadful curse," the woman said sympathetically. "To not be able to fulfill your desires and cravings. I can only shudder at the thought."

"So, can you help?"

"Of course."

"How much will it cost?"

"Free."

Vena and I shared a look.

"Why is it free?" Vena asked.

"I don't need money. I'm rich enough for several lifetimes. Since I'm assuming it was one of my kind who committed the atrocity, I'm happy to lend a hand. When can you come?"

Vena smirked. "Anytime."

"Good. And your name?"

"Vena."

"A beautiful name. I'll text you the address. We can fix this problem right away."

Vena thanked her and hung up. "Did you hear that, babe? Your water gun is going to squirt again. Let's go."

I cringed but still said, "I'm going with."

"Okay, but why? I thought you wanted to bake."

"I do, but you remember what happened at Enticed, right? A little fae energy and you were on the table and I'm scarred for life. What if there are other people around? You need a censor."

She tried to wave off my concern, but Cross agreed they shouldn't go alone.

"Vivian is still out there," Cross said. "And Anchor will be distracted."

"Then hurry up. My man's muff missile is overdue for a visit to Pound Town."

"Give me a minute." I hurried to the master bedroom and pulled a cute tote bag from one of the closet shelves, silently thanking Cross' personal shopper for the forethought. I grabbed an empty spray bottle from my vanity, added water, and stuck it in my bag.

Payback, Vena.

We piled into the red SUV, and Cross drove to the address the guy had texted Vena. I made Anchor sit up front with Cross because I didn't trust Vena and Anchor in the back seat together.

"This is going to be great," Vena said when we were on the road. "Anchor, what position should we try first once we're home?"

I glanced at Anchor and saw he was looking out the window, his face flushed.

"Vena, stop teasing him."

"I'm not. This is a monumental occasion. I've been waiting for years."

"Days," I corrected.

"Feels like years. And I can't just lay there in missionary and take it."

Cross choked on air, and Vena twisted in her seat to look at me.

"I should get Mom's book."

"No. Do not pull out the Joy of Sex again."

"It's a family treasure, Everly. My grandma passed it down to my mom. Technically, I would just be collecting my inheritance."

"You don't need it," I said.

"But I need inspiration. What about the snake charmer position? Or the backward swan dive?"

"You're making those up," I said.

She shrugged. "Inspiration comes from many different places."

"How about quietly in your head?"

She made a face at me but stopped talking.

Just outside the city, we started passing through the neighborhoods with massive homes built for the rich, mainly fae. Cross stopped at one with a gate and pressed the call button.

"What do you desire?" a feminine voice asked.

"Vena is here," Cross said. "She is expected."

The gate rolled open, and Cross drove up the hand-laid brick driveway to a sprawling three-story home with a large portico lifted high by Grecian columns.

A fae stood by the door, waiting for us as we parked. She wore a flowy, opaque gown that clung to her unfettered curves.

"Welcome, friends," she said when we made our way over to her. "Which of you is the afflicted?"

"We are," Vena said, taking Anchor's hand.

"I am truly sorry for all that you've suffered. Desires aren't meant to be suppressed. Come in." Her gaze shifted to me as I stood beside Cross. "And you are?"

"Their friends. We're here for emotional support."

"Excellent. Recovering from this curse will not be easy for either of them. They will likely need your help throughout the process."

She led the way inside. Our footsteps echoed in the huge foyer, and I tipped my head back to look at the painted ceilings depicting debauchery that rivaled Grecian Art.

Cross' fingers twined through mine, the only thing that kept me moving forward as I stared at everything.

"I've prepared this room for you," the fae said.

I returned my attention to where we were and saw her open the door to a lushly appointed room with leather lounges rather than sofas or chairs.

"Come in. Make yourselves comfortable. Tell me more about the curse and the person who cast it."

While Vena explained, I looked around the room. Books and pretty objects I couldn't identify filled the shelves. Most of the items looked like they were from another world. On a pedestal near the front of the room sat a shiny blue globe.

"You've done well on your own," the fae said. "It will go much faster now that you're here. Give over to what you desire."

I felt a pulse of something hit me, igniting an instant need inside of me. The heat receded as my necklace thrummed, and a cooling wave washed over me. However, the heat didn't entirely disappear.

Cross' thumb stroked over mine.

As I turned to look at him, thoughts of how he'd made me feel this morning swam through my head, and I saw the responding hunger in his gaze.

"Very good," I heard the fae say. "Yes. Excellent. I know it's still soft, my pet, but the attempt counts. Now, off your knees.

Although your mouth is lovely, you will tire yourself too quickly like that. Switching positions means a new attempt."

My cheeks slowly heated as I realized the help my friends were getting. Another pulse hit me, heating me again. I watched the darkness flicker to life in Cross' eyes, and the effect from my necklace wasn't enough to stop me from thinking of being on my knees for *him*.

He groaned. "You're tempting me, Everly."

"I know, my pet," the fae said. "It's frustrating when it won't go in. Try a new position."

Another pulse hit me, followed by a protective wave that didn't touch the growing fire inside me. The veined webbing started around Cross' eyes, and his fangs made an appearance before he turned away from me.

When the next pulse hit, I saw something moving inside the globe.

"What is that?" I asked. My voice sounded breathy and a little whiny.

The fae woman walked so silently over the tiled floor that her sudden appearance beside me should have startled me, but it didn't. The need I had for Cross was starting to overshadow everything.

"It's a relic leftover from my world," the fae woman said. "It amplifies a fae's natural ability so even creatures such as were-wolves and vampires can feel us. Without it, your friends would have to suffer the curse even longer."

"You don't know Vena," I managed. "She is very driven."

"I believe she's not the only one. If you need a separate room for a time, you may use the one beside this one."

I opened my mouth to tell her that wasn't necessary but found myself tossed over Cross' shoulder.

With his hand planted firmly on my ass, he moved us to the other room before I could protest. The second he righted me, his mouth was on mine.

CHAPTER SEVEN

TIME HAD NO MEANING. ONLY CROSS' TOUCH DID. MY MIND WAS in a haze that only sought pleasure. Even after Cross had satiated my need for him, I desired more.

Desired.

The fae had kept using that word.

"I think I've orgasmed five times already," I said breathlessly. "Why do I need more?"

Cross' eyes maintained their inky blackness even as he pushed away.

"I love your eyes," I said.

"I love everything about you," he said.

"Then come back here. I need you."

He shook his head as if to clear it, and his eyes slowly returned to normal with only a flicker of black. I whined and held out my arm for him to rejoin me on the lounge.

"We've been here far too long," Cross said. "I think the relic's power is finally wearing off. We should go while we can."

"One more orgasm."

"You'll have plenty of them in the future, I promise. Let's check on Vena and Anchor and leave."

Hearing Vena's name and the resulting concern I felt made some of the haze disappear.

Cross dressed, then helped me to do the same. My limbs were too shaky to work properly. He held my hand and led me to the door. Opening it, he looked out and motioned for me to follow him.

We hurried toward Vena and Anchor's room, but he hesitated when we reached it.

"What's wrong?" I asked.

"I can feel the globe's sensual magic through the door. It's not nearly as potent as it was, but I would rather get you home before I succumb to its power again. Stay here, all right?"

Exhausted, dehydrated, and completely drunk on multiple orgasms, I nodded and sagged against the wall.

He was reaching for the door when a series of grunts and groans sounded, followed by a cry. It wasn't one of pleasure. It was pure frustration coming from Vena.

Cross knocked on the door and then inched it open. "I'm coming in."

"I wish Anchor could come. In me," Vena whined.

After an aggrieved sigh, Cross slipped inside. Vena would owe him big time after this. I would make sure of it.

I heard Cross say, "Get moving." A bit of shuffling and another whine followed it.

"I am moving," Vena said.

"Not against him," Cross said.

More shuffling and another whine, but soon enough, Vena and Anchor stumbled out, looking like they barely survived a battle. Vena's hair was sticking every which way, and Anchor looked dazed.

"Only 435 times to go," she mumbled. "At least, I think. I might have lost count."

After watching my friend stumble like she was drunk, I

grabbed her arm, and we leaned on each other as we made our way outside.

"What time is it?" she asked. "Or should I say day?"

I glanced at my phone. "It's nearly dinner time. We've missed lunch."

It hadn't felt like we were in there so long, but then again, being under the fae's influence was like a drug. I'd lost track of time and even reason beyond a physical need.

"I'll let you and Anchor sit in the backseat together if you promise not to maul each other."

"Too tired," Vena said, climbing. "And thirsty."

"We need a drive-through for water," I said as Cross helped me into the passenger seat.

"No. I need sugar, too," Vena said. "Get me the biggest soda out there. Maybe two for Anchor. I worked him hard."

"I'll get both for everyone," Cross said, getting in behind the steering wheel.

No one else talked until after we had our drinks. I looked at Cross, worried because he hadn't ordered anything for himself. Not that soda or water was his drink of choice. I touched my neck where he'd left more than a few love marks but no additional bites and shivered lightly at the remembered feel of his lips there. Although the fae's influence was gone, my desire for him remained. Definitely not as urgent, but still…

He reached over and set his hand on mine.

"Are you all right?" he asked softly.

"I am. Are you? Do you need to stop somewhere? Or do you…" I blushed, unable to finish the offer.

His eyes flickered black.

"Shepard might forgive once, but I don't believe he'd forgive a second time."

I studied Cross' profile and wondered if Shepard would give Cross a hard time for the first bite. Turning my hand, I held

Cross' and didn't comment. Rather than speculate how Shepard would react, I wanted to focus on the moment.

As soon as we arrived, Anchor helped Vena out of the SUV and into their car with a promise that he'd have her call me first thing in the morning.

He waved goodbye, and I followed Cross inside. No one was working on the first floor, and everything in the kitchen looked set up when I glanced through the door.

"We need to decide on a supplier," I said tiredly.

"But not today. Come on. Let me feed you before I put you to bed."

The way he said it started all sorts of yummy thoughts. He seemed to know, too, because he suddenly picked me up and darted to the second floor with me.

"Behave, Everly," he said tenderly. "I'm still hungry for you, and it would take very little to break my fragile control."

I considered him. "I like seeing you lose control, though."

He groaned, kissed my forehead, and led me to a stool. "Sit. I'll cook for you. How does a BLT sound?"

"Phenomenal."

I watched him move around the kitchen, enjoying the simplicity of our time together. When it was time to eat, he playfully fed me.

Outside, the light started to fade.

"I'm starting to worry about Shepard," I said.

Cross had his phone out and sent a text before I could stop him. When it buzzed, he chuckled and pocketed it.

"I promise he won't let another night pass without you."

"What did you say to him?"

"That he was starting to worry you, and if he wanted to keep his claim on you, he needed to rectify the situation."

"That's not fair, Cross. He's putting out fires Orphia is setting, not playing out there."

Cross shrugged. "His priority is you, not the pack. He shouldn't need a reminder."

"Since you're not being nice, I'm going to shower and go to bed early. You can come help me."

"That doesn't sound like a punishment if it's meant to be."

"We'll see."

I teased Cross the entire time I showered, telling him he could look but couldn't touch. He loved every second of it and couldn't take his eyes off me. And I adored the appreciation and joy in his gaze and his relaxed smile as he helped me brush and blow dry my hair.

When I closed my eyes, I was in his arms.

But when I opened them again the next morning, I was in Shepard's.

He was sound asleep beside me. The room was dark, but I could tell from his soft, steady breaths.

As tempted as I was to check the time, I stayed where I was, comfortably in the little spoon position, and dozed for a while longer. I knew exactly when he woke up because his arms tightened around me.

"Good morning," I said softly.

"Good morning." He nuzzled my neck, kissing me right where Cross had bitten me. "Did he hurt you?"

"No." I hesitated a moment. "I liked it. Are you mad?"

"No. As long as you're okay, I'm okay." He sounded completely relieved and accepting.

"I've missed you."

"I missed you too. I'd rather stay with you like this and let the rest of the world deal with its own stupidity, but Cross reminded me you have your heart set on opening a bakery, and that can't happen if Orphia and her vampires take over." He exhaled heavily. "He's an ass when he's right and knows it."

Laughing, I turned in Shepard's arms.

"How long do I get your company today?"

"If I'm lucky, the whole day. Cross and Doc are taking the lead."

"And what would you like to do today?"

"Spend time with you. Just the two of us if we can get away with it."

"I'll do my best to accommodate that," I said, tipping my head to kiss his chin. "Any chance you know how to open the window to let a little light in?"

I felt him roll away, and a second later, the window shades opened enough that I could see Shepard standing beside the bed in nothing but a snug pair of underwear, like a model. What he wore wasn't fancy but showed off his muscular backside and a nice package in the front.

When I stood, he hugged me to him and breathed deeply.

"Are you okay?" I asked, running my hands up and down his back.

"I'm always okay when I'm with you."

We stayed in the locked embrace for a few moments until he finally pulled away. He still looked tired.

"Why don't you sleep some more?" I suggested.

"I'll sleep for a few more minutes while you get ready, but I'll be fine. Don't worry about me."

I hugged him again and headed to the bathroom to get ready. When I emerged dressed for the day and my hair pulled into a ponytail, I found the bed made and the bedroom empty.

Leaving, I found Shepard in the living room, which had changed slightly. Someone had rearranged the furniture, and we now had a television.

Shepard held the remote in his hand and was watching breaking news.

"What's going on?" I asked.

"Another fae was brutally murdered. The method of killing was the same as the first one. They're thinking it's a serial killer."

Another? Then I remembered Cross had been reading an

article about the death and one of the fae servers at Enticed had mentioned it.

Shepard turned off the television and put down the remote. After everything he had to deal with because of Orphia's videos, I didn't blame him for turning off more negative media.

"Since you're up, what do you want for breakfast?"

He followed me to the kitchen and sat at the island. "Whatever you are making is fine."

"How hungry are you?"

"Very."

I decided on something filling and delicious, and Shepard watched me pull out the ingredients.

"Cross mentioned, without going into detail, what happened at the fae's house. I didn't have a chance to talk to Anchor since he and Vena went straight to bed when they got home. They looked a little rough. Are you all right?"

"Rough might not be the right word. Used is probably better, but not in a bad way. I've never felt anything like that before. I know what the usual draw of a fae feels like from working at Blur, but this was different. It was intense, and I felt drugged even with my necklace fighting it. Like being in a fog and unable to feel complete. It's hard to describe."

He nodded. "That's what Cross said, too, which isn't something otherworlders typically feel when around fae. Those older fae relics were made in their realm where they can access their full power and can be dangerous. I've already spoken to Effora about ensuring it isn't used again."

"What did she say?"

I caught his disgruntled eye roll and knew the answer. Effora evaded like she always did.

"She's been calling several times a day but never to help or answer questions."

I reached over and rubbed his arm for a second. He captured my hand, gave it a grateful squeeze, then let go.

"What are you making?" he asked.

"Eggs Benedict. Does it sound good?"

"Wonderful. Can I help?"

I shook my head. "I've made it enough times that it doesn't take me long. But if you really want to help, I'll tell you when to toast the English muffins."

"Deal."

His phone rang, and he groaned when he looked at the screen. "It's Effora."

He tapped the speaker button and placed the phone on the table.

"Hello, Effora. If this is about your scheme for the sexapoloosa you keep trying to get me to come to, I'm not interested."

"You know how to wound me, Shepard. But this is actually about the information you need."

"What kind of information?" he asked.

"Would you be interested in what kind of underwear I'm wearing?"

"Effora, I'm two seconds from hanging up."

She laughed. "It was a trick question. I'm not wearing any."

"Goodbye." He was about to press the end call button when Effora said, "I know Orphia's location."

"Where is she?"

"I'm happy to tell you, darling. But over lunch."

He looked liked he wanted to reach through the phone and strangle her.

"Effora, we don't have time for your games. Humans are dying. So are your people, according to the news."

"And I need lunch. I'm not asking for much. And lunch is a few scant hours away. We can even meet at a neutral location."

Shepard pinched the bridge of his nose. With a sigh, he let his hand drop. "Where?"

"You know that charming restaurant where we had the little meeting with Hugh?"

"Yes."

"I'll have a private room booked. We can discuss everything there. Let's say noon?"

"Fine."

He hung up, shoved his phone an arm's length away, and focused on me. Although he smiled, I could see the frustration he was hiding.

"I can see she's getting to you."

"I hate that she found a way to pull me away from you."

"How about I tag along to the meeting and keep you company?"

"You're willing to do that?"

"Of course."

He stood and came around the island to hug me from behind as I used the pot filler faucet.

"You smell so good," he said, kissing the top of my head.

"Even with Cross' scent on me?" I wanted to slap myself for actually saying that out loud. They were getting along, and I didn't want that to stop.

Shepard chuckled and ducked in to kiss the side of my neck where Cross had bitten me.

"Yes. Even with his scent on you. It's part of you now. He's part of you."

I glanced back at Shepard.

"Are you mad?"

"No. I accepted Cross as a part of our lives a long time ago. As long as he doesn't do anything to hurt you, which I know he never will intentionally, then I'm willing to share. Whatever it takes to be a part of your life."

I nodded and started cooking. Shepard stayed close, watching me and finding ways to be helpful until I had a plate of food ready for us both.

We sat at the island and ate together, chatting companionably, then cleaned up. The morning's peace wrapped around me like a comforting blanket, and I never wanted to leave it.

Unfortunately, my life never seemed to be peaceful for long.

Shepard and I were on the couch, watching a talk show together, when his phone rang again. Vena's name flashed on the screen, and with a sigh, Shepard answered on speaker.

"Hey, King Alpha, Lord of the Otherworld."

"Just Shepard, Vena."

"That's not nearly as prestigious."

"I think it is," I said.

"Hey, sister from another mister. Did you climb Mount Shepard this morning?"

"You're a little extra spicy already, considering how you were yesterday."

"Yesterday was insane, but a good night's sleep worked wonders. Not on the undercarriage, though. That's going to need some time. Which is why I'm calling."

Sometimes, the line of Vena's thinking scared me.

"I needed a distraction and scried," she continued. "The crystal found a bigger nest again."

"How do you know it's bigger?" I asked.

"I'm going to take the higher road and not fall victim to your setup there. It's the vibrations of the crystal. The more it vibrates, the bigger it is. I have to go. This conversation is giving me the tingles, and it's still uncomfortable down there. Love you both!"

The line went dead, and Shepard looked at me.

"I already told Cross...I think Miles tested malfunctioning charms on her as a baby."

Shepard chuckled and shook his head. Then he sent a text to Doc and Cross to check in with Vena.

Not long after her call, my phone pinged with a group text from Miles. They hadn't found any information yet, but Curran was helping them acquire more books that might have the information they were looking for.

"That's good news," Shepard said, reading over my shoulder.

"Good news would have been, 'We found the cure to vampirism and know where Orphia is.'" I sighed and rested my head on Shepard's shoulder again. "Or even a text from Effora canceling her lunch invitation. What are the chances that she actually knows where Orphia is?"

"Honestly, I'm not sure, which is why I can't ignore her. We know that fae had an agreement with vampires, so perhaps Effora has her own contacts who are willing to reveal where Orphia is."

After glancing at the time on my phone, I stood and held out my hand to Shepard.

"Let's head out a little early then. The sooner we ask our questions, the sooner we can get out of there."

The smile that tugged at his lips as he took my hand warmed me, as did the playful way he tugged me into his lap for a quick kiss.

Fifteen minutes later, as we pulled out of our parking lot, I glimpsed the structure on the roof.

"They're making good progress," Shepard said, noticing my attention. "Cross gave me a tour of the rooftop last night. It's going to be nice once it's done."

"I haven't been up there yet."

"Hopefully, this will go fast, and we can check it out after."

I nodded and sat back to enjoy the ride, hoping whatever information Effora had wouldn't change that plan.

CHAPTER EIGHT

Two men in suits waited by the private entrance to the restaurant, even though it wasn't yet officially open.

"I'm curious," I said as Shepard parked. "How much does renting one of these rooms cost, especially when it's not open?"

"Depends on what's needed. If it's full service for a small group, maybe ten grand."

I cringed, remembering the dinner Cross and I had here, then accepted Shepard's hand as he helped me from the car. His expression was neutral, but I wondered what emotions I'd smell on him if I had his nose. Nerves? Dread? Probably both.

Shepard held my hand as we walked toward the entrance together. One of the men opened the door for us as we approached. Inside, two more suited men waited near a private room to the left. One of them tapped softly on the door before opening it and letting us inside.

Shepard, ever protective, moved to enter the room first but stopped mid-step in the doorway. His body blocked my view, but not the sensual pull I felt. It wasn't as strong as when Cross and I had been near that relic, but it was stronger than being next to a fae at Blur.

A hum of energy spread out from my necklace, protecting me enough to control my desires, but I still felt a teasing edge of it.

"You're just in time for lunch," I heard Effora say, explaining the pull I felt. "Do you like the presentation?"

"No," Shepard said, sounding strangled.

Curious, I peeked around him, and the view had me cringing.

Effora was sitting *on* the table, leaned back on her hands, her heels braced along the edge. The clothing she wore—a whisper of an ouvert bra and a crotchless thong—was sheer, leaving nothing to the imagination. A loose silver chain connected her exposed nipple piercings to a large jeweled belly button ring. The stone in that thing was as big as Shepard's thumbnail, reflecting a rainbow of colors.

An empty plate and bib rested on the table right in the V of her legs.

Unfortunately, I now understood the view my gynecologist had to witness, and I wasn't a fan of it.

I glanced at Shepard and saw the extreme flush he wore as he stared at the ceiling. The man was completely adorable when embarrassed, and I was beginning to understand Vena's obsession with shy men.

"Please put clothes on," he said.

"I'm wearing clothes," Effora said, "and I don't remember inviting a third party."

I shrugged at her, pushed Shepard into the room, and closed the door behind us.

"Where Shepard goes, I go." I took his hand and led him to the head of the table, the farthest away from her display. He pulled out the chair. Before I could sit, he took the seat and pulled me onto his lap, using me like a shield.

When Effora saw her efforts were in vain, she discarded the plate and stood.

"Let's get to the point of this, Effora," Shepard said as he ran a hand up and down my back. "You said you have information on Orphia's location. Where is she?"

Effora's pale blue eyes narrowed briefly, and I felt another way of desire hit me. Then another and another. My necklace thrummed as it worked to suppress the effects of Effora's allure, but she was queen for a reason.

Waves of need pulled at me. I angled myself into Shepard and tucked my face against his shoulder. Whether to hide from Effora or breathe him in, I couldn't be sure. His hand settled on the back of my head, not trapping or dictating but cradling it. My breath caught, and I tipped my head to kiss his neck. He shivered beneath me.

"Effora, stop what you're doing," Shepard said.

"Why, when I can feel your delicious reaction to her? I think she needs more assistance. Once you're finished with her, you can finish me while she recovers."

Understanding what she was doing, I tried to resist the waves of sensual magic battering at me. Ducking my head against Shepard's chest, I focused on my breathing and his pulse. It was racing, proving he was struggling too. His hands wandered slightly, and he kept pulling them back.

Was it because Shepard affected me or because of Effora's magic? I reached up to touch my necklace, wondering why it wasn't blocking more. Had Asherah oversold its strength to Cross? Humans had taken it from me once before. It wasn't blocking fae allure, and it hadn't blocked Vivian.

"Why isn't my necklace working?" I murmured.

"Oh, it is working. It was simply made by a weaker fae than myself," Effora said.

"How many fae are stronger than Asherah?" I asked, fighting the need to kiss Shepard as my necklace sent a cooling vibration against my skin.

"Fewer than fifty, perhaps. She is one of the most exceptionally gifted in making charms, though. Not as gifted as I am, of course."

"Then you're the traitor," I said. "Why are you helping Orphia?"

The waves of need immediately stopped, and I lifted my head to look at her.

Her gaze narrowed on me. "That is a serious accusation. Explain yourself, and take care of what you say next, human."

Shepard growled as he held me, and I subtly patted his chest.

"I'm wearing a protection necklace made by an exceptionally gifted fae, and yet it did nothing to stop Vivian from attacking me because of the necklace he wore. Meaning he had something more powerful—and by your own admission, you're the most powerful fae in the area."

"I *am* the most powerful of all the fae living in the human realm. And Asherah is *one of* the most powerful fae in the area."

"Are you saying someone else made the necklace for Vivian?"

She lifted one shoulder and sat at the table, dragging a glass of red wine to her.

"I'm tired of your secrets, Effora," Shepard said. "You wanted me to come here to discuss Orphia, but you won't answer even the simplest questions. What are you hiding?"

"I'm not hiding anything." She looked away, which was uncharacteristic of her. And the way she was clutching her wine glass was a little odd.

"I'll let you feed off Shepard if you answer our questions," I said.

Her head whipped around to look at me. The eager glint in her gaze intensified as Shepard held me tighter.

"But I want them *all* answered. No secrets. No holding back."

Effora's gaze remained locked on Shepard, a slow smile curving her lips. She set her glass on the table and leaned back against the chair as if she had no care in the world that her breasts were on display.

"Do you agree with your future mate's offer? Will you allow me to feed?"

"I will," he said.

I'd been lying, which I was sure he knew, and hoped he was doing the same. Yet, as Effora continued to search his gaze, I began to get a little nervous that he was serious. After all, with so many people dying, what was a little sex to stop it?

"All right." She elegantly crossed her ankles. "Ask your questions."

"Tell us the truth about Adriel and Vivian. How do you know them? Are you helping them? What's your relationship with Orphia? Where is she?"

"I have no direct association with Orphia. Her representative approached my mother centuries ago, offering his help in procuring the humans we desired. Back then, times were not as... free as they are now, and humans were more resistant to embracing the pleasure we could offer." Her gaze grew wistful. "Their resistance made the pleasure that much sweeter."

And suddenly, I understood her driving obsession with Shepard.

"Who was the representative?" I asked.

Her gaze shifted to meet mine briefly.

"You've already guessed, haven't you? Adriel.

"Vampires are capricious by nature. Blood dominates their thoughts, and they will betray their own to get it. Adriel was different. Twisted, yes, but he had a measure of loyalty that overrode his bloodlust.

"His loyalty and his desire for his pet endeared him to my mother. She gifted him with his second form. After she left this world, Adriel continued to assist my people until a few weeks ago.

"I've known him most of my life. Played with him a few times. He was entertaining and had unique tastes. But of one thing, I am certain—he hated Orphia. He never spoke of it in detail, but I believe it was because she was the one who converted his pet. He hated the control she had over him.

"When he came to me after Orphia threatened us all at the meeting and asked for a protection necklace, I gave it since I knew he wanted it to protect his lover, not her.

"Other than the necklace, I have not helped Adriel or Vivian."

"And Orphia?" I asked. "Have you helped her?"

"Absolutely not. That woman is a bane to the existence of all Otherworlders."

"How?"

Her gaze flicked between me and Shepard.

"Speak your mind, Effora," he said. "I haven't hidden anything from Everly and see no reason to start."

"I don't *know* anything, but her obsession with obtaining the rings leads me to believe she means to open the portals to my realm. Since her people are why we closed them, her purpose cannot benefit us all."

"In that, we agree," Shepard said, "which is why we need to find her and stop her before she obtains your ring and Cross'. Where is she?"

"Judging from what Adriel said, Vivian is called away often but never for long, which means she's in the States. Nearby. Within a night's drive since Vivian had to see her in person and always managed to return to Adriel the same night."

"She's in the States and nearby?" I questioned. "That's not a location. That's an area."

"I gave more information than just a location. On that, we can agree. I fulfilled my end of the bargain. You will fulfill yours, Shepard."

"Gladly," he said, turning slightly to wrap his arms around me and nuzzle my neck. The desire I had been holding back pushed through my defenses as I threaded my fingers through his hair.

"This was not the deal," Effora protested. She stood and stepped toward us.

"The deal was that you could feed," Shepard said, lifting his head. "I didn't say you could have sex with me."

"You tricked me!" Anger flashed in her eyes.

"Still want to feed, or shall we leave?" he asked, starting to stand with me.

"No. Sit. Just... I need this. At least, take off the necklace."

"She will keep it on," Shepard said. "It's her protection."

"I don't need your fae allure to kiss Shepard. I would do it gladly."

Effora huffed. "I'll take what is offered. But I swear there will be consequences if you trick me again."

Effora breathed deeply, and I felt the wave of desire hit me. I gasped and ran my hands up Shepard's chest.

Beside us, Effora gently pulled on her nipple chain and moaned.

"Focus on me," Shepard said softly before his lips met mine.

He kissed me hungrily, his mouth hard and demanding as his hand drifted from my waist to my hip. Gripping me, he pulled me closer, settling me over his blatantly urgent need. I whimpered into his mouth, moving against him as another wave of magic hit me. His hand moved upward, cupping my breast, kneading it until the nipple pebbled, then pinching it until I cried out in his mouth.

My release, with only that, shocked the hell out of me and left me breathless. While I panted for air, he trailed kisses down my neck. I held onto his head as he nuzzled me and kept my eyes closed. I didn't want to know what Effora was doing. Based on the sounds, though, she was taking care of herself.

Once her low moan filled the room, Shepard cupped my face and kissed the tip of my nose.

"It's time to go, sweetheart."

I opened my eyes and gazed into his golden ones.

"Can you walk?" he asked.

When I nodded, he stood and set me on my feet. Once he

knew I was steady, he kissed my cheek and led me out of the private room without either of us looking directly at Effora, who was once again on the table.

The guards outside the room were missing, and I wondered if they'd joined the ones outside to avoid Effora's allure. Instead of heading in that direction, Shepard tugged me into another private room. He held me close and rested his head against my forehead.

"I need a moment before we leave," he said.

I wrapped my arms around him and hugged him through his steady breaths. He suddenly stilled.

"Are you okay?" I asked.

He placed a finger to my lips and looked at the door. He hadn't closed it tightly behind us. Through the small gap, I heard the indistinct murmur of Effora's voice. Although I couldn't make out the words, I could hear the tone. She was annoyed or angry. Because of Shepard and me or something else?

I waited in silence as Shepard listened to whatever she was saying. Several minutes after her voice faded, he slipped from my hug and took my hand.

"Let's go."

I didn't ask him what he had heard in case other people were around. It wasn't until we were in his SUV and on the road that I asked.

"Effora got a call from Vivian," Shepard explained. "It sounded like he was asking for help to avenge Adriel's death. In return, he'll give her what she needs."

"What does she need?"

"I don't know, but we need to find out. She made it sound like she didn't have any direct contact with Vivian, yet he called her private number."

Shepard made a good point.

"How are you going to find out?" I asked.

"I'll need to follow her."

"Do you think she knew we were in the room? She was pretty annoyed she couldn't have her way with you. Maybe she wanted you to overhear so you would follow her."

"Doubtful. She sounded and smelled angry, not deceitful."

"Then be careful. You'll have to watch your back from not only vampires but the fae as well. Would she betray you to aid Vivian, though? She really wants to have sex with you."

"She is loyal to no one but herself."

"That makes me even more worried for you."

Shepard pressed the phone button on his steering wheel and called Cross.

"How did it go with Effora?" Cross asked when he answered.

"Bad as usual. But she confirmed what we'd already guessed—Orphia is nearby. She also had a conversation with Vivian that I wasn't meant to hear. Can you tail her? I think she's going to meet up with him soon. I need to know why and what he's promising her in return for her help."

"What about Everly?"

"I'll take her home and stay with her. I'll also send out a message with more information for you and Doc. Get the team leaders involved if you have to."

"Understood." Cross disconnected.

When we arrived at Cross' place, a man from the construction crew stopped us to ask about the third floor. Shepard seemed to know what he was asking, so I left it to him and went to the second floor.

I realized I couldn't keep thinking of this as Cross' place. It was our place now. After sleeping with him, I was fully committed. But thinking of it as home didn't sit right either. But why? We'd been through so much together. I didn't doubt him or our relationship. Why was thinking of this place as home such a struggle then?

The answer was simple once I was honest with myself.

I was afraid that because I'd slept with Cross and was starting a business with him, Shepard would feel like he didn't have a place in my life. Which was ridiculous if I thought about it. Shepard and Cross were working together. When I was worried about Shepard, Cross messaged him to hurry home. *They* were acting like a team.

The problem was me. I needed to figure out what I wanted our life together to look like and then have an actual conversation with them about it.

Making a face, I shook my head and went to relax on the couch. Shepard found me in the same spot a few minutes later.

He smiled as he sat next to me. "I have to hand it to Cross...he has great taste."

"It's a comfy couch, isn't it?"

"I meant you."

CHAPTER NINE

I blushed at Shepard's words. Beside me, he chuckled and opened his arms in invitation. I snuggled in, loving being held by him.

"Are you okay with what happened with Effora?" he asked.

"Honestly? Most of it tested my patience and turned my stomach."

"Most of it?"

"She had a plate and bib between her legs, Shepard. That's just crass."

He made a thoughtful sound. "If you'd been on the table, I don't think I would have found it crass."

I snorted.

"What else bothered you?" he asked.

"That she was chummy with Adriel and Vivian. The people in her circle reflect her character."

"True."

"And I hate that she keeps panting after you. Especially right in front of me."

His hand, which had been stroking my back, stilled. "Oh?"

I lifted my head to look at him. "She knows you're mine. You might be fine with sharing me with Cross, but I'm not okay with sharing you, Shepard. Especially not with her."

He growled softly, grabbed me, and flipped us, pinning me underneath him.

"Do you have any idea what it does to me when you show a hint of possessiveness?"

"The gold in your eyes gives me a good idea."

He continued to watch me, and I caught on to what he wanted. Something I was ready to give.

"You're mine, Shepard." I wrapped my legs around his waist and hooked them over his firm ass. "And I acknowledge it's hypocritical for me to be possessive and ask for monogamy when my heart belongs to two people. I'm sorry for that."

"I love you the way you are. I love *you*."

Stroking his cheek, I leaned up and gently kissed him. "I love you, too, Shepard."

"I've waited so long to hear that."

He kissed me tenderly. It melted me and brought back my thoughts from earlier.

He pulled back and studied me. "Your scent just changed. What are you worried about?"

"Worry is a strong word. I'm never going to be able to get away with anything with that nose of yours."

A small smile tugged at his lips, and he kissed me lightly again. "Talk to me."

My stomach did a little flip with nerves.

"You said you can accept Cross in my life. Will that change once we're mated?"

A tremor ran through Shepard's body, and I watched flecks of gold appear in his irises.

"No."

"Okay."

I leaned up and kissed his chin. Then, his Adam's apple. He swallowed hard, and the tremors increased.

"What do you mean by okay?" Even as he asked, I could hear the desperation in his voice.

"Okay, as in, I'm ready, Shepard. I can't imagine my life without you in it."

"Everly, do you know what you're doing?"

I playfully licked the column of his throat. "If you have to ask, I guess I'm not doing a good job convin—"

His kiss was savage in its intensity, and I would have forgotten where we were when he reached for the edge of my shirt if not for the sounds of a nail gun.

Tearing my mouth from his, I caught his hand and said, "Not here."

He lifted me. I saw a blur of color, and then we stood in the master bedroom.

"Will this work?" he asked.

I glanced at the closed door and nodded.

He growled and kissed me hard. His hands shook as he tugged my shirt off over my head roughly. He caught my wince.

"Sorry. I'll try to control myself," he said.

"Don't. I want the wild part of you, Shepard. I love knowing I make you lose control. But there's no rush. I'm not going anywhere. I promise." As I spoke, I reached for his shirt and eased it up his torso.

A shiver ran through him, and he reached for the material. His nails had grown, and he used them to tear his shirt off and tossed it aside.

"If I get too rough, tell me."

"I think I might like it a little rough."

His growl turned into a groan as he shook his head, his golden eyes flickering.

"Everly..."

I gripped the waistband of his jeans. "Why don't you let me help with these so you don't wreck them?"

The rest of his clothes disappeared before I could touch the button, and then his mouth was on mine again, kissing me hungrily as he backed me toward the bed.

He gripped my arms as he slowed our fall onto the mattress, and I could feel his nails. But he was careful as the heat of his body settled over mine. He wasn't rough. He was perfect. Each touch. Each kiss. He stoked my need for him until I was begging to feel him inside of me. And when he finally entered me in one slow stroke, I moaned his name.

I looked up at him, meeting his golden gaze and felt…different. Connected in a way I'd never felt with him before. Then, he started to move.

He unmade me with his thorough love and showed me how I would never be able to live my life without him. As I found my release, his canines scraped the place Cross had bitten me, intensifying my pleasure. He didn't break the skin, though. His rhythm increased until he suddenly withdrew and found his release on my stomach.

Heart racing, I attempted to catch my breath and rein in my confusion as he rained kisses all over my face.

Leaning on his forearms, he captured my face.

"Forever, Everly," he said. "It means we have time. And, as you said, there's no rush. I know you want to finish school and open the bakery. Although I'm desperate to see you carrying our child, I won't put my wants before yours. When you're ready, I'm ready."

"Thank you," I murmured, lifting my lips to catch his.

He stayed with me until we both breathed normally. Then he picked me up and carried me to the shower. We washed each other and talked about little things until his stomach growled aggressively.

"Ready for food?" I asked.

"Can I choose what to eat?"

The flash of gold in his eyes had me shaking my head.

"I think I better choose. How does a sandwich sound?"

He helped me dry and followed me to the kitchen once we were dressed. Then he sat at the island as I pulled out ingredients.

"Don't think I'm ignoring you. I promised to send out texts, but you distracted me." He winked at me, which did things to my pulse.

"I'm so sorry I distracted you. I'll make sure not to do it again."

He let out a soft growl, and I laughed.

"In all seriousness, Shepard, I know you have a lot on your plate. I'm not going to be upset if you need to work. I'm proud you care so much about your pack and other races."

A soft smile played on his lips. "Thank you."

"Get to work. I'll have food ready soon."

Cross returned home just as I finished making our late lunch. He sat down at the table with us.

"Did Effora meet with Vivian?" Shepard asked.

"Not yet, but I have people watching her. They'll report any movement."

"Thank you."

"Not a problem." Cross leaned over and kissed me on the cheek. "Anything new?"

Before I could answer him, my phone rang. "It's Vena."

I answered it on speaker so I could keep eating.

"How can you be so calm, Ev?" Vena demanded after my hello. "We need to do something. Now."

"What happened?" I braced for news of another Orphia video or a new protest.

"Are you serious right now? Don't you watch the news? The producers are thinking of canceling *The Other House* because of the protests. Despite the DOS's announcement that the were-wolves are helping, the network doesn't want to promote contro-versial content. Can you believe that shit?"

I let out a relieved breath. While I'd hate for our favorite show to get canceled, worse things could happen.

"It's all because of Orphia and her hate videos. The show will be pulled if public opinion on wolves doesn't change. What are we going to do, Ev?"

"We? I don't think *we* can do anything."

"Is Shepard with you?"

"I'm here," Shepard said between bites.

"This is a dire situation. I need your full attention and cooperation."

"I'm listening."

"You'll need a multifaceted approach to rebuilding the werewolf public image—from media exposure to grassroots canvasing—and it all needs to be done swiftly."

"While I think Vena is going overboard—" Cross started.

"It's not going overboard to save something you love."

"—I do think she has a point. On my way home, I saw groups of protesters outside more businesses, and I heard there was trouble at the Shadow Trade market. The mood is turning. People are embracing the fear Orphia was instigating in her videos. Public opinion is swinging."

"Swinging like an ax," Vena added. "So, what are we going to do about it?"

Shepard looked thoughtfully at his half-eaten sandwich. It had to be hard to know that people who didn't even know him hated him and his pack. People who didn't know how much he did and sacrificed for their safety.

I placed my hand over his. "I can do the cookie class for werewolf mates. It's not much to tip the scales, and it'd only be for a few people, but the kitchen is operational."

"Orphia's vileness is spreading past D.C.," Vena said. "We're talking national and worldwide. A dozen women making cookies for wolves isn't enough."

"It has merit to be more, though," Cross said. "If it gets media attention."

"I'll call Hugh and see if he has any ideas," Shepard said.

"Good," Vena said. "Call him now."

"Vena, let Shepard finish his lunch first," I said.

"Wolves eat fast. I've seen Anchor. Timed it even. Two double cheeseburgers gone in four bites. Makes you think about them eating other things, right? Like things downsta—"

"Bye, Vena." I ended the call.

Shepard shoveled in the rest of his meal and stepped away to make a call. Rather than listening to a one-sided conversation, I asked Cross to give me a play-by-play.

"Hugh was about to call Shepard," Cross said quietly. "He agrees something needs to be done before public opinion sways too far. It will be hard to regain the trust once it's gone, and the humans need the wolves."

"True," I said.

"He's proposing to do a spotlight to show how coexistence is possible, using me and Shepard as an example."

"Really? That's good for Shepard and the werewolves, but what about you? Publicly declaring yourself as a vampire when your kind is still living in the shadows is kind of scary. For every person who believes werewolves are a threat, more will see you as a bigger threat. You'll be putting a target on your back for every vampire hunter out there."

Cross' slow smile didn't amuse me, but my annoyance amused him. He pulled me into his arms and kissed my cheek.

"Everly, your concern is precious to me, as is your answer, even when I don't take it seriously. Since I woke up to this endless life, no one has cared about me as much as you do. Thank you."

I huffed a sigh. "You make it really difficult to stay mad at you when you say sweet things like that."

He chuckled and kissed my nose.

"Actually, I'm very surprised you know vampire hunters exist."

"Pfft. Before I crash-landed into your cave, I thought vampires were more mythical than real. That didn't stop certain hunters from chasing them as obsessively as Vena chases treasure. We met a few in passing through her connections. I thought they were crazy."

"Like Vena," Cross murmured.

I poked his side lightly.

"For believing in something that regular people didn't know was real," I clarified. "But now everyone knows, thanks to Orphia's videos. Those vampire hunters will look to fulfill their life's ambitions.

"I don't mind that Orphia put her face out there, but I don't like the idea of you doing the same. How will people differentiate between a good vampire and a bad one?"

"We'll find out. Sounds like Hugh wants us to go to the studio tomorrow."

Shepard hung up and turned toward us.

"You make a good point," he said, proving he'd also been listening to our conversation too. Or at least partially. "And I think that should be the point of tomorrow's segment—how I figured out Cross wasn't bad."

"Can you do that without Cross showing his face? You know he needs anonymity to stay safe."

Shepard smiled slightly as his gaze swept over me in Cross' arms.

"He does, but not for his safety. For yours. Since you're staying here with Cross, I won't risk protesters showing up at his door."

"That's unlikely to happen," Cross said. "I've already sold the business to Vena. Everything is legally in her name."

"You what?" I demanded, pulling back from him.

He quickly kissed my forehead and released me. "Let me explain. I would have rather put it in your name, but she and I agreed it was better to put it in hers so nothing could be traced back to you if my involvement in the business is discovered."

I wanted to say she'd only done it for the money, but I knew better. When it came to her love for me and her love for money, I knew I would win. She'd do anything for me, including putting her name on everything so I could safely remain a silent partner. I was more than her best friend, and she was more than mine.

Grabbing my phone, I sent Vena a text.

Me: I know what you did. Sisters by choice. Sisters for life.

She sent back a crying emoji followed by hearts.

"Aren't you worried she'll sell the place once it's profitable?" I heard Shepard ask.

"She won't," I said. "This is our dream, and she won't forget who made it possible. Vena is loyal to a fault. It gets her into trouble more times than not, but she won't abandon anyone she considers her people. Ever."

I went to Shepard and took his hand. "Please don't do anything that will end with either of you two hurt. Hugh's job is to keep the peace between the races *for the benefit of humans*. Not for wolves and vampires. Don't forget that."

Shepard wrapped me in a hug.

"Hugh isn't Effora. He won't sacrifice everyone around him to benefit himself or the people he works for. He understands the dangers of alienating the wolves. We're the only line of defense against the vampires."

"Maybe you were centuries ago," Cross said. "But the world has changed. Humans have evolved. Their technology has evened the playing field enough that my kind can't hunt as freely as they used to. Why else would Orphia want to open the portals?"

I felt Shepard sigh before he kissed the top of my head and released me to look into my eyes. "He's a bit of an ego killer. Are you sure you need to love him?"

"You know you're starting to love me, too," Cross said from behind me.

Smiling, I stood on my toes to kiss Shepard on his lips.

"I'm as sure about him as I am about you," I said.

"Aw," Cross said a moment before shouting, "Group hug!"

I was crushed between two hard bodies and felt Shepard trying to push Cross away without hurting me while Cross laughed. Slipping out from between them, I grinned at the pair as I watched them scuffle playfully.

Shepard walked away first and started cleaning up our dishes. He left shortly after to check in at the pack house and his people before meeting with Hugh in person.

"What would you like to do?" Cross asked after I started the dishwasher. "Your wish is my command."

I laughed. "I don't need any wishes fulfilled. You have already done that for me. How about a quiet evening? I could go for one of those. Maybe a little creative baking time, too. I should have asked if there was a cookie wolves favored the most."

"I suspect their tastes vary like humans."

It sparked an idea. "That's perfect."

"What is?"

"That everyone has varied tastes. What if I don't pick the type of cookie for the class? What if the woman can choose her favorite cookie? By her making her favorite, not only can the wolf smell a potential mate but also what kind of preference she has.

"I mean, it's only a cookie, so it will hardly represent her whole palette. But it's a start. Gives a sliver of insight into a person. Like what if they were a coconut lover and you hated coconut?"

"I see what you're getting at. But you would need to plan supplies for nearly every cookie conceivable."

I shook my head. "When the women sign up for the class, they can request the cookie they want to make so I can have the ingredients ready for them."

"Sounds like a win-win."

The idea excited me. Everything was coming together, except it was all just talk until I put the idea into motion.

"You have a laptop here, right?" I asked.

"In the study."

While the details were running through my head, I wanted to organize them and create a sign-up form.

Sitting behind the desk, I opened the laptop and laughed at the desktop screen. It was a selfie of Shepard sleeping and Cross pretend-kissing his cheek.

"Does Shepard know about this?"

Cross nodded with a wink. "He wasn't happy at first, but you know he can't say no to me for long."

I shook my head at him, loving that he was playful with Shepard. His relaxed approach had probably helped win Shepard over.

Creating a new document, I flooded it with ideas. Cross helped fill in where needed. By the time we were done, we had a list of things we would need, a promotional image for social media posts and ads, social media accounts, and a form for class sign-ups.

I leaned back, happy with our work, when a slice of pizza appeared in front of my nose. It smelled delicious and helped me realize I skipped dinner.

"When did you get this?" I asked Cross.

"It was just delivered. I didn't want to disturb your progress. But I think it's time for dinner, a little mindless television that people seem to love to watch, and then bed."

I closed the laptop and grabbed the slice of pizza. Following him out to the living room, I saw he had the box of pizza on the coffee table in front of the couch. We settled in, and I curled up against him, feasting, cuddling, and watching a mindless movie.

The movie didn't even matter. Just having a normal evening was exactly what I needed.

CHAPTER TEN

"How long are you going to sleep?" Cross murmured as he kissed the side of my neck.

I shivered at the memory of his bite there and tilted my head to give him better access.

"Mmm, you're teasing me again, Everly. But I promised Shepard all I would do is wake you."

"I'm not awake yet," I said, keeping my eyes closed. "I need a few more kisses."

He chuckled and nipped my collarbone. Nothing to break the skin but enough to make me reach for him. My hands skimmed over material instead of a bare chest.

Slightly disappointed, I opened my eyes. A slash of light from the partially open curtains illuminated the room enough to see that his eyes were dark but not veined as he smiled at me.

"Good morning, beautiful. I need to meet Shepard at the TV station in an hour. Would you like to come with to watch, or would you rather spend the day here with Vena and Anchor? Fair warning…Vena is fully recovered and keeps begging Shepard to lift his sex relic ban so they can have another go."

"I love that girl, but I'm not ready to witness that again. Ever. I'm sticking with the two of you today."

I stood and saw I was wearing a long, silky nightgown. "Pretty sure I didn't wear this to bed."

"Do you remember going to bed?" he asked.

"I remember falling asleep on your shoulder and then... nothing."

He grinned. "You're cute when you drool."

"Stop," I said, covering my ears. "I'm perfect when I sleep. You're ruining my illusions."

His laughter followed me into the bathroom. He didn't, though. I wasn't sure how I felt about that.

I showered and dressed in something that looked business casual. When I emerged, I found Cross waiting for me. He looked incredible in the blue pin-stripe suit and paisley tie with color accents complementing his hair.

He caught my stare and turned slowly in a circle so I could see the exquisite cut of his suit that molded to his firm body.

"I like you in a suit," I said when he faced me again. "I like you in jeans. And I like you in nothing at all."

He kissed my cheek and stood back to examine my clothes. The shirt accentuated my chest, which wasn't hard to do, but it also flattered my waist and hips.

"You look delicious," he said. "Are you ready to tease Shepard?"

"Tease? How?"

"You'll know when you see him."

Cross and I met Shepard at the TV station.

When I saw Shepard in his suit, I almost forgot how to walk. While Cross had a classic, elegant look, Shepard looked like a professional athlete in his well-tailored suit, and I couldn't stop staring.

Hugh and the producer for the nationally syndicated news show were also there and noticed our arrival when Shepard excused himself. He said a quick hello then left with Cross to introduce him to the producer, Aggie, a very anxious woman with bright red lipstick and short dark hair. They listened as she went over what they should expect.

On the way over, Cross said Hugh had chosen this show because the anchor wasn't cutthroat when she asked personal questions.

"Just answer the truth every time," Aggie said. "Denise can smell a lie a mile away, and she'll pry further. Normally, I wouldn't give anyone this advice. It doesn't make for a good show when she's not prying into your personal business, but I understand the need to reveal a different side to the story and set the record straight."

Aggie walked us over to the set, which had three large cameras controlled remotely by an operator. She pointed at a dark window above our heads, indicating where the director, switchboard, camera, CG, and teleprompter operators were located.

I knew about half of what she said. The other half was over my head.

The audio person placed microphones on Cross and Shepard and had them sit on a sofa together. An assistant poured them glasses of water. I stood back in the shadows, out of the way and watching everything.

Shepard caught my gaze. I pointed to him and fanned myself. The corner of his mouth curved. Cross leaned over and said something softly to Shepard. Whatever it was, it had Shepard's eyes flickering with gold.

Denise arrived two minutes before the floor director called out the warning to start the recording. She greeted Shepard and Cross and took the chair across from them. I recognized her, but I had never watched her show before. She always looked fussy and judgmental, even though people praised her for her casual interview approach.

The floor director started the countdown. My stomach churned with nerves when they went silent at two.

Denise looked at the camera and smiled.

"Good morning, and welcome to News for You. Today's guests might surprise you. We have Shepard Ulv and Brodier Cross with us. Gentlemen, thank you for joining us today.

"Now, just so viewers understand who you are, Shepard, you're the head of the werewolf organization in D.C."

Cross immediately hid a smile behind his hand. Shepard ignored him.

"Head of an organization sounds like some kind of mafia or crime boss," Shepard said bluntly. "That's not who I am. I lead the pack in D.C."

Her eyes narrowed on him. "How exactly is your job different from a crime boss? You make hits on the people you're paid to kill, don't you?"

My mouth dropped open. If I'd stood any closer, I would have succumbed to the temptation to slap her. Hugh appeared beside me, and he shook his head when I glanced at him. How was this woman not cutthroat? Where was her casual approach?

"Make hits?" Shepard echoed. He laughed. "No. There's no organized killing. There are no payments—nothing like that. The videos released have grossly misrepresented what my pack actually does. And what vampires do, for that matter."

"How so?" she asked.

"Vampires feed on humans, plain and simple. In centuries past, they would kill indiscriminately. My kind was meant to stop them from killing the entire human race.

"However, as humans and technology evolved, vampires could no longer kill everything in sight and leave a trail of bodies without persecution. They've learned how to hide what they do. Now, they feed on the weak and the unwanted, those alone in the world who would never be missed.

"Look around the city. Where are the homeless? Four weeks

ago, you would have seen them in doorways, parks, or the subway. Today? They're gone."

She pressed her lips together and nodded as if contemplating the case. "Where are they?"

"The unlucky ones have already been converted. The lucky ones didn't survive and were dumped in mass graves we discovered a few days ago."

Hugh muttered something under his breath, and I knew he wasn't happy with Shepard for revealing that.

"The surge in the vampire population and the rising number of people they're killing forced us to increase our efforts to remove them from our city to protect its people."

Her eyes lit up as if she had snagged him on a hook. "Isn't it bold of you to take this task on yourself? What gives you the right to be judge and jury and take a life?"

"This isn't about being judge and jury. This is about protecting humans the way we have been for centuries. We've always taken care of humans. It's at the forefront of everything we do. We have seen firsthand towns wiped out by vampires when their numbers grow too big."

"But is it your right to regulate it?"

"Is it their right to feed on humans? To kill them? Is it their right to convert unwilling victims, causing either vampirism or death?"

"We're not talking about their rights but yours. By what right are you taking this role?"

I could see Shepard's face getting redder. If Denise had any sense at all, she would realize she was poking the bear…or, in this case, a wolf.

Shepard locked gazes with her. "Can you run faster than any car you own? Hear your rapid breathing and smell fear? See at night to hunt those who can't?

"If not, you're not qualified to protect your fellow humans from creatures who can do those things. Creatures who don't need an invitation to enter your home. Creatures who are only holding themselves back until they can amass the numbers they need to take control and make you their living feeding bags... make you their slaves."

Her eyes widened for a moment before she leaned in. "This seems to be an emotional topic for you. Is killing vampires perhaps personal? Do you hold a grudge?"

Shepard looked ready to explode, and Cross didn't look so amused anymore.

"Will you tell the people who witness a vampire suck their loved ones dry within seconds that they're being too emotional?" Shepard reached for his mic, but Cross caught his hand.

"I thought we were here to share the truth," Cross said to Denise. "Is this reporting or pandering for more views?"

Denise carefully composed her expression. "Just because one person says something is true, doesn't make it true. I'm asking the questions our viewers have asked. And the truth is that Mr. Ulv doesn't have the *right* to kill anyone. He is not the authority. We have a government body for a reason."

"And that government body is backing Mr. Ulv." Cross' gaze shifted to Hugh, and he nodded in his direction. "The person to ask is right there. I believe he was introduced to your station manager, something I know you were informed of. So this isn't about discovering the truth."

Rather than acknowledge his words, she asked, "You are a vampire, are you not?"

He nodded. "I am."

"What is your opinion of the wolves savagely killing your fellow vampires?"

"It's a good thing."

She blinked. "Good? Doesn't that mean he should kill you too?"

"He won't. The recent videos released by Orphia Prince have raised concerns because it appears werewolves are killing innocent vampires. I'm here to clarify that the majority are not innocent.

"Because I understand the threat my kind poses to humans, Shepard and I have formed an agreement of sorts. And while Shepard and I are...let's say friends, few of my race are as rational as I am or have the capability of friendship. Most are driven by a single desire—to feed on fresh human blood. Especially those who are newly turned."

"Are you saying it's okay for wolves to kill?"

"I'm saying wolves are doing what they were made to do. Hunt and kill vampires."

"Is this like saying just because a leopard has spots, it's okay for them to kill their prey?"

"Isn't that your point as well? Vampires have the right to feed on humans because they have the teeth to do so?"

Cross withdrew a pamphlet from his pocket and held it up toward the camera. "This is an informational pamphlet being handed out on the streets by people working for Orphia Prince. If you would care to open it, it clearly states that vampires need blood to survive. What it doesn't clearly state is how they feed or how many humans die because of their manic bloodlust while feeding."

He set the pamphlet on the table and pushed it toward Denise.

"Across the world, there are agencies that manage species populations. Bans on killing certain creatures—elephants and fairies, for example. And licenses to keep certain populations low —such as bears and snakes.

"Exactly," she said. "*Licensed* killing."

Shepard's flush, which had started to fade, roared to life again.

Cross cut in before he could say anything. "I don't understand why you think a piece of paper from the Department of Other-world Security stating Shepard's people have the authority to hunt vampires will hold more authority than what was already broadcast. Or perhaps you only believe the truth you speak. I must warn you, though, just because one person says something is true, doesn't make it true."

Denise sat up straighter at having her words thrown back at her.

"For the sake of argument," she said, "let's say the werewolves are legally hunting vampires. Even regular hunters know not to kill the weak or young."

"Exactly. Yet, that's what the vampires do, do they not?" Cross held up his hand to stall another question. "I'm simply explaining the current circumstances, which are quite bleak and will only worsen if you don't let the wolves do what they were made to do. Stop the protesting, get out of their way, or be prepared to have a vampire suck you dry."

Cross cocked his head to the side. "I'm willing to do you that favor now if you think it will help your views."

She rapidly blinked at him, and he shrugged like it made no difference to him.

Cross let out a sigh. "The concerns your viewers have are valid. As I said, the majority of vampires are not innocent. For the few that are, I think there should be a better way to deal with this matter. However, reform will not happen today or even this year.

"What you see now, a vampire sitting next to a werewolf, has never been done before. And it took a lot of patience and understanding to make it happen. Though he and I can coexist peacefully, not every wolf and vampire can. Shepard and I are an exception to the rule. But that we are here together proves that change is possible with time. A lot of time."

Denise's gaze shifted to Shepard, noting his fisted hands.

"It doesn't exactly look like a peaceful meeting."

"You're the one who upset him, not me. He quite likes me. Want me to prove it?"

Cross moved fast and kissed Shepard full on his lips. Shepard's fragile control of his temper broke. He moved as fast as Cross and hit him hard across the jaw.

"Shepard!" I whispered harshly.

He immediately cringed and muttered an apology to Cross. Then he took off his mic and walked off the set.

Cross chuckled and straightened his jacket as if nothing had happened.

"See?" he said, looking at the camera. "If any other vampire had tried that, they would be dead. Yet, here I am. I am an exception."

Denise gaped after Shepard, then pasted a smile on her face. "Well, that was an insightful interview. Coming up after the break, we'll look at how fairies are making a name for themselves at a metal sculpture garden."

The camera light flicked off, and the floor director gave the all-clear.

"What the fuck was that?" Denise shouted, but someone was already ushering Cross toward me, and in short order, we were all being escorted out of the studio.

"The show will air at our three o'clock slot today," Aggie said as she led us and Hugh outside, then shut the door on us.

Hugh looked exasperated and a little worried. "This might have backfired on us. I'll be in touch."

When Hugh walked away, Cross turned to Shepard with a playful smile. "Well, that was fun."

Shepard let out a soft growl then kissed me on the lips. "Better."

Cross shook his head with a laugh, and Shepard went to the SUV with us since he'd arrived with Hugh.

Once we were on the road, I said, "I don't know what lies that producer fed us, but Denise wasn't out to reveal any truth."

"Shepard guessed right that we were there for views alone, which is why I kissed him. We weren't giving them the drama they wanted, so I gave another kind to ensure the interview will air."

"Hopefully, they won't edit it down to just the kiss scene," I said, knowing that it was probably already uploaded to their social media sites as clickbait.

"They won't. Our disagreement with her will be the build-up they need for the kiss scene to make sense."

"Can you please stop referring to it as 'the kiss scene?'" Shepard muttered.

I turned in my seat to look back at him. "It was sweet until you hit him."

"I thought you didn't want to share me," Shepard said. "That includes with him. Tell him to keep his lips to himself, or he'll get a black eye next time."

"I like that he already assumes there's a next time," Cross said with a chuckle.

I wanted to grin at them but put on my best scowl instead. "This only works if you two respect each other's boundaries."

Cross snorted. "He'll appreciate that kiss when public opinion sways his way because of it. But I promise there will be no further surprise kisses." He waited several seconds to add, "I'll warn him before the next one."

"Asshole," Shepard muttered under his breath, but there was no real heat to it.

"Do you think there will be any fallout because of the interview?" I asked.

"Hopefully," Cross said. "That was the whole point. But this time, it should be in the werewolves' favor."

CHAPTER ELEVEN

By the time we arrived home, Shepard was on the phone, coordinating the hunting parties for the new nest Vena had located that morning. He also updated Doc on how the interview recording went.

Cross and I made lunch while he talked, and we discussed Bites and Delights planning while I ate.

Once Shepard hung up, I handed him his sandwich.

"Thanks. How does a watch party at the complex sound? Lisa overheard what happened during the recording and wants to turn it into something positive. It's short notice since the show will air this afternoon."

"I'd love to come," I said.

"You're invited too, Cross. If you can keep your lips to yourself."

"I'll do my best to resist."

My phone buzzed with a group text with Miles and Vena.

Miles: Check this out!

A picture of a book page came through with the text. The

paper was old and yellowed. On it was a drawing of a stone circle with what looked like a circular hula hoop standing upright in it.

The phone buzzed in my hands.

> **Vena: We need hints. What are we looking at?**
> **Miles: It's an ancient rendition of a fae portal. And guess what? It says they're found all over the world.**
> **Vena: Focus, Miles. You're there to find information about the relic Grandma and Grandpa Hunter were looking for and a cure for vampirism.**
> **Miles: Mom and Dad are sifting through GGH's research history to check all the books they looked at before they disappeared. They're hoping we're missing something that will make it easier to figure out what exactly GGH were looking for or where they went last.**
> **Vena: Is there anything we can do to help? Anywhere you need us to check?**
> **Me: We won't be checking. Shepard's people will.**
> **Miles: Nothing yet. I'll let you know if there is.**

"You're frowning," Cross said.

"Vena's bored and going to get in trouble soon if you don't give her something active to do."

"Is she asking about that sex relic again?" Shepard asked.

"No, but that might be a good distraction if you can afford to lose Anchor for a few days."

"I'll talk to him after the watch party and see what he thinks. If it wasn't about the relic, what was it about?"

"The other relic—the one Grandma and Grandpa Hunter were looking for. Miles found a book with a picture of a portal in it, and it says they're found all over the world. He got excited, and Vena reminded him what he was supposed to be looking for."

As I spoke, I sent Vena a private message.

**Me: It's the first time he's excited about something. Be
supportive. Remember what he's been through!**

**Vena: I realized that after I hit send. I'm the worst sister
ever.**

**Me: You know you aren't. Just tell him good job and ask
some questions about the portals. He needs to get lost in
some research and forget for a while.**

She sent me a thumbs-up.

Setting my phone down, I glanced at Shepard. "Should I make
something for the watch party?"

"You don't have to," Shepard said. "Lisa will take care of the
details. But if you *want* to, you can. Everyone will gladly eat
whatever you make. I swear I feed the entire D.C. population
rather than a house full of wolves and their families."

I looked through the cupboards and refrigerator to see what I
had. "How about bacon-wrapped watermelon?"

Shepard nodded his approval, and the pair of them talked as I
prepared the shareable. It was mostly about Denise, what people
would think of the show, and the protesters. I noticed a hushed
conversation as well, but it didn't last long.

Once I finished the bacon-wrapped watermelon, we headed
to the pack house. He escorted us to the empty dining room and
took my appetizer to the kitchen while Cross and I looked
around.

The large room was ready with a projector pointed at one of
the walls. Someone had positioned the tables in their normal
checkered rows, but they'd turned all the chairs toward the
screen. It reminded me of a comedy club setup, which seemed
fitting since the interview had been a bit of a tragic comedy.

When Shepard returned, he said he needed to talk to a few
people and would be back in a few minutes. I glanced at Cross, a
little nervous about him being there without Shepard present. He

flashed his signature smile at me and distracted me with Bites and Delights conversation.

A few people arrived early and started scoping out the snacks on the side tables. Lisa appeared from the kitchen.

"Get your sniffers out of there," she said. "More is coming." She bustled back into the kitchen.

Vena and Anchor walked in not long after.

"What did you make?" she asked.

"Bacon-wrapped watermelon."

She made grabby hands. "Give me."

"They're in the kitchen with Lisa. She already scolded people eyeing the snacks that are out. Are you feeling lucky?"

Vena's gaze darted to the kitchen door, and I smirked, seeing her hesitation.

"Let's grab seats in front," she said. "I can't wait to see the interview. Heard Cross went off script."

"The entire interview went off script," Cross said.

Vena picked out a table, and we sat down. As more people showed up, Vena said hello to nearly everyone. It obviously hadn't taken long to find her place in the pack. Everyone seemed to like her. Some of them even laughed with her at an inside joke they shared.

How did they have inside jokes already?

Was I a little jealous? Yes. But I was also happy for her. Joining any kind of group came with complications, but it seemed like everyone accepted Vena.

I smiled at her and marveled at how our lives were changing.

Shepard arrived a couple of minutes before the show's scheduled air time.

"Can I have your attention?" He waited a moment for the room to quiet. "This interview didn't go as planned. We'd hoped for an unbiased interview, but that wasn't the case.

"I still think Cross and I made some good points. But one thing is very clear after this interview, and I will say it now for all of you to hear and understand: The world is changing, and we need to change and adapt with it. Coexisting with vampires will become normalized. If we can't adapt, we will be shunned like the vampires have been in the past."

Shock rippled through the room, and Shepard held up his hands.

"I'm not saying you have to befriend vampires, and I'm not saying we will stop hunting them. I'm saying there will be change. Not all vampires are killing humans. Some might deserve a chance to prove themselves.

"Make peace with it. Because peace is our goal."

He stepped aside and nodded to the projector operator.

Shepard dragged a chair over to our full table and sat next to me as a commercial came on for fake coins to put out for fairies.

He reached out to hold my hand. As his thumb stroked over my skin, I wondered if he was nervous about his pack's reaction to Cross' kiss. He'd obviously told a few people about it if Vena already knew.

The room quieted as the opening segment of the show played. When Shepard and Cross appeared, a few of the pack cheered, but Lisa quickly shushed them. The producer hadn't cut anything out of the recording, leaving it just as it was with a few enhancements, like up close shots of Shepard's ticcing jaw, a few eye rolls by Cross, which I'd missed, and a slow replay of the kiss and the punch that followed because, in real-time, it was a little hard to see what had happened.

A few women chuckled at the kiss while the men mostly frowned, but when it came to Shepard's punch, they laughed. Shepard squeezed my hand lightly in an unspoken apology.

The segment didn't end after Shepard walked off set, but it didn't show what Cross had said about being an exception, either. It cut to a shot of Denise saying there was obviously more to the hate werewolves had for vampires than they were willing to let on.

"What the hell is that supposed to mean?" Vena asked.

"She made us look like we're the problem," Bear said angrily.

Shepard stood as the grumbles increased.

"Like I said, I didn't expect the interview to be pretty, but Cross kept his cool when I didn't, and he made some valid points. The fact that a vampire said vampires are dangerous and killers will hopefully hold more weight than having me say it.

"Hugh is already running damage control. Trust me when I say he wasn't happy with how we were set up for this interview. We're not liars. He was ready to tell the truth and thought Denise was ready to hear it. A miscalculation on his part that he promised won't happen again.

"But let's focus on the positive. We're more than a novelty TV show, and the world now knows it. We've officially stepped out of the shadows. Change always comes with a few bumps, but we can handle it.

"Now, who wants some of this amazing food your mates provided?"

The mass exodus from the chairs was a little chaotic, and Vena jumped into the fray without hesitation. Shepard left to talk to a few people. The conversation turned lighter, and rather than scowls, I saw smiles.

"He's quite the motivational speaker, isn't he?" Cross asked.

"He is. But so are you. Come on, let's make a plate before Vena eats all the bacon watermelon."

Being at the complex with Cross didn't feel as weird as I'd thought it would be. Shepard had chased him out of bed the last time he was inside. That'd also been the last time the three of us slept in the same bed together. I wondered if it would ever happen again because I'd kind of liked it.

"You're distracting us both," Cross said as he added a finger sandwich to my plate.

"What do you mean?" I asked, looking around for Shepard.

He was on the other side of the room, staring at me while

someone talked to him about something that needed big hand gestures.

"We both have noses. What were you just thinking about?"

"None of your business. Will you carry that plate to our table for me or surrender it?"

He carried it, and I sat next to Vena, who was scrolling through the comments regarding the werewolf "breaking news."

"A lot of haters, but more are questioning vampires now. Someone said they tried to go to one of the Night Club meetings, but the people who came to meet him looked sketchy, so he bailed. Finally, people with common sense."

"Um...aren't we waiting for a call to meet up with sketchy people?"

"Yes, but it's different for us. We're using common sense to ferret out the truth while staying safe. Right, babe?"

Anchor gave her a doubtful look, and she pouted.

"You're supposed to support everything I do and say."

"I do. I just doubt your ability to keep yourself safe."

"That's why I have you," she said, hugging his arm.

He flushed and took another bite of his food. At the same time, an alert sounded on her phone. It was the ominous one she'd set up for Orphia.

"Don't do it," I said. "Don't be a mood killer."

She was already tapping on the notification to open the link to a video. I made a face when I saw Orphia and her fake, chilly smile.

The room quieted as we all listened to Orphia's rant.

"You may have seen the recent interview between a vampire and a werewolf. Don't be fooled. It was staged to suppress the truth about the prejudice werewolves have against vampires. It was blatantly obvious in the way the leader of the werewolf organization treated the supposed vampire at his side.

"And I say 'supposed' because a wolf would never willingly sit next to a vampire. The vampire would be dead within seconds.

Other than the so-called vampire's speed, there's no proof he is one. He might be a werewolf or even an infamous vampire hunter with a fae charm, enabling him to move faster than a normal human. After all, vampires can't walk around in daylight, which was when the show was pre-recorded."

She then gave the address of the pack complex and suggested that those who wanted the truth protest until Shepard explained his unjustified hate and duplicity.

"I'm going to kill her," Vena said.

"You might need to stand in line," Cross said, glancing around the room.

People had gone from contentedly eating food to looking like they were about to shred clothes and turn into wolf form.

"Protesters are going to start arriving by the bus loads," Vena said.

Shepard muttered a soft curse and ordered more guards to surround the building. "Do not engage if they are peaceful. We call the police first because they are trespassing. If they turn violent, we detain them quickly and carefully. I don't want to see any bruises on them if we can help it. Understand?"

The responding chorus of growls seemed to indicate that they understood since Shepard let them go without another word. He came over to us after.

"You should leave now. I need to stay and ensure nothing happens that will make this situation worse."

I hugged him. "I'm sorry."

"Not your fault, but thank you. Once everything is under control, I'll come to you." He shared a quick glance at Anchor, who nodded.

Vena caught it. "Wait. I'm leaving, too?"

"Just for tonight," Anchor said.

"The protesters have been peaceful so far."

"That doesn't mean they'll remain that way," Shepard said. "Stay with Cross and Everly for tonight."

"But I have knives."

"Yeah, I think that's why they want you to leave," I said. "You might be the triggering factor."

Her mouth dropped open for a second before she said, "Fine. I'll go with the babysitter."

"Anchor will join you later," Shepard said.

Vena grinned. "Yay. Come soon," she said to Anchor, then looked at me. "Get it? Cuz he can't yet."

I shook my head at her.

Vena patted Anchor. "Only 399 to go, babe." She took my arm and ushered me to the door. "Cross' whole place is soundproofed, right?"

I sighed as we walked out to the SUV.

"Shotgun," Vena called, running to sit in the front as I moved to the driver's seat.

"It truly is like babysitting," Cross said, climbing into the back with a half grin.

When we were halfway down the driveway, I asked, "They'll be okay, right?"

"I should think so," Cross said. "Nothing about the protests so far has indicated it will get violent, and Vena found a few people turning in our favor on social media."

"And if not, our guys are badass wolves that will tear out throats for breakfast," Vena said unhelpfully. "Can we do a marathon of *The Other House* tonight? Maybe if we watch a lot of them, the producers won't cancel the show."

I agreed since it was barely after four o'clock, and I didn't want to think about the protesters. Watching *The Other House* with Vena would be like living at our old house before life turned complicated and dangerous.

"And you'll make peanut butter popcorn?" she asked.

"One batch and no dropping any on the new couch."

"Deal."

After we arrived home, Vena helped herself to a pair of my

pajamas, and we both changed. I made the popcorn with Cross' help as she turned on the TV and navigated the menu. She and I settled on the couch together. It was just like old times.

Cross sat in a comfy leather chair next to us, asking a question about the show now and then but content to just hang out with us.

When I couldn't keep my eyes open any longer, Cross quietly told Vena to claim a guest room when she was ready. He picked me up off the couch and carried me to our room.

*   ·   ☾   ·   *

WHEN I OPENED my eyes the next morning, I knew I was no longer snuggling with Cross. At some point in the night, they had switched.

"Morning," Shepard said sleepily and hugged me even closer to him.

"Morning. When did you get here?"

"A few hours ago."

"Is everything okay at the pack house?"

"For now. Hugh wants Cross and me to do another spotlight interview in a few days to explain our relationship and the kiss. Especially my reaction to the kiss." He sighed. "Not looking forward to it."

He mumbled something about a troublesome vampire and nuzzled into my neck.

The door flew open, and Vena bounded into the room with her hand over her eyes. "Cover your privates!"

Shepard groaned. "The ass didn't lock it."

She waited a beat. "Are your bits covered? If they're not, I don't care. I've seen too much at wolf run night. I'm immune."

"What? What's wolf run night?" I asked.

She dropped her hand and grinned. "It's when the moon is

full, and the guys all strip down and run. I've never seen so many mate masts in my life. You have to come next time."

"If I say yes, will you go away?"

"No. I have juicy news."

"What?"

"Shross is shipping!"

Shepard glanced at me, confused. I returned the look.

"It's too early for this, Vena. What is Shross?"

"It's Shepard and Cross. A fan group is shipping them as a couple. You should see the fan art they have already. It's spicy."

CHAPTER TWELVE

SHEPARD GROANED AND HUGGED ME TIGHTER AS VENA BOUNCED on her toes and told us about Shross.

"No, this is great news," Vena said. "It's something light and loving and *not* about how either of you are murderers. It's about adapting and rolling with the punches, like you said, Shepard. We need to encourage your fans instead of coming across as a hard-ass this time. Be the gentle Shepard who likes to snuggle Everly."

He leaned back enough to look at me. "Is she making any sense to you?"

"Of course I am," Vena said before I could answer. "Yesterday, you gave the viewers angry Wolf Boss and walked off in a fit. Not a great public image. Meanwhile, Cross was calm and kissed you to prove a point. It's shitty they cut out his explanation of the kiss, by the way.

"You need to be the calm one too. Embrace your relationship with Cross and focus on that instead of trying to convince the public that they're in danger and Orphia is evil. People want drama, but they don't want to believe they're going to die. They're like Everly. They'll ignore that shit until it's biting them in the neck."

"Hey," I said.

"Sorry, babe, but it's true. Avoidance is your M.O. until you can't avoid it anymore. That's the general public, too. So give them something they don't want to avoid. Show them your bromance in all its glory. Being loved by the public in any form will mean Orphia's hate campaign will lose its foothold."

"Unfortunately, she's making sense," I said.

Shepard sighed. "Do you have any other news to share?"

"Nope." She continued to stand at the end of the bed, not taking the hint.

"Go away, Vena," I said.

She grinned, blew me a kiss, and said, "I'll send Cross in so you three can work on your cuddle puddle."

"Our what?" Shepard asked, but she was already out the door.

"Cross is still home?" I asked.

"Yeah. He gave up his spot to work on a few things when I got here and make us breakfast."

The words were barely out of his mouth when the door opened and Cross walked in carrying two plates.

"Breakfast is served, my darlings."

Shepard grumbled something as I sat up. Whatever it was had Cross grinning and reminded me of the moments before the show started yesterday.

"What did you tell Shepard yesterday before the show started that made his eyes turn gold?"

"How sweet the scent of your desire was when you saw him in a suit and that you'd worn the blue lace panty set he'd picked out."

Shepard's hand skimmed over my lower back, and I felt him tug on my sleep shorts to check. He groaned and told Cross to come back later. I quickly reached for the omelette he'd made me.

Laughing, Cross handed it over. "And deny Everly nourishment? Never."

"I heard Vena tell you the good news," Cross said, handing Shepard his plate as he sat up. "We're officially a couple."

"That's not good news. Why do humans accept lies so readily? You should have kept your lips to yourself."

Cross looked at me. "And what do you think? Should I have kept my lips to myself?"

"I think you attempted to save an unsalvageable interview. When's the next interview? Please tell me it won't be the same lady again."

"Hugh is still working on when, but it'll be Denise again," Shepard said around a bite of his food. "Hugh claims he's been assured it won't be another attack."

I thought about it and shook my head. "You embarrassed her yesterday, and she was mad when you walked out. I'm betting she's holding a grudge."

"I agree," Cross said.

"Vena thinks you guys should stop trying to convince the public of the vampire threat. And I agree. I think you need to convince them with your actions. Maybe not more kissing, though. But if you do, Vena will want to post about it on your fan page."

"What do you have in mind?" Cross asked, sitting on the edge of the mattress next to Shepard. I caught Shepard's side glance and knew Cross was purposely provoking him.

"You and Shepard shared a lot about the dangers of vampires yesterday. But you missed a very key trait. Hugh needs to make sure this next show is live so nothing can be edited out. Then, once you're on the air, you need to compel Denise."

"I like the way you think," Cross said.

"I'll let Hugh know," Shepard said. He reached over to set his plate down and grabbed his phone from the nightstand to call the liaison.

Situating myself better, I dug into the omelette. "Thank you, Cross."

"My pleasure."

"Do I get one?" Vena asked, peeking back inside the bedroom.

"Anchor is already making you one," Cross said.

Vena took a quick photo of Cross sitting by Shepard.

"That better not get posted," I called.

"This is for the greater good," she said, her voice growing distant as she ran to the kitchen.

"Don't worry," Cross said. "I blurred right before she took the picture. But she might be on to something. A few candid photos might work, but I won't allow it in our bedroom."

"Aw! It's blurred," she shouted. "You did that on purpose, Cross."

He grinned and waited until Shepard finished with Hugh. From the one-sided conversation I could hear, it sounded like Hugh was on board with the idea.

"Hugh agreed," Shepard said when he hung up. "Denise will not be warned ahead of time."

"Hopefully, she'll change her tune," I said, then finished the last bite of omelette.

Cross took my plate and left. While Shepard made another call to someone, I got ready for the day, wanting to spend some time with Vena.

Last night had been fun, and I missed our time together, even though we still talked and texted every day. And I saw her most days, too. Still, it was different. I missed having her to myself twenty-four-seven.

Grabbing my phone from the nightstand, I kissed Shepard on the cheek as he continued talking to Doc on the phone. Then I slipped out of the bedroom, closing the door so he could have a little privacy.

"I'm not sure if I like Shross," Vena said to Anchor and Cross. "What about Cropard?"

"I think it doesn't matter as long as people get behind us," Cross said.

Vena sat at the table, her focus on her phone. She scrolled with one hand while using her fork with the other to absently eat.

"Do you want to see the fan art?" she asked Cross. "You should see the size of your dueling swords."

Cross stepped over to look. "Impressive. But I'm not sure how I could walk with something like that. My tailor would charge extra for sure. Taking my inseam would be salacious."

Vena snickered.

I sat next to her and peered at her screen and the many, many pieces of art that flooded the page. From hyper-realistic to manga, the variety and imagination of the images impressed me.

My phone rang. Taking it from my pocket, I saw it was Miles.

"Hey, Miles," I said. "You're on speaker."

"Good. Are Shepard or Cross with you?"

"Both. Cross is right here, and I can get Shepard."

"I'm here, too," Vena said. "Thank you for asking."

Shepard emerged from the bedroom just as I was about to get him.

"What's going on?" he asked when our gazes swung to him.

"Miles is on the phone," I said.

"You found something, didn't you, Miles?" Vena demanded. "Spill it."

"While Mom and Dad were following Grandma and Grandpa Hunter's research trail, I was combing through the dwarven archives for anything vampire-related. I found two very interesting things. The first is about a relic that has the power to pull an entire race into the portal."

"An entire race?" Vena questioned. "What if they were halfway around the globe?"

"Wouldn't matter. It's that powerful, and it's why the portal was closed. From what we've pieced together, it was made by the fae originally to steal humans. Vampires were angry about it and called for a treaty.

"But the important part is that it's a relic that can influence all creatures."

Vena's mouth dropped open. "Like what Grandma and Grandpa Hunter were looking for."

"Exactly. We just don't know why they were looking for it or who wanted it."

"What's the source of this information?" Cross asked.

"An old book in the dwarves' archive. It's so old it looked like it was about to turn to dust. We had to be very careful turning the pages. But it talks about the relic. I also found information in it about the first vampire and first wolf created, which is the second interesting thing. It chronicles how much power it took to create the original curses."

"Can you send us pictures of the pages?" Shepard asked. "I'd like to see it."

"Already done. I can send you what I have. So many pages are already beyond reading."

"Does the book say anything about breaking the vampire curse?" I asked.

"No. But I suspect if it took immense power to create, it would take even more power to break. You'd have to ask the fae queen."

I wrinkled my nose at the thought.

"Thanks, Miles. You did good," Vena said. "Let us know if you find anything else to help prove vampires are bad and were-wolves are good."

"You got it."

After he hung up, he sent images of the book pages. The ink on the age-yellowed paper had faded to almost nothing.

"I bet Mom and Dad are already talking to Curran about making a copy of the book and preserving the original," Vena said.

"That's not a bet I'd take because you'd win," I said, adjusting the contrast so I could read it better. "Do you think sharing the vampire origin story would help?"

"Doubtful," Shepard said. "It would only make the fae look bad, which would cause more unrest."

"Which would play into the chaos that Orphia wants," I said.

Shepard nodded.

"Then I say we stick to our original plan to show what Cross can do," I said.

The group agreed.

Shepard drummed his fingers on the back of his phone, and I knew he was considering calling the fae queen.

"Do you think Effora will answer honestly about breaking the vampire curse if you call her?" I asked.

"Unlikely," he said. "But I owe it to all the people Orphia is converting against their will to try."

He stood and moved away from us to make the call, only to return a few seconds later.

"She didn't pick up, which is unusual."

"Is she still mad about us tricking her at the restaurant?" I asked.

"When it comes to getting what she wants, she doesn't hold grudges," Cross said. "And Shepard's unattainable desire is something she would do anything to have."

"He's right," Shepard said. "She always picks up when I call, even when she's occupied with a meal."

I snorted. "That's when she especially likes to answer. What does a fae queen do when she's not having sex with anything that has a peg?"

"Or a hole," Vena said. "I don't think she's picky."

"True," Cross said. "As for what she does…it's not much. She doesn't lead her people like Shepard does. Fae live independently of one another. Even families. Once a child is old enough, they're left to their own devices. It makes feeding easier."

"Has she met with Vivian yet?" Shepard asked Cross.

"No, but my people are watching closely. A group of humans arrived at her place last night and haven't left."

"How large of a group?" Shepard asked.

"Twelve."

"Ooh, orgy," Vena said.

Anchor pulled her into his lap, a possessive move that I attributed with Shepard and Cross, but not Anchor, and not something past-Vena would have liked. But I watched my friend melt into the cuddle and pull Anchor down for a kiss.

"Aw," I said. "That's so sweet."

Anchor flushed and immediately pulled away, which earned me a scowl from Vena.

"Payback for bursting into my room this morning."

She pouted but didn't argue. Instead, she went back to scrolling on her phone.

"Wait," Anchor said, watching over her shoulder. "Go back."

She did, and he looked up at Shepard.

"Turn on the news."

The reporter was just finishing a feel-good piece about a little girl helping a fairy caught in a net. She'd proudly shown the camera her bandaged finger, which the fairy had bitten.

"And she still thinks they're cute?" I muttered.

Vena grinned at me.

A second later, the news switched over to another fae murder. Officials called it a serial killing since the stab wounds were identical to *three* other victims.

"Three?" I said, looking at Shepard.

He was already dialing someone, though, and he looked worried as he paced farther away from us. Serial killers concerned me, a human. But Shepard wasn't human. Why he was worried clicked into place, and I looked at Cross.

"A human couldn't kill a fae, could they?"

"Not usually. Perhaps if they had help, but even then..." he shook his head.

"So what could kill a fae?"

"Werewolves, other fae, and vampires," Cross said. "Some minor races are possible, too, but they would have no reason."

"You think this is Orphia stirring up shit, don't you?" Vena said, leaning forward on Anchor's lap.

She wasn't fooling anyone, not when Anchor flushed and gripped her hips so she would stop wiggling.

"Yes." Cross looked at Shepard, listening to his conversation for a moment. "So does Hugh."

Vena let out a noise that was between a squeal and a screech. We all swung our gazes to her—even Shepard, who was saying goodbye to Hugh—as she bounced on Anchor's lap. His eyes were nearly rolling back in his head at her aggressive movements.

"It's them!" She poked her phone screen and set it on the table, calming before answering on speaker. "Hello?"

"Is this Aneva?" A man asked.

"It is."

"Great news. We have room for you and your guest if you are still interested in attending a Night Club meetup."

"We are."

"Excellent. Are you free tonight?"

"Actually, we are."

"Great. I will send the details to this number. Be sure to wear something red to show your support of the vampires. It will help the bus driver identify you."

"Where is the driver taking us?" Vena asked.

"Unfortunately, I can't say. As you know, the wolves are killing innocent vampires. We keep the location a secret to protect the vampires and their supporters. I hope you understand."

"I do. It makes sense."

"I'm so happy to hear that. We'll see you tonight, Aneva.

Thank you again for your support of the endangered vampires. Together, we'll end the wolves' oppression."

She disconnected the call. "Looks like I got a date with my bestie tonight."

A new message pinged her phone. Cross read it. "The pick-up spot isn't too far away."

"I don't know if I have anything red," I said.

Vena made a disbelieving sound. "Trust me, you do."

When I raised a brow at her, she smiled. "Do you really think you could get a wardrobe filled with clothes and not have something red? You're cohabitating with a vampire. It's their color." She pointed to my necklace peeking out from the collar of my shirt.

I automatically placed my hand on it, feeling the rubies.

"Now, back to what's important," she said. "Are we thinking Shross, Cropard, or maybe Crosh?"

Shepard shook his head. "I'm going to make a few calls in the study."

Cross grinned and patted Vena on the head. "Good girl."

She grinned back until Anchor softly growled. Facing Anchor, she cooed, "Aw, do you feel threatened by the big, bad vampire?"

Anchor stood with Vena in his arms.

"Cross, you need to call me a good girl more often." She cackled as Anchor took her to their room.

"That's one way to get rid of her," I said with a chuckle.

I started picking up our plates.

"I can do that," Cross said.

"You cooked for us. The least I can do is clean. Maybe you can help Shepard coordinate the details for tonight. I know you'll both worry. It will help me feel better too. While I know I have you and the pack, as well as the necklace, which I'm charging up before we go, I don't want any hiccups."

"You know I'll get to you if anything happens, right?"

I nodded. "That doesn't stop my stomach from knotting, though."

He took the dishes from me and gave me a one-arm hug, pressing his lips to my temple.

"If anything ever happened to you, vampires would be wiped clean from this earth."

He kissed me one more time and released me. "I'll coordinate with Shepard." He placed the dishes in the sink and headed to the study.

Not wanting to know details since I would overthink everything, I took care of the dishes, then baked until the apartment smelled like lemon tarts.

Vena appeared just before I was about to start lunch. Her hair was a tangled mess, and her shirt was inside out.

"Did you even bother to look in a mirror?" I asked.

"It smells like sunshine and summer in here."

"It's lemon."

She breathed in and sighed. "The scent of energy. Need some of that."

I slid her a plate with a tart on it. "Only one. Lunch will be soon."

"What are you making? Whatever it is, I need two. And my man needs three. He worked hard. Still no launching of the pocket rocket, but we only have—"

I held up my hand. "Don't want to know."

She pouted.

"And to answer your question, I'm making SOS," I said.

She squealed and hugged me to her.

"I'm only making it because you love it so much."

"What's SOS?" Anchor asked, emerging from the bedroom in a neater state.

"Shit on a shingle," Vena said happily. "I want more shit on my shingles."

"I remember," I said.

Cross and Shepard joined us at the table just as I started setting out plates. I sat between them and listened to Cross explain how they would handle the meetup tonight as we ate.

"You'll have your phones so we can track you easily," Cross said. "But if anything feels wrong, leave. We want to save lives, but not at the cost of yours. Do you understand?"

Vena and I both nodded.

"Since the meetup time is just before dark, we don't expect any problems at the pick-up location. Most likely, it'll be thralled or compelled humans."

"Or humans who are on team suck-and-slave," Vena said.

"That too," Shepard said. "There might also be friends of vampires watching, which is why we'll be close enough to see you, but we'll stay out of sight."

"Once we know the actual meeting location, we'll come for you and start asking questions," Cross said. "You're not there to get the information yourselves. You're only there to find the location. Understood?"

"I feel attacked. Why are you only looking at me?" Vena asked with false innocence.

Shepard's phone rang before he could respond.

When he saw the name, he put it on the table and answered it on speaker.

"Lover, forgive me for missing your summons," Effora crooned. "It was an oversight that I'll immediately correct. Where and how would you like me?"

CHAPTER THIRTEEN

VENA AND I SHARED A MUTUAL CRINGE AT EFFORA'S WORDS.

"I'd like you right where you are, and how I'd like you is honest," Shepard replied to her.

"Mmm, sounds interesting. Do you want to know how I'm touching myself?"

Vena pantomimed gagging, and I nodded.

"I want to know what you know about a fae relic that can pull an entire race into the fae realm."

She was silent for a moment. "Pardon?"

"A very old fae relic, Effora. It's rumored to be why the treaty was created in the first place."

"The fae made it so they could pull all the humans into the fae realm," Vena said. "The vampires got mad—I wonder if that's where the story about Vlad the Impaler comes from. Maybe he wasn't killing people but the fae who stole his meals. Anyway, the fae agreed not to use it, and here we are, all happily living in the same world. What happened to the relic?"

"I don't know what relic you're referring to."

Effora was brash and abrasive most of the time. Haughty the

rest of the time. She was rarely nervous, but that was exactly how she sounded. Shepard heard it too.

"I think you do know," Shepard said, "and you're worried. You should be. The Hunters, a well-renowned pair of treasure hunters, were hired by a private party to find the relic over a decade ago. They went missing after that. What are the chances they found what they were sent to find?"

She was quiet for a long moment. Vena opened her mouth to say something, but Shepard silenced her with a look.

Effora huffed. "The chances are high. Why else would the bitch want the rings or be willing to reveal her kind to the world after centuries in the dark?"

My stomach dropped as I understood what she was saying. Orphia was the one after the relic. She was the one responsible for Grandma and Grandpa Hunter's disappearance. I glanced at Vena and saw her anger.

"Once she has all the stones, she'll open the portals and send us all back, Shepard," Effora said. "We can't let that happen."

"All the fae? Or all otherworlders?" I asked.

"Why leave anyone to compete for a food source? If the fae and werewolves are gone, the vampires have free control over the humans."

"Is that why she's starting to kill fae now too?" Vena asked. "Why not wait until she has the rings?"

"Never question the motivations of a fanatic. The bitch will do everything in her power to satiate her blood lust. Lust is a powerful motivator."

"If you have suggestions for stopping her, we're listening," Cross said.

"As you know, we love our relics. I have something here that might help. Might. I make no guarantees, but it's yours if you want it. You'll need a human to transport it. It's not dangerous to humans, but it is to our kind.

"It should help you locate Orphia and destroy her."

"When can we have it?" Shepard asked.

"Immediately if you'd like. I'll be home all evening."

"We'll come right away," Shepard said.

She sighed audibly, her mood shifting. "If only that were true. Your coming is something I dream about, Shepard. It would be abundant and delicious."

I reached over and hung up on her.

"Let's get this over with," I said. "I'll be the human handling the artifact to make sure she doesn't grope you again.

Shepard grinned at me. "I was hoping you'd protect me."

"While you're doing that, I'll scout the pick-up location for later," Cross said.

"Anchor and I will stay here," Vena said. "Make sure you're really loud when you all come back so you don't walk into anything you don't want to see."

I rolled my eyes at her then left with Shepard.

"You heard Effora's voice when you asked about the portal relic," I said once we were in his SUV. "She's hiding something."

"I think you're right, but I don't know what. Which is why we're going to her place, despite her lying to us when she said she had Orphia's location. I want to know what she's up to, and I think we'll get more truth from her in person than over the phone."

"As long it's only the truth we get more of," I said.

Shepard reached over and took my hand in his. "It will be okay. She's a nuisance, but she's not stupid. She won't alienate her allies, especially now that we know what Orphia wants to do."

We reached a gated entrance manned by fae guards. They took one look at Shepard and waved him through. The mansion that came into view looked like something out of a fantasy book. The white stucco between the glass walls and windows made it look like it belonged in the clouds with the blue summer sky as a backdrop, not on earth with the rest of the dwellings.

Shepard parked in front, and I looked up at the two massive steel and glass doors that had to be two stories high. While he got out, I silently thanked Cross for being discreetly rich.

"Ready?" Shepard asked, opening the door and holding out his hand.

I nodded and walked up the sweeping portico with him.

Shirtless fae men opened the doors at our approach. My necklace thrummed against my skin, shielding me from their pull. Inside the furnished entryway, I saw another shirtless man waiting.

He inclined his head to Shepard. "Welcome back. Queen Effora is in her boudoir."

"Tell her we'll stay here," I said. There was no way I was going deeper into the house.

"Please sit. Relax. I will inform the queen." He indicated the high-back chairs at a small side table decorated with a mixed flower bouquet.

I sat at the edge of the chair, and Shepard stood next to me as the man walked up a grand glass staircase. It gave the illusion he was walking on air, and I was sure I'd break an ankle or neck if I tried to use them.

He returned several minutes later. "Queen Effora will be down in a moment. Would you care for a libation?"

"No, thank you," I said. I didn't trust Effora wouldn't spike it with something and steal Shepard.

Shepard declined as well.

Eventually, Effora appeared wearing a ridiculous scrap of dressing gown that was as see-through as her glass house. Her nipple and belly button rings and chains slid against the sheer fabric with each step.

Once she reached the bottom of the steps, she smiled at Shepard. Her gaze barely flicked to me.

"Hello, darling," she said to Shepard. "Do you desire anything?"

"The relic."

"I was hoping for more, but you continue to tease me, Shepard. Very well, come with me."

"We're in a hurry, so can you have someone bring it to us?" I asked.

Her eyes narrowed on me. "As I said, it requires a human. My staff is fae. If you want it, you'll have to follow me."

Thinking of all the ways I'd ask Shepard to strangle her if she was lying, I reluctantly agreed.

We followed her down a white hallway, her hips swaying dramatically with each step, the fabric not covering the dimples above her rounded cheeks. I tried to look away, but it was almost like looking at a pendulum.

With each step farther into the house, the pull of fae magic grew until I had my hands fisted by my sides, keeping myself from jumping on Shepard. Judging by his fisted hands, he was having the same issue.

Effora stopped at a door with a guard standing outside of it. "Open."

As soon as the door opened, I felt a familiar pulse. The globe's magic swept over me, washing away my resistance to the desire riding me.

"Shepard." The whining, desperate plea ripped from my lips without thought.

He growled softly.

"None of that in the hallway. In we go."

With a nudge, she pushed us into the room. We both stumbled and reached out to steady ourselves on each other. That simple contact shattered what restraint he'd been holding onto.

He was there, touching me. Kissing me. The slide of his tongue against mine was unlike anything I'd felt before, and I moaned into his mouth.

"Oh, I found that relic you mentioned, Shepard," Effora said, sounding far away even as I felt her hand trail over my back. "You know, the sex relic at the house your friends went to. I confiscated it. So, thank you for bringing it to my attention."

She unclasped my bra through my shirt.

"That should feel better, doesn't it?"

It did. My skin felt so hot and tight. I needed all my clothes gone and a few dozen orgasms.

I reached for Shepard as he broke off the kiss to pull my shirt off. The air on my skin felt so good that I moaned. He returned to my mouth, ignoring my loose bra in favor of my lips as his fingers threaded through my hair, coaxing me closer.

"Oh my," Effora gasped, sounding delighted. "You are well endowed."

He ripped his mouth from mine to growl savagely at her, and I drunkenly noted her hands on his pants. The button was undone, and the zipper was calling my name. In a trance, I eased it down and palmed his hard length.

The pained, desperate sound he made before he focused on my mouth again barely registered.

"It seems my abilities, enhanced by my ring and the power of the relic, are enough even for you to lose control, Shepard. I think I just discovered the fae version of Viagra. One hit, and you'll stay hard for hours.

"It's a pity you chose her, though. We could have been good together. I hope she's worth it."

"She is," Shepard breathed against my lips.

"Then take her. I can feel what you want. Show me what it's like for a wolf to mark his mate."

"Show me," I echoed, mindlessly tugging at his shirt.

I needed more skin contact. His hands needed to be everywhere. So did what he was packing. My hand slipped into the waistband of his underwear and wrapped around his heat. He groaned into my mouth, and the next thing I knew, we were lying on a pile of cushions.

"I need you," he rasped.

"Yes," I breathed.

"I can't...it won't..."

"Stop fighting it," Effora said. "If she's truly your mate, she will accept everything you are. Even the animal side of you."

Shepard snarled at her and looked at me with gold eyes.

"Tell me to stop if it's too much."

I nodded even as I realized it would never feel that way. I needed him too badly.

He stripped us of the rest of our clothes, flipped me like a pancake, and pulled back on my hips until those were up in the air. He bit my ass cheek roughly enough that I gasped and arched my back. His fingers swept through my wet folds before he positioned himself and thrust into me.

I cried out in relief and fisted the pillows as he set a brutal pace. What lingering awareness I had of the room and our audience faded completely.

Occasionally, I would hear Effora's voice, but her words didn't register. Sometimes, her touch did, especially when Shepard drew me upright from behind and she brushed a fingertip over my nipple. When he bit into my shoulder, she touched my clit to help me through the pain with an orgasm.

After that, though, the only thing that existed was Shepard and his ravenous appetite for me. We had sex on the pillows until they were damp with our sweat, then against the wall, then on the rug with me on top of him, then in the bed.

It went on forever. I was thirsty, and my bits were starting to chafe, but I couldn't stop reaching for Shepard.

Then, suddenly, that extreme need started to fade.

Shepard came inside of me again with a groan, then rolled us to our sides without pulling out. I was glad he didn't. I was pretty sure I wouldn't survive. Everything was aching in a combined pleasant and unpleasant way.

"I'm not sure if I should hate her or thank her," he murmured as he wrapped me tenderly in his arms.

"Both," I breathed, unable to open my eyes. "I'm so thirsty. What time is it?"

I felt him move and hissed out a breath when he withdrew.

"Are you all right? Was I too rough?"

"No. Just a little too thorough. How many times was that?"

"I don't know. I couldn't stop. It looks like she left with the sex relic. Stay here, and I'll grab our clothes."

I couldn't have moved even if I'd wanted to.

When I heard him curse, though, I lifted my head. He was sifting through our trail of clothes and looking around at the floor.

"What's wrong?" I asked.

"My ring is gone."

I struggled to sit up, and he hurried over to help me. In seconds, he had us both dressed.

"Hang tight, sweetheart." He went to the door, yelling for Effora. He didn't leave me, only poked his head into the hallway. Then he came back, his strides long and hurried.

"What's going on, Shepard?" I asked as he handed me his phone and picked me up.

"That's what I'd like to know. I think she took my necklace and ran."

The seriousness of what had happened hit home. Effora had used the sex relic and Shepard's need to mark me as a distraction to steal the ring.

"Call Cross," Shepard said as we left the room.

As soon as I opened his phone, I saw several unread messages from Cross.

Cross: What's happening? Why is Everly bleeding?
Shepard: Something to do with connecting to the relic.
A small amount of blood. She's fine. I'm not. This is
going to take hours.
Cross: Keep me posted.

Cross: Don't forget about the meetup.
Cross: If I don't hear from you soon, I'll find you.

"She messaged him," I said.

Shepard glanced down at the messages. "He sensed when I marked you, and she used my phone to keep him from coming here. I bet his last message is why she finally took the relic and ran."

Shepard growled. "I hope Cross lets me kill her before he kills me."

I dialed Cross' number on speaker.

"Everly is fine. We're on our way back," Shepard said as soon as Cross answered.

"Vena's waiting impatiently," Cross said.

In the background, I heard Vena say, "I'll go without Everly if I have to."

"We'll be there in twenty," Shepard said.

I hung up the phone and noticed the absence of even the slightest fae pull. The place was completely empty.

"What is Effora going to do with the ring?" I asked after we were back in Shepard's SUV.

"I don't know." Shepard cursed and slammed his hand against the steering wheel. "I fucked up. We shouldn't have gone there alone."

I ran a soothing hand down his arm. "Anyone with us would have been in the same situation. Who knows what would have happened then?"

He looked at me, his gaze going from angry to tender to guilty.

"I'm so sorry."

"The only one who should apologize is Effora."

"No. Not that. I mean, losing the ring is not good. But I mean…fuck, Everly. I shouldn't have marked you like that. Not here. Not in front of her.

"I was so out of my mind. And so were you. You didn't consent to any of this. I'm so sorry."

He looked miserable, and his hurt tugged at me. "I don't regret you marking me, Shepard. Yes, I wish it would have happened any place other than at Effora's house, and definitely not with her there and touching me, but I'm okay with what happened between you and me. I love you."

He tugged me to him, hugging me. "I love you so much. I swear I'll make this right. She'll pay for today."

His body trembled from the force of his emotions. I hated that Effora did this to us, but I meant what I had said. I wasn't upset with what we'd done, only that she forced something that should have naturally happened.

"Switch places with me," I said.

"What?"

"I'll drive while you make the calls I know you need to make."

He nodded, and we quickly switched spots. As I drove, he kept his hand on my thigh and made two calls. One to Hugh, letting him know what had happened and the seriousness of the issue. One to Doc since he was second in command and needed to know.

I peeked in the rearview mirror at my shoulder, since it throbbed, and saw the two puncture wounds from Shepard, not dissimilar from the ones Cross had given me. They hurt a lot more, though. I didn't say anything since I didn't want him to feel worse than he already did.

When we arrived home, Shepard told me to wait and hurried around the car to help me out.

"Does anything hurt?" he asked.

"Yes, but in good ways, not bad, okay?"

He nodded but didn't look convinced, so I captured his face between my hands and pulled him down for a quick kiss.

"Shepard Ulv, I will have dreams about what we did together

today. Dreams that will wake me up desperate to do it again. Am I lying?"

A tremor ran through his body as his eyes filled with gold.

"No," he said roughly.

"Then stop apologizing for showing me an amazing time and focus on figuring out why that sexed-out lunatic took what she did."

He exhaled heavily and was a little more his controlled self as we went inside.

Cross was in front of me the moment I opened the door to the second floor. He gently pulled the collar of my shirt, revealing the bite mark. His eyes flashed black at Shepard.

"She's bruising. You promised not to hurt her," Cross said.

"It wasn't his fault," I said. "It was Effora's. She had that sex relic there and used her powers with it. We didn't stand a chance, and I'm just grateful I can walk."

"No, it's my fault," Shepard agreed with Cross. "I should have never taken you there, Everly."

"Are you saying you were willing to go by yourself and be Effora's sex puppet?" I asked.

Cross lifted me and started through the apartment.

When Shepard went to follow, Cross paused and softly snarled a warning. Worried that Cross was already mad at Shepard before he even knew about the ring, I lightly grasped Cross' chin and turned his head toward me.

"Shepard wasn't mad at you when you bit me. Be nice."

Cross' gaze swept over my face.

"I was careful."

"You weren't under the influence of a sex relic at the time."

"When I was, I knew not to bite you."

He turned away from Shepard, and I motioned for him to wait there. I'd talk to Cross first and calm him down before Shepard told him about the ring.

CHAPTER FOURTEEN

CROSS SET ME ON MY FEET THE BATHROOM AND HELPED ME REMOVE my shirt. His gaze raked over me, taking in every light bruise before settling on the mark on my shoulder.

"Shepard's already feeling guilty. Please don't make it worse."

I saw the moment Cross relented in his anger. With a defeated exhale, he kissed my red, injured skin gently before sucking. The sensation almost made my knees buckle. Cross held me upright as he took one more sip and closed the wounds. The pain subsided nearly instantly.

He kissed the skin again and pulled back to look into my eyes. The black had receded, only leaving his beautiful amber eyes.

"Thank you," I murmured. "You know that bite would have happened eventually, right?"

"I know. But I wanted to be there so I could make the pain go away. I never want you to suffer."

"I was too out of it to feel much pain," I said. "Are you still mad?"

"No. I love you and only want what's best for you. Shepard and I know we both have a piece of your heart."

He reached over and started the shower.

"Did you get the portal relic?" he asked as he helped me remove the rest of my clothes.

"No. Every word out of that woman's mouth was a lie. Shepard wants to kill her, and I don't think I would stop him."

"Did she hurt you?" Cross asked, black slowly consuming his eyes.

"Physically? No. Mentally. I'm not sure yet." I made a miserable sound. "Vena's right about me avoiding what I don't want to face. And I don't want to face Effora's part in what happened in that room, but I think I need to so you understand why Shepard was out of it.

"Do you remember how it felt when that fae controlled the relic? Well, with Effora controlling it, I had no hesitation. None. I didn't care that she was there, talking to us, giving us suggestions. Or touching me."

My face flushed scarlet, and Cross made a soothing sound.

"I'm sorry you went through that. I will not rest until I've dealt with her. Until then, I think after what you've been through, you'll feel a fraction better after a hot shower."

It sounded exactly like what I needed. I'd scrub off the sweat and Effora's touch.

Cross took off his clothes as well and followed me inside. He gently washed me, giving me soft kisses whenever he saw a bruise from Shepard's grip on me.

"I promise I felt nothing but pleasure. Honestly, I think I completely lost the sense of who I was. I only wanted…sex. And Shepard was the same. He growled at her when she touched him at first, but once he was inside of me, he didn't notice her at all."

Cross kissed my forehead and shut off the water.

"I can smell how nervous you are, Everly. As long as you liked what he did, I promise Shepard is safe from me."

When he was done, he wrapped me in a fluffy towel and cuddled me on the bed. Shepard came in a moment later, looking at us. I patted the space beside me.

Once he lay on my other side, Cross said, "Tell me what happened."

"It was a setup. She used the sex relic to distract me and take my ring."

I could see Shepard's fury and touched his cheek.

"It's not your fault."

He closed his eyes.

"Rather than blame yourself, you should ask yourself why Effora would risk your anger," Cross said. "Do you think she's working with Orphia?"

Shepard shook his head. "Effora might be speaking to Vivian, but I think that's as far as her connection with Orphia goes. And I think the only reason she's still dealing with Vivian is because of his hate for Orphia. But then again, she said she had a relic that would help us, which was obviously a lie. As far as I know, it wasn't in the room she took us to. I'm not sure what to believe anymore."

"I can't see Effora working with Orphia," Cross said. "We were there in the room to smell Effora's distaste when Orphia came onto the video call. I don't believe that was faked."

"Why would Effora want the ring then?" I asked. "When you told her about the portal relic the Hunters were looking for, she sounded pretty mad about Orphia wanting to open the portal. The safest place for the rings is with the bearers so they're not all together."

"They aren't all together. Not yet. Orphia has Curran's stone," Cross said. "That's it. If Effora is working with her, that would mean she also has Effora's stone and Shepard's. Effora isn't foolish enough to put that much power into Orphia's hands. But, even if she were, I still have my ring and won't surrender it easily."

Shepard scoffed. "If Everly were taken, you would give it in a heartbeat."

Cross' hand smoothed over my arm. "Perhaps it would be wise if you didn't attend tonight's meeting."

"I disagree. We can hope Effora isn't working with Orphia, but she *might* be. Which means we need to find Orphia fast to stop whatever magic trick she thinks she's going to pull.

"And before you say that's exactly why I should stay locked in this room, I want to ask both of you how much more danger I would be in if Orphia opened the portals."

Shepard sighed and wrapped his arms around my middle, pulling me flush against him and out of Cross' arms. Cross inched closer until we were touching again. It was nice getting a group hug.

"How much time until we need to leave?" I asked.

"You should start getting ready," Shepard said.

"But you probably need to shower again," Cross added. "It would be best if you didn't smell like us."

"All right." I quickly climbed over Shepard and regretted it immediately. Everything between my legs ached. "While I'm doing that, Shepard can tell Vena to shower, and Cross can get me pain relievers and some electrolytes."

I held up my hand to forestall their worry. "I'm not in real pain, but I think it would be better if I weren't walking with a hitch."

Their slow smiles of understanding had me shaking my head and retreating to the bathroom for a second time. I'd just wrapped a clean towel around me when Vena knocked on the bathroom door.

"Oh, sister from another mister, I'm here to raid your closet. Can I come in?"

"Come in," I said.

Vena rushed into the room and hugged me enthusiastically.

"Welcome to pound town, Everly! I heard you're walking with a hitch and need some pain relievers. So tell me, what's he working with? Are we talking a rolling pin or more like that juicer I picked up?"

I rolled my eyes at her.

"I'll take that eye roll as a rolling pin. Lucky ducky."

I grabbed a red shirt decorated with white macarons from a shelf and tossed it at her.

She easily caught it and stripped off the shirt she was wearing.

"You showered first, right?" I asked.

"Of course. I washed all the delicacies Anchor was nibbling on. Let me tell you, the Vena buffet was open for business today, and he ate well."

The only reason I didn't scold Vena was because I needed her distraction. I didn't know what we were heading into. Even though I put on a brave face for Cross and Shepard, I knew this had the potential to backfire on us.

After we both wore red shirts, I hugged her. "Love you."

"Love you, too. Let's go kick some vampire ass."

"No, no ass-kicking. We're just the bait."

"I know, but let me just pretend a little, okay?"

Shepard was getting off the phone when we left the bedroom.

"Hugh is downstairs," he said. "He'll set Vena up with a body cam so the DOS can get the footage they need."

Both Shepard and Cross looked like they wanted to hug me— either that or lock me in a tower so I wouldn't get hurt. But I blew them each a kiss and followed Vena downstairs. They trailed behind us, keeping their distance so we wouldn't smell like them.

Hugh and one of his security were ready for Vena. They hid the camera in a pair of red-framed glasses that matched her shirt color.

They tested it over their high-tech system before giving us the go-ahead.

"Always go for the safe route," Hugh said. "You know the

danger this meetup poses. My team and I might not be able to get to you in time. If you need to bail, do it without hesitation."

We nodded our understanding.

"You won't be able to take your own car there," Hugh said. "The seat fabrics hold scents. Instead, we have a driver with a ride-share logo on his window. He's right outside and ready for you."

After a quick breath to steel my nerves, which didn't really help, Vena and I walked out to the car.

Once we were both seated and buckled, the driver took off.

"Are you ready?" I asked Vena softly.

"Yep. And I got my lucky knife ready, too."

Thankfully, I didn't have to focus on what problems lay ahead of us since Vena began chirping in my ear about everything and nothing, and that's when I realized she was just as nervous as I was. She was just showing it differently.

I glanced over at her and smiled.

She smiled back at me. "I always called your girls Thelma and Louise, but now we're really being them."

"Yeah, but we get a better ending."

The driver pulled over. "I'm letting you off here. The spot is just down the road. Less than a block. You'll see it."

We thanked him and got out.

Vena glanced at her phone and flashed me the picture included with the instructions. "We're looking for a 'No Loitering' sign that's been graffitied on."

Heading down the road, we found the sign easily.

"Now what?" I asked.

"We wait."

I glanced at the time and saw it wasn't yet seven. We'd made it with five minutes to spare.

Vena and I stood under the sign, trying to blend into our surroundings. I was positive we were going to get a ticket for loitering literally under the no-loitering sign, but a party bus pulled up at the appointed time.

The door swung open, and music and the swirl of disco lights spilled out. The man driving wore a powder blue leisure suit and a blonde, curly wig.

"Aneva and guest?" he asked.

We nodded.

"Your chariot awaits." He gestured to the bus. "Before you board, I've been asked to hold your phones for you. Don't worry. They will be in a box on the dashboard the whole time. It blocks the signal so our location stays between us. This minor inconvenience keeps our vampire friends safe from their persecutors. We take their safety seriously."

Vena handed her phone over first and got onto the bus. I was a little more hesitant but knew I couldn't turn back if I wanted my normal life back. The one where my parents and grandma were safe. Getting on the bus was a necessary step in that direction.

Handing over the phone, I got onto the bus and blinked at the lights as they flashed in my eyes.

Vena patted the seat next to her. It was a silver glitter pleather that reflected the bouncing lights.

"Feel free to partake in the libations," the man said, pointing to the complimentary champagne, soda, and water. "I have a couple more stops, then we'll be on our way."

He closed the door and sat behind the wheel.

"Do you mind turning down the music just a little?" Vena called up to him. "I've got a brewing headache."

"Roger that." The seventies disco music turned down slightly.

Vena and I didn't talk as he headed into the suburbs and picked up a man from a random corner who was wearing a red ball cap. When he got on and saw us, he smiled and complimented Vena's shirt.

"First meeting?" he asked, sitting next to us.

"Yep," Vena said. "And you?"

"Same. I'm nervous and excited. I'm really hoping I'll find a vampire sponsor who wants to convert me."

Vena nodded. "We're nervous and excited, too." She leaned toward him and lowered her voice. I watched the driver's gaze flick to her. "It was a little creepy being the first ones on the bus. We're glad you're here."

The ball cap guy's smile turned reassuring. "Yeah, I bet."

The suspicion in the driver's eyes faded.

"We have seven stops today," the driver said. "Twelve people in total. Enough to fill the bus. Feel free to help yourself to the drinks."

The ball cap guy had no problem doing so and opened a cola as Vena chatted with him.

He wanted to be converted because he just found out he had advanced-stage pancreatic cancer.

"I'm so sorry," Vena said. "If either of us ends up getting a sponsor, we'll try to talk them into taking you on, too."

"I appreciate it."

The sorrow on my face was no lie. I'd never considered how many people attended these meetings because they saw it as a way to live.

When we pulled alongside the next stop, no one was waiting, and the driver quickly got on the phone.

"I think we have a no-show," he said into the phone. He listened for a moment. "Yeah, I know. Sorry, bro. If you can fill the spot, I'm game." Another pause, where he looked up at us. "You guys good back there?"

We all nodded.

"Yeah, we have plenty of drinks yet," he said to the person on the phone. "And I can always break out the snacks. It's up to you. All right. Later."

He hung up and started driving again.

"They're going to try to find a replacement. These meetings

are hard to get into, as I'm sure you know, so it's not fair to the people waiting when we have no-shows. If you ever can't make a future meeting, call ahead."

"Will do," Vena said at the same time the ball cap guy said, "Got it." When the driver looked at me, I smiled and nodded.

"You're a quiet one," the driver said.

Vena laughed. "She's dying to ask questions but is too shy."

"Ask away. It'll make the time go faster."

I subtly reached over and pinched Vena even as I asked, "How hard is it to get a sponsor?"

"Yeah," the ball cap guy said. "I want to know too."

"Not hard at all. I promise. We tend to have more sponsors present than attendees to ensure you find someone you vibe with, you know?"

"How many meetings do people usually need to attend before they connect with a sponsor?" the ball cap asked.

Vena and the guy chatted with the driver while he drove back into the city to pick up another person. When the newcomer boarded, the mood on the bus changed. She was snippy to the point she sounded angry. When asked why she was going, she told Vena to mind her own business. The ball cap guy defused the situation slightly by complimenting her red scarf.

Vena and I shared a look as the driver headed out to the suburbs again. It didn't make sense to do all the weaving around he was doing. I desperately wanted to look back to see if Cross and Shepard were following us, but I knew better.

The next stop was empty, too, and I began to suspect these weren't no-shows but a way to waste time as the sun sank lower in the sky.

Vena and I eventually took a bottle of water from the cooler. So did the angry woman. As the driver continued his so-called "route," he made a call each time there was a "no-show" and added another pickup.

By the time the person on the other line agreed it was too late to add more, we had thirty minutes until sunset and seven passengers in the twelve-person party bus.

Vena and I chatted with them casually, asking generic questions about why they wanted to attend the meeting. The mood of the bus was generally upbeat except for the one woman.

"How much longer is this going to take?" the woman demanded. "If you'd just given the location, I could have been there already instead of putting up with this bonding bullshit."

The conversation halted as we all stared at her.

The driver laughed nervously. "We'll be there in fifteen minutes. Don't worry. How about I turn the music up?"

He blared it, so conversation wasn't possible. While the woman seemed content, the rest of us weren't.

Twenty-four minutes later, we pulled through the gates of an abandoned hospital outside the city limits. Two men waited by the weedy, overgrown front entrance as the driver parked the bus.

The sky was more grey twilight than blue.

Dusk was upon us, and Vena and I were headed into a vampire meeting.

Nothing good was going to come from this.

CHAPTER FIFTEEN

THE DRIVER OPENED THE BUS DOOR, BOUNDED OUT, AND WAVED US outside. "Welcome. Don't let the digs scare you. We have to operate under secrecy for everyone's protection. Please watch your step. This place has been abandoned since the fifties."

"Is this the old insane asylum?" the hat guy asked.

"It is. Lots of really cool old stuff in there."

"I heard it was haunted," a woman said. "I saw it on a ghost hunter show a few years ago."

"I can guarantee it is not. In fact, our meeting room is set up so you don't even know you're in an abandoned building."

Vena grinned, loving this "adventure."

I shoved my trembling hands into my pockets so I wouldn't give my fear away. Going to a vampire meeting was bad enough. Attending one in an abandoned insane asylum? No amount of sweet bribes was going to make this better once it was done.

However, it *did* help that other buses were showing up. Part of me found comfort in "safety in numbers," but the other part knew that meant there would be more victims if things went south.

Our driver opened the main doors and led us through an old

entryway that had all the creep factors. Broken tiles scattered the floor, along with decaying pieces of lobby furniture and enough cobwebs to turn a horse into a mummy.

Vena and I would be in so much trouble if this were a horror movie. Like cast extras, we dumbly followed a stranger down a dark hallway…into a place my gut said we wouldn't be able to escape from. To meet vampires!

Vena snaked her arm through mine, an excited smile plastered on her face as she pinched my inner arm in warning. Taking the hint, I tried to slow my breathing.

The driver opened the doors to a large, slightly less terrifying room lit with several lamps.

"How do you have electricity here?" Vena asked.

"Generators." He gestured to a table with a notebook on it. "Please sign into the guest book, then have a seat. The meeting will start soon."

He and the other bus drivers congregated around the doors, repeating the same thing to attendees that continued to file into the room. We stood in line and signed the guest book, which was nearing its last page. It was a testament to how many people had become victims.

Someone clapped loudly as we were following the people in front of us toward the seats.

"Welcome, new friends!" a familiar peppy voice said. The neatly dressed man didn't fit the dismal surroundings. "Please sit, and we'll get started. I know you all have questions and are eager for answers."

I realized he was the person who'd spoken with Vena on the phone.

When the room settled, he smiled. "Welcome to the night life! Who here came to find a sponsor?"

About half the people in the room raised their hands.

"And who is here to support the vampire cause? To be an ally to persecuted vampires?"

The remaining people raised their hands, including Vena and me.

"You all are in the right place, and we will celebrate this unity in just a few minutes, but I want to introduce you to our beloved queen and leader, Orphia Prince. She is the driving force behind our efforts and has saved countless vampire lives from those genocidal maniacs, the werewolves. We owe her gratitude and obedience."

I felt Vena bristle next to me. I placed a calming hand on her arm.

The man turned on a large screen, and Orphia's face stared back at us.

"Hello and welcome," she said, all diplomatic smiles and faux warmth. "I'm so glad you've joined us this evening. Vampires need your help. We cannot survive without the support of people like you, so thank you all for being here.

"We have lived in the shadows for so long. The wolves murder our kind without hesitation or motive. Humans fear us because of the lies they have been told. Yes, we consume human blood to live, but we don't harm our donors. We source our blood ethically, ensuring the safety and wellness of our donors so they're able to donate again in the future.

"Humans have no reason to fear us. It's all propaganda pushed by the wolves. We've been slaves to the fae, always having to find them food but never for ourselves.

"It's time we end this tyranny. For those who are looking for a sponsor, I applaud you and your bravery. Know that this is a great time to become a vampire because we are close to winning the freedom we deserve. We will show those who dare to oppress us that we are more than the fabled shadows they think we are.

"For those who are here not to convert but to support, I applaud you as well. We need allies like you. Please fight these injustices alongside us.

"In order to fight these injustices, I want you to know who to watch out for. These people have done everything in their power to push us down. They've killed countless vampires in brutal mass attacks."

A slide show of people I knew came on the screen. Cross, Shepard, Anchor, Doc, and…

My face flashed on the screen, along with Vena's. We looked at each other in wide-eyed panic.

"Sorry about this, Ev," she said a second before she pulled a pin from the cuff of her shorts and stabbed my leg with it.

I jumped to my feet, calling attention to us. Vena yanked me back to my chair, but it was too late. If we hadn't been recognized before, we were then. People turned to look, and recognition flashed in their gazes.

"We're not enemies of anyone," Vena said, holding up her hands. "We haven't even finished college yet."

She sounded so dumb and clueless that it convinced a few. Not the guy on the stage, though.

"Bar the doors!" he yelled.

We watched the drivers run out of the room, and I turned to look at Vena.

"Breathe, Ev," she said softly. "We'll be okay."

An alarm went off. Not the emergency kind but like a timer.

"If you're here to find a sponsor, please stand," the man said. "Our benefactors have arrived."

The side doors, which had been closed, opened suddenly, and people poured in. The first one inhaled deeply, and his eyes went black. He grabbed the first person standing.

"Welcome to the night life," he said a second before biting into the man's neck.

The room exploded into chaos as vampires swarmed the people standing and started a frenzied feeding. Those of us sitting remained glued to our chairs in shock.

I was so focused on the spectacle that I was unprepared for

the hands that closed around my arms and lifted me out of my seat.

"Orphia wants to speak with you, Everly," a woman said with manic glee in her voice.

"Fuck you!" Vena yelled, springing to her feet lashing out with her lucky knife.

The woman dropped me and gripped her bleeding arm. Her eyes were pitch black, and the surrounding skin was a web of veins as she looked at my best friend.

"Orphia isn't interested in you, though." She opened her mouth, hissing at Vena and showing her teeth a second before she lunged.

Vena dodged and swung out with the knife, again. This time, the woman avoided it and smiled slowly.

People were screaming and crying. The scent of blood laced the air. Panic and fear boiled inside me. Desperately, I scanned the area to find a way to help Vena. Overturned chairs lay scattered everywhere. So I picked one up and hit the woman across the back like I was a professional wrestler.

Unlike a pro, when she turned toward me unaffected, I dropped the chair in fright and held up my hands.

"I'm sorry. I shouldn't have done that. Is there any chance I can have a do-over?"

The vampire woman laughed in a cruel and creepy way and slowly shook her head.

"That's too bad," I said as Vena took the opportunity to stab her in the back, right into her heart. The woman gasped and stumbled a step with the knife still embedded in her.

Vena dodged around her and grabbed me. She dragged me around feeding vampires and backed me into a wall.

"Didn't you bleed?" she asked.

I looked down at my thigh where she stuck me and didn't see anything.

"I don't know. Aren't your glasses working?"

"I don't know." She pulled a small knife from her bra strap. "We can't risk it."

Without another word, my best friend for life nicked me with her blade.

The squeal I made was similar to a pig being led to market. And the reaction of the vampires around us was instantaneous.

Several heads whipped our direction, and all I saw was a sea of black eyes. I grabbed onto Vena's shirt as she stood in front of me with her tiny, backup blade ready.

Suddenly, the main door burst open, and more people rushed in. The familiar faces of Shepard's men almost made me cry. They moved fast, peeling off their clothes and shifting into wolves as they began their attack. The other people who rushed in didn't shift but moved just as lethally as the werewolves. They beheaded vampires faster than I thought humanly possible, but not with the blurred speed of an otherworlder.

Then Cross was in front of us, his fangs out as he grasped a vampire by his neck and tossed him like he was a wet towel into the fray. He spun around and grabbed me.

"Where are you hurt?" he asked.

Vena pointed to my neck as she stuck to the wall beside me.

Cross' mouth was on my skin a moment later, suctioning softly. I wrapped my arms around him and melted into the safety of his embrace as he lightly fed and closed the wound.

"I might kill Hugh later," he whispered as he hugged me tightly to his chest. "I'm sorry we weren't here sooner."

Wrapped in his arms, I didn't witness the carnage in the room, but I heard it. People's dying screams echoed around us, and then everything went quiet.

"If you're human, please stand," Hugh said.

Cross released me, and we turned to take in what was happening.

As some of the survivors stood, another group of people filtered in. They carried blankets and medical kits and began walking among the bodies scattered on the floor, checking for pulses. Some bodies were headless. Some were heartless. Between them, people were crying and crouched low, covering their heads. The ball cap guy wasn't one of the survivors. His life-less eyes stared up at the cobwebbed ceiling.

The angry woman was there, though. She slowly stood with several others. She didn't look so angry anymore. Her eyes were wide and filled with fear.

"What was that?" she asked in a shaking voice.

"The feeding frenzy you just witnessed, or the werewolves who stopped the vampires from killing more of you?" Cross asked.

"I don't know," she burst into tears.

Cross sighed and turned her toward one of the medical people. They were sorting everyone out, dealing with those who were bleeding and giving blankets to those who were falling into shock.

Hugh spoke above the noise. "We can provide medical treat-ment at no cost to you. You can also refuse treatment. The right is yours. However, everyone must give their statement regarding what happened here once we move you to a safe environment. Please bear with us until then."

The medical people treated the survivors one by one and escorted them from the scene. Anchor and Shepard joined us as they tugged back on their clothes.

"Are you all right?" Shepard asked.

"Fine."

"I'm fine too," Vena said. "Where's 'my good job, Vena' for keeping Everly safe."

"Good job, Vena," Cross said as Shepard's gaze swept over me.

Hugh called Shepard's name.

"I have her," Cross said. "Go."

Shepard gave me one last longing, regret-filled look and jogged away.

A small group of men and women who had infiltrated with the wolves returned. I wasn't sure where they had gone or who they were. They didn't wear the DOS uniforms, yet they had swiftly mowed down vampires. I would have suspected they were undercover DOS agents, but they had a unique vibe, almost like they didn't belong...yet did.

"Who are they?" I asked, pointing to the group.

"Vampire Hunters," Cross said.

Vena's expression filled with awe. "They're here? I want to talk to them."

She grabbed Anchor's arm and pulled him over. We followed them across the room, hearing one hunter say, "We cleared the building. There were only a few hanging behind."

"Thank you," Hugh said. "Make your escape before news crews invade."

"Wait," Vena said to them. "How do you become a vampire hunter? Is there a test?"

"You just have to be quick and a little crazy," a female hunter said with a laugh. "And good with a knife."

"That's me!" Vena said. "I'm in. How do I sign up?"

Anchor groaned when the lady handed Vena a card.

Vena stared at it as if she'd just received a golden ticket.

"Good luck with that," I said to Anchor.

Hugh stepped over to me. "I'm really sorry we were delayed. I had to make sure everything was by the books, and I needed as much evidence from the glasses cam as possible. We need the world to see Orphia's deception for what it is. Hopefully, we'll be able to save more lives."

"Evidence is great, but what about answers?" Vena asked. "I thought the goal was to come in and ask questions. The guy on the stage was human."

"Not everything went as well as we'd hoped." He took the glasses back from Vena. "I'll be in touch to get each of your statements, but you can go while I deal with this. It'll take a while."

I stared after him in disbelief as he walked away, and my gaze again caught on the pancreatic cancer man. My whole body started to shake with residual adrenaline and anger. Yet, the need to cry burned my eyes.

"Everly, look at me."

My gaze found Cross'.

"Tell me what you need," he said tenderly.

"To leave quickly."

He took my hand, and as we headed out at a hurried human speed, I saw personnel walking in with armfuls of empty body bags.

How many lives could have been saved if things had happened differently? If people had shown up sooner? If they'd taken at least one of Orphia's people alive?

Outside, we veered to the bus to grab our phones, which were still in the box. Some of the other people had already claimed theirs. I glanced at the phones left as Cross grabbed mine and saw the lifeless bodies in my mind again.

A van with a city news station logo on it pulled in. A reporter and camera person hurried out, and Cross and Anchor steered us toward the vehicles.

"Wait. Can I interview you?" one of them called to us.

I shook my head as Vena said, "Sure."

A man put a heavy camera on his shoulder and nodded to the reporter.

"What happened in there?" the reporter asked Vena as Cross continued to lead me to the SUV.

"What about Vena?"

"Anchor has her."

Behind us, Vena said, "Vampires just slaughtered people who were there to support them. No hesitation. No consent given. That's all I have to say."

"Wait," the reporter said. "Where are the vampires? Tell me more about what you witnessed."

I glanced back and saw Anchor and Vena moving toward his car and Shepard jogging our way. The camera person filming the reporter caught sight of Shepard and did a double-take.

Cross helped me into the backseat and looked up at Shepard.

"If you're in back, you're focused on her," he said.

Shepard nodded and got in next to me. My shaking grew more pronounced as he wrapped his arms around me and kissed my temple. I felt Cross' gaze on me as he drove and knew they were both worried about me. I wasn't acting like I usually did. No complete meltdown this time. What did that say about my life? Too much was happening.

I tried to tell myself the trauma of the night hadn't been for nothing...that even though we hadn't caught Orphia or any of her people, we had footage that should stop her from luring in more innocent people. At least for a little while.

Still, the images from tonight would run on a loop in my mind for a long time, along with the sounds of the screams and cries.

I shivered.

"We're almost home," Shepard said.

Home wouldn't fix what was wrong, but it was a haven I needed to regroup. When we finally arrived, I headed for the shower and stripped off my blood-stained shirt. I was pretty sure it was splatter from vampires hitting arteries on victims.

I shivered again.

Cross followed me, turning on the water for me. His gaze swept over me as I washed.

"Want me to join you?" he asked.

I nodded.

A second later, he was behind me, naked and rubbing his hands over my back.

"What happened tonight?" I asked.

"Hugh was being cautious. He kept the team back until the

meeting started, worried that the incoming vampires would scent the werewolves. He didn't want to tip them off."

Cross let out a heavy breath. "Even though my scent would have blended with theirs, he asked me to stay back as well because I'm too recognizable."

He grabbed a scrubby and soaped it up.

"When your identities were revealed, we rushed the building, but those precious seconds gave them the advantage. My heart stopped beating when you bled the second time. I thought—"

His arms wrapped around me from behind. The hold wasn't sexual. It was desperate.

Turning in his arms, I met his dark gaze.

"I would have killed everyone in that room if anything had happened to you."

I believed him. The webbing around his eyes was the darkest I'd ever seen.

"Nothing happened. I'm here. I'm fine. Shaken up. Angry we didn't get what we needed after all that risk, but fine."

He kissed me gently as the bathroom door opened, and Shepard walked in without a stitch of clothing.

Seeing them both naked at the same time sent a little jolt of panic through me.

"Is there room for one more?" he asked.

"I knew your aversion to Shross was just a front," Cross teased, his anger bleeding away from his expression as his sexy smile appeared. "Don't worry, Everly. Despite the kiss I gave him, he's not my type. I think it got him curious about what I have to offer, though, since I've seen what he has to offer you. First impression was that it wasn't much, by the way."

"It was cold the morning you stole my towel at the Hunter's house," Shepard said. "And I'm not here to look at you."

"So you claim. I'll save you the trouble and embarrassment. You have a pinch more girth, and I have a smidge more length. Otherwise, we're fairly evenly matched."

"I'm not looking at you. Get out. It's my turn." His gaze locked with mine, softening.

"What? No cleaning train?" Cross asked with a laugh.

He kissed my shoulder and strutted past Shepard with a grin. Shepard's soft growl didn't stop until Cross wrapped a towel around his waist and disappeared from the bathroom.

"It's more than a pinch," he muttered as he joined me.

I grinned, grateful for and loving their distracting banter, even as Shepard grumbled about Cross' poor eyesight.

When I finished helping Shepard wash his back, he wrapped me in a towel and carried me to the bedroom where Cross was waiting. He already wore the shorts he favored for "sleeping" with me. I climbed into bed and surrendered my towel while Shepard put on a pair of shorts as well.

"That blank wall needs something," Cross said as his arms wrapped around me from behind. "Something soothing. Something to inspire a good night's sleep."

As Shepard set his arm over my waist and kissed my forehead, I hummed my agreement.

Cross had impeccable taste. Whatever he chose would be beautiful.

CHAPTER SIXTEEN

I woke with a stretch and felt Shepard's hand stroke over my side. His fingers lingered on my hip, tracing small circles.

"Good morning, mate," he said, his voice a low rumble. "Do you want any pain relievers again?"

"Morning," I murmured as I considered his question and realized how sore I was. My thighs ached when I moved my legs, but so did my shoulders. "I'm not sure yet. I think moving around will help."

"I promise not to be so rough next time."

Thoughts of the previous day filled my head. I hated that Effora had tricked us and that Orphia was one step closer to getting what she wanted. How many more days until my family returned?

I opened my eyes to stare at Shepard even as I felt Cross move behind me.

What in the hell was I going to tell my parents? Vampires are real, they're trying to take over the world, and, oh, by the way, I'm in a committed relationship with one. And a shifter too.

"Why did that upset you?" Cross asked, kissing my shoulder.

"Did you like it rough or are you upset that you're stuck with Shepard for life? I can help with both."

Shepard shot Cross a dirty look.

I laughed, thankful we could still find humor.

"I'm not upset about being your mate, Shepard," I said when my laugh died. "I realized that what's become very natural for me to accept might not be easy for others to accept. Normally, I wouldn't care what other people think, but this?" I sighed.

"You're worried about your parents," Shepard guessed.

"A little. They're good people, and I don't think they'll have a problem with the fact that I'm dating a werewolf or a vampire—well, maybe a little about the vampire, but that's only because of the bad reputation and current news.

"But the key part is that it's an 'and' instead of an 'or.' I don't know how they're going to feel about their only child having two husbands in a state that doesn't allow polygamy."

Shepard's eyes flashed gold, and if I were to guess, Cross' had gone black as well.

"Trust us to make good impressions when you're ready to introduce us," Shepard said. "Maybe say we're friends first so they can get to know us, and we can go from there."

"Once they meet us, I think they're going to embrace us like you have," Cross said.

Having their unconditional support helped ease some of my fears. They snuggled me until I heard the bedroom doorbell.

"I give Vena ten seconds before she attempts to break down the door," Cross said.

"I'll say five," Shepard said.

Cross and Shepard both chuckled.

"What are you laughing about?" I asked.

"It took less than three," Cross said.

"I thought this room was soundproof," I said. "How did you hear?"

"The vibrations of her ramming into it," Shepard said.

I pulled up the covers. "Open the door before she hurts herself."

Shepard padded over to the door with a stretch and opened it. "Did you hurt yourself?" he asked Vena.

"No," she said, rubbing her shoulder.

"Next time, wait for someone to open the door," Shepard said.

"I didn't hear the doorbell, so I wasn't sure if you heard it."

Shepard slid back into bed, and Vena grinned at us.

"A little Supernatural Everly Sandwich again? Anything interesting happening under those covers? I need a S. E. S., too, but with a V in the middle. Get it? Cuz my name starts with a V, and it's in the middle cuz—"

I chucked a pillow at her. "Nothing is happening here. Get your mind out of the gutter."

She frowned. "I knew you weren't having kinky sex. Seriously, Everly, you need to try it. I need to live some of my unfulfilled fantasies through you. I mean, you got both. A vampire and a wolf. The first time that's happened in history. Get on it so you can give me the deets."

I heard Anchor say her name from the living room.

"Don't worry, babe, my S. V. S. will stay unfulfilled. At least by people, but sex toys are still game, right?" she called.

He didn't answer. She grinned. "He loves me."

"Is there a reason you're here this early?" I asked.

"Yeah. Your men have been holed up in here with you, and we need to talk about what happened last night."

"You mean how you cut Everly in a vampire nest?" Shepard asked. "I thought we agreed a pin poke in the thigh."

"I did do that, and it didn't work."

"It worked. We were delayed," Cross said.

"Oh. Sorry about that, Ev. But we need to talk about how Orphia has all our pictures and shows them to new recruits. How long until the protesters know that Everly and I are public enemy numbers one and two for vampire oppression, along with all the werewolves and Cross."

"I'll call Hugh for an update and see about what we can do," Shepard said, slipping from the bed and revealing a bit of my bare hip in the process.

Vena grinned. "Nice bruise, Ev. I know how you got that one. I can even tell you the page number of that position in The Joy of Sex."

"Get out before I ask Cross to toss you out."

She shrugged and followed Shepard out the door.

"Was there anything that happened at the meeting we don't know about?" Cross asked me.

"Not that I can recall. It all happened very fast."

"Many things happened fast yesterday."

"Yeah, they did."

"You seem okay, and you say you are, but I'm not sure many people would be if it happened to them. Both at Effora's house and at the meeting. And it all happened in one day."

"It did. And I'm not okay with what Effora did or the people who were killed. But like Vena said, avoidance is my specialty. So, I'm going to focus on what I am okay with. I'm in an amazing relationship with the two men I love the most in the world. My dream of opening a bakery is coming to life because of the people who love me. And my best friend is going to try to become a vampire hunter.

"I'm not actually okay with that last one, but that's life, right? Some good and some bad, all mixed up together."

He wrapped me in his arms and kissed the top of my head.

"Don't change, Everly. You're perfect the way you are. And I promise I will never stop hunting Orphia and Effora for what they've done. They will pay."

"Don't go looking for trouble, Cross. It tends to find us anyway."

He let me escape to the bathroom where I let the warm water

wash away the past, the doubts, and whatever future fate had in store for me. When I was so pruned that I had no choice but to turn off the water, I went to explore the closet and find something fun to wear.

Cross spared no expense on the closet or what it contained. The array of suits his side contained had me shaking my head until I noticed a few jackets on the other side that looked larger in the shoulders. Curious, I peeked through drawers and found clothes that looked like they belonged to Shepard. Mine were neatly in the middle of theirs.

Smiling, I dressed and headed to the living room to find Cross, Shepard, Vena, and Anchor all staring at the TV.

"What's going on?"

"It's a press conference with the mayor," Vena said. "Most of what he said is PR bullshit, but he's finally telling people about the attacks and to not attend Night Club meetings."

"He has to. There's proof now," Anchor said.

The chief of police took the podium after the mayor. "As you saw from the footage, vampires are not the friends they would have you believe. We are actively pursuing leads on Orphia Prince's whereabouts and working with the DOS to arrest her and her ring of vampires.

"Again, do not attend Night Club meetings, and be aware of your surroundings. Even in the daytime, there are those who will aid Orphia and her movement.

"We've set up a hotline to call if you have information regarding Orphia and her people."

The camera cut to a news anchor in the studio. "Our thoughts are with the families who lost loved ones last night."

Rather than going to a commercial, footage of the aftermath of last night's carnage rolled as the anchor continued to reiterate what the mayor and chief of police said.

"For your safety, do not attend any vampire support meetings at this time." The anchor turned to a co-anchor, a grin replacing his serious expression. "Stew, I heard there's going to be a lot of monkey business in town."

Stew grinned. "You know it. The zoo is holding their annual celebration—"

Vena reached over to grab the remote and turn off the TV.

"I can't keep sitting here. I need something to do," Vena said, standing. "You said Effora just up and left her house, right?" She looked at Shepard, who nodded. "And you have people watching it, waiting for her return?" Cross nodded. "Then let's go stir up some trouble and see if we can get a reaction out of her."

"What do you have in mind?" Shepard asked.

"A house raid for relics that pose a threat to humans."

I snorted. "You just want the sex relic."

She held a hand to her heart as if I'd wounded her, then grinned.

"I mean, that would be a nice perk, but I'm serious about stirring things up. Now would be the perfect time. Think about it. Effora took Shepard's ring—"

"You know?"

"If Anchor knows, I know," Vena said.

"I told key members of my pack for the pack's safety," Shepard said. "However, if word spreads that I lost the ring representing the leadership of our Alphas for as far back as anyone can remember, I'll need to answer to the pack delegates, and that's a distraction we can't afford right now."

"Oh." I hadn't even considered that when Effora stole it. I'd been more focused on what Effora planned to do with it.

"Anyway," Vena said, reclaiming all our attention. "Effora took Shepard's ring to either give to Vivian or keep for herself. If she gave it to Vivian, that probably means Orphia has three of the four stones and will try for Cross' next. If she didn't give it to Orphia, I think she'll try to use it to lure Shepard into having sex with her.

"Since we all think that Orphia and Effora aren't working

together, she probably didn't give the ring to Vivian and is going to try for Shepard. So dangle your carrot by doing a house raid. I'm betting she has cameras all over the place, especially in that sex-fest room."

My stomach churned at the thought, and I looked at Shepard.

"She wouldn't record anything," Shepard said. "It could be used against her as evidence of how fae use humans. Effora and her people are smart enough to hide what they do. But I'll call Hugh about sending some agents to raid the house."

"I want in on the raid," Vena said.

Anchor and I said "No" at the same time.

"Where is your sense of adventure?" she asked him with a pout.

"We don't need a relic," he said. "Nothing needs to be rushed."

"Says you. I have needs for some serious penetra—"

Her phone sounded with her Orphia alarm, and I'd never been so grateful.

Cross pulled me to his side with a chuckle.

"How did you manage to live with her for so many years?" he asked me quietly as she looked at her phone.

"Lots of distractions," I said. "And bribes."

"And rules," Vena said absently. "Guys, you're not going to believe who commented on the mayor's press conference." She looked up at us. "Vivian, the cat lover. His user name is a little on point. There's a linked video promising the truth about the real power struggle between werewolves and vampires."

She grabbed the remote and mirrored her phone to the TV so we could all watch as she clicked the link.

Vivian's face came on screen. His long black hair was pulled back, showing more of the black makeup he liked to wear. Even though he looked the same at first glance, he wasn't. The crazed look in his dark eyes had an extra edge to it. He looked like a man pushed to his limit.

A shiver ran through me.

Cross' hold on me tightened comfortingly as Vivian's lip curled in a sneer.

"Orphia, the self-proclaimed leader of the vampires, wants you to believe she's my kind's champion and unsung hero. She's not. She's a power-hungry cunt, who has drunk an infant or two dry for an appetizer.

"Shepard, the Alpha-king of the werewolves, wants you to believe werewolves don't have a mindless grudge against vampires. Oh, they do. It's in their DNA. Literally. Werewolves were created by the fae to protect what the fae craved most—humans—from vampires who were slowly culling the number of their favorite meals.

"Wolves were made to kill vampires. Made to kill…us." Vivian smiled, showing his fangs, and reached up to tug his hair free. In doing so, we all saw the blue ring he wore on his thumb.

Shepard growled, and I grabbed his hand, holding it in mine.

"Vampires kill humans. Fae feed off of human desires. And werewolves have to breed with humans to make more little baby werewolves.

"Do you see the problem? Otherworlders all want a piece of the humans. But these days, we vampires aren't allowed to drain our victims dry as we want. We're forced to fight over the scraps we're allowed.

"And Orphia isn't happy about that. But she has a plan.

"She intends to cleanse this world, sending all otherworlders back to the fae realm except for the vampires and the humans. All she needs are four little stones and one powerful relic. Once she has it, she will unleash a feeding frenzy to rival the last one the humans call the black plague.

"You think we're not dangerous? Watch and learn the truth."

He reached off-screen and pulled a young girl toward him. She didn't utter a word as he roughly tipped her head and bit down hard.

I closed my eyes and buried my head in Cross' neck, only hearing the wet noises as Vivian fed.

The TV clicked off, and the sound stopped.

"Holy shit…" Vena breathed.

Lifting my head, I looked at Cross. His concerned gaze met mine. I saw the worry he had for me and more.

"Not all vampires are monsters," I said softly.

"No, but Vivian is," Vena said. "And he just confirmed what we'd been guessing. I mean, it all lines up with what we know. Orphia's drive to get the rings. A private party contacting my grandparents about finding a missing relic. They disappear after reading the book that contains information about the rings…and the portals to the fae world."

We all shared glances. Shepard looked like he was about to explode.

Although we'd guessed it, hearing it confirmed felt different. More real. More imminent.

"I still say we raid Effora's house," Vena said. "They hoard relics. Maybe the one Orphia is looking for is there."

"Doubtful," Cross said. "She wouldn't have left it behind, and she wouldn't hand it over. She would never agree to leave the human realm."

"If she doesn't support Orphia and her plan, why give Vivian the ring? And why does Vivian still have it?" I asked, trying to make sense of it all. "I don't understand what his angle is. He basically called Orphia out and exposed her plan. How does that benefit him? How does it benefit her? Does he plan to give the ring to Orphia, or is he up to something else?"

Shepard stood and walked over to the window to look out as Cross answered.

"If this was just about having humans to feed on, I'd say he would give the ring to Orphia even if he's angry with her. She was the one to turn him, after all. But the only person Vivian has ever been interested in is Adriel, not the humans they fed on. I doubt he'd give Orphia the ring just for a feeding frenzy."

"Then what was the point of getting the ring from Effora?" I asked.

"Stirring the pot," Vena said with a shrug. "It's what I would do if I were Vivian. Make everyone chase after things while he's living his best life feeding off people."

It still wasn't adding up for me. Cross said Vivian only cared about Adriel. How could he be living his best life without Adriel?

"It's his revenge," I said, suddenly understanding. "He's getting back at the wolves for what happened to Adriel. He was wearing Shepard's ring so that the packs know Shepard doesn't have it anymore."

Shepard's phone rang. He pulled it out of his pocket and answered it.

"Yeah?" He was still looking out of the window. Had I not known what just happened, I wouldn't have thought much about the call. But his already stiff shoulders tensed further.

"I understand." He ended the call.

"What was that about?" Vena asked, but Shepard was already answering another call.

This time, he walked into the study and closed the door.

"Did you hear anything?" Vena asked Anchor and Cross.

"The first call sounded like a pack delegate asking about the ring and warning him there could be challenges," Anchor said. "Not sure about the second one."

"You mean challenges from idiots like MC?" Vena made a barfing motion, which made me want to sympathy barf for real.

CHAPTER SEVENTEEN

I FLED TO THE KITCHEN TO MAKE BREAKFAST AND TO ESCAPE Vena's fake puking, but she followed me.

"What are you making?" Vena asked.

"Something simple for Shepard," I said. "I have a feeling he is going to need to leave soon."

"I'll take whatever it is, too. Even your simple is better than most things. I'm not dissing the cooks at the pack house, but I miss your cooking."

"I can't tell whether you're buttering me up for something or if you're actually being sweet."

"I'm always sweet."

Both Anchor and I snorted and shared a conspiratorial smile as he joined her at the island.

"Hey. I *am*," Vena reiterated.

When I arched a brow at her, I noticed that Cross wasn't in the living room anymore and hoped he had slipped into the study with Shepard.

Losing the ring the way Shepard had was bad enough, but having to face challenges for his alpha spot because of it was worse. Would he need to face more guys like MC, who played dirty?

The title he held in the pack didn't matter to me. I loved him for who he was, not his position of power. Yet, I knew that losing it would be a crushing blow to him, and I hated that I was so… human.

Grabbing my whisk, I beat eggs.

Vena watched me. "Ah. It's your frustrated egg-beating technique." She smiled at Anchor. "You're about to have the best, fluffiest eggs of your life."

What could I do to support Shepard? Make his meals? Have his babies? That was hardly very—

I froze, my mind going back to all the unprotected sex at Effora's. My panicked gaze went to Vena as I counted back in my head.

"You're freaking out," she said, standing. "Why are you freaking out?"

Realizing I was out of the danger window, I sagged with relief even as I picked up my phone to send her a text.

"Don't read this," I said to Anchor as I typed. "And I don't care if he's your other half or not. You keep this to yourself, Vena. Sisters before misters."

I hit send, and her phone pinged.

"Sorry, babe," she said to Anchor. "Close your eyes."

Me: Order condoms.
Vena: You gave me a heart attack for nothing!
Vena: But I was wondering how long it would take you to think of that. Ordered you a case yesterday.
Vena: It'll be here tomorrow. Multi color, flavor, and texture because I love you.
Vena: The box in the order that says "beast buddy" is mine. You can open it if you want to broaden your horizons.

Me: You have issues.

She grinned at me like a lunatic.

Ignoring her, I went back to cooking. By the time I had the frittatas ready, the study door opened.

We all looked expectantly at Shepard and Cross as they sat at the island.

"Well?" Vena asked. "What's going on?"

"No challenges yet," Shepard said. "But there are plenty of people threatening to."

I slid a plate in front of him.

"Thank you, Everly."

I rubbed his shoulder consolingly before making another plate.

"Do you need to get back to the pack?" Vena asked.

"I will, eventually. There will be a lot of questions that I'll have to answer."

"Blame it on Effora," Vena said. "It's her fault."

"Unfortunately, that's just an excuse that wouldn't buy me sympathy points. My duty is to protect the ring, and I failed it. Any pack member has the right to challenge me, and I don't begrudge them their anger. My failure rests on my shoulders alone."

"Our shoulders, too," Anchor said. "Your pack is loyal to you. No one from our house will challenge you."

"Is there anything we can do to help? I asked.

"Actually, I think there is. I need to show the rest of the alphas I'm taking the loss of the ring and my alpha responsibilities seriously. It's time to shut down Blur indefinitely."

"What? Why?" Vena asked.

"How is that going to help?" I asked.

"The other alphas always questioned why I ran Blur when I have responsibilities to not just my pack but all the packs. Honestly, it was never a problem. The alphas mostly manage their own territories, and I have a good team to oversee things at Blur and in the pack when I can't.

"I think it rankled others that my pack didn't need micro-managing. Closing Blur will be an olive branch and prevent them from issuing any immediate challenges, which would be a distraction our people can't afford."

"Okay. What do you need us to do?" I asked.

"Call Griz, and help him clear out all perishables. Anchor, you'll need to grab everything we need to close out the book-keeping."

"You'll reopen, though, right?" Vena asked, looking more upset than I would have thought.

"We'll see how things turn out. It was a great bonus income for the pack house, but we won't hurt without it. While you're clearing out Blur, I'll meet with Hugh in person. We need his help to flush out Vivian. Orphia will know he has the ring and go after him, whether he plans to give it to her or not. I'd rather take it back from him than her."

He looked at Cross. "Will you go with Everly?"

"Always."

"Watch your back while you're out there. We can't afford for you to lose your ring as well."

Cross smiled. "If Orphia were capable of taking my ring, I would have lost it centuries ago. She won't risk trying to take it directly again."

"Sounds like there's a story there," Vena said.

"Yes, and it's not suitable for children. Go get ready," Cross said.

Vena looked like she was going to bristle, but Anchor smacked her ass and turned her toward their room. She was so shocked—and happy—that she actually went.

"Am I a child too?" I asked.

Shepard chuckled, kissed my forehead, and promised to keep

in touch. Then he escaped from the house, leaving Cross to answer me.

"No, you're not. But I'd rather not share that part of my history with you. It's in the past, and no longer who I am. I would prefer to remain as I am in your mind."

I hugged him and rested my head against his shoulder. "Okay. If you don't want to share it, then don't. You're right in that it doesn't matter. It's in the past. And if you're trying to let go of it, then there's no point in bringing it up again."

"Thank you."

He helped me clean up, and by the time we finished, Vena and Anchor emerged from the bedroom. His face was flushed, and she was grinning.

"No details," I said, pushing her toward the stairs before she could say anything.

Anchor drove, which was a good thing since protesters still stood in front of Blur despite it being before ten in the morning. I looked away, fearing someone would recognize me before we turned the corner.

When we pulled in, Griz's car was already in the employee parking lot. He got out as we parked.

"Are we going to have a problem with them if we go inside?" I asked him.

"We should be in and out before they even realize we're here," Griz said, unlocking the back door for us.

The kitchen already smelled like stagnant water and old oil. Thankfully, we never left any food out and always emptied the garbage cans at closing, or it would have been worse.

Griz sighed. "Everly and Vena, you two pack up the perishables in the main fridge. I'll clean the kitchen. Anchor, you take the office upstairs. Cross, can you check over the bars and throw out anything perishable in those refrigerators? Give it a wipe down as well."

We all split up. While Griz cleaned, Vena and I started

packing boxes with stuff from the kitchen fridge. Some of it needed to be thrown out already, but most of it was still good. Once we had several boxes waiting by the back door, we checked the storage room.

"I think everything will be good in here for a while," I said. "Let's take what we have out to the SUV."

Propping the door to make it easier for us, Vena headed out with the first box. As I was picking up a box from beside the door, I heard a shout and looked up. A group of protesters descended upon Vena, who was standing at the back of the SUV with the tailgate open.

"Werewolf lover!" someone yelled.

A man ripped the supplies from her arms and started throwing the contents at her. Dropping the box I was holding, I ran into the chaos, yelling her name, then Anchor's.

I briefly lost sight of her as I reached the outer ring. The guy whose shirt I pulled on in an attempt to get him to move turned on me and shoved me back. I stumbled and fell on my ass hard enough that it felt like I broke my tailbone, and all the soreness of the sex-a-thon I had with Shepard came roaring back.

A booming growl filled the air.

Everyone stopped moving.

I twisted around to see Anchor storm out of the building. He knocked down people like they were bowling pins and he was the ball. Those still upright backed away in a hurry, giving me a clear view of Vena on the ground. She was sitting awkwardly, holding her arm.

My friend, who barely ever cried, had tears in her eyes.

She looked up at Anchor. "I think my arm's broken, babe."

"It's okay. I've got you now," he said, picking her up gently. Any softness he had was for her alone because, when his gaze swept the crowd, it held pure murder.

"Do you see the man at the top of the building?" he asked.

Everyone turned to look at the building, but there was no one there.

"Thanks for looking right at the security camera," he said. "Everyone here can expect a call from the police."

"Who are on their way," Cross said, appearing beside me to help me to my feet. He faced away from the camera and flashed the protesters his black eyes and fanged teeth.

The crowd scattered.

"Did you have to do that?" I asked as his face went back to normal.

"It was for their own good," Cross said simply. "Maybe they'll think twice next time."

"You can't fix dumb," Griz said. "I doubt it did any good."

"I'm going to take Vena to the hospital," Anchor said. "Can you give the police the footage?"

He didn't wait for an answer because, of course, we'd do what was needed. I watched as he gently put Vena in the passenger seat of the SUV and secured her seatbelt. He ran to the driver's side and hopped in.

"I hope she's okay," I said.

Cross rubbed my back for a moment.

"I'll get the footage and let Shepard know what happened," Griz said.

While he did that, Cross and I cleaned up the mess in the parking lot and resumed clearing out Blur. The police arrived just as Cross and I put the rest of the perishables in the back of Griz's car.

He handed over the footage. "You can see they started it, and everyone's faces are clear."

"Once we ID them, do you want to press charges?" an officer asked.

"I'll leave that up to Shepard, the owner, and Vena, the woman who was hurt," Griz said, passing Shepard's business card to them.

The police asked a few more questions and took all of our names, along with Vena's information.

After they left, Griz locked the back door and walked us to his car.

"Thanks for your help. I'm sorry it turned out like this."

"It's not your fault," I said. "I can't believe they would attack Vena like that."

My thoughts drifted to Pam for a moment. She had been thinking about leaving Blur because of the attacks. What if it would have been her instead of Vena?

At least Vena was scrappy. She'd wrap her arm in a cast and come out swinging. But the others? I wasn't so sure. Maybe Shepard had been right to shut down Blur even though it was sad. It felt like one more thing was lost in this stupid war Orphia had started.

"It'll be okay," Cross said as he opened the passenger door for me.

"Will it? What if our bakery is attacked next?"

"Then we'll repair and move on. Don't let other people's hate and misinformation dictate what we do. Our bakery has a mission, after all. One that will hopefully unite people. It might not happen overnight, but it has to start somewhere. Where better than a place filled with love and cookies?"

"You're right. But it still sucks."

"It does. Let's head back and wait for Vena and Anchor. Does she have a favorite treat you can make her?"

I nodded and got in so Griz could drop us off at home.

"Oh, I forgot to tell you," Cross said as we walked upstairs. "The sign is ready. It should be installed tomorrow."

While I still felt the thread of excitement, I wondered how long it would take to find Orphia. Would we have to deal with her for weeks or years? Would she be like the villain in a movie franchise that kept returning movie after movie?

At the top of the stairs, Cross drew me into a hug and released me into the kitchen. He even handed me my whisk and tied a new apron on me.

"Kiss the Vampire?" I asked as I read it aloud. "Isn't it supposed to say 'Kiss the Cook'?"

"If you insist," Cross said, kissing me.

I grinned at his playfulness, especially after everything that happened.

He straightened the apron as if unable to stop touching me yet. "It's just a reminder for you. I'll always know to kiss the cook."

"I'll always know to kiss you as well. Out of curiosity, did you get one that says 'Kiss the Wolf'?"

"No. I'm getting him something better. He's going to love it."

"I have a feeling he won't."

Cross lazily shrugged and sat at the island to watch me work.

"Where are my gnomies at!" Vena yelled from downstairs, announcing her arrival just before lunchtime.

I heard Anchor shush her and one set of footsteps on the stairs. He appeared at the top with Vena in his arms. She was grinning like it was Mardi Gras and she was half a bottle in.

"A clean break," he said. "They gave her some pain meds. Too strong in my opinion."

"I told 'em it didn't hurt, but they didn't listen to me."

"They were listening," Anchor said. "The whole emergency room was listening."

"Oh-oh," I said, beating him to the couch where I had pillows and a blanket waiting for her. "What did she do?"

"Nothing," he said with a flush as he set her down.

"That doesn't look like nothing."

"That's what she said!" Vena yelled.

"Ah," I said, understanding.

"That's what she said next!" Vena dissolved into a fit of laughter, which ended with her wincing and whining to Anchor that her arm hurt. But once he was within reach to soothe her, she pulled him in for some huggles like an octopus.

"Would you like lunch on the couch, or should I pry her off of you?" I asked him.

"Lunch here is fine," he said.

"Yeah, I'm hungry too," Vena said. "But you're going to have to feed me, babe. I broke my pumping arm. Why that arm? I can feed myself with my left, but I can't get a decent rhythm on you with it. Here, let me show you."

I stopped in my tracks, turned around, and marched right back to Vena.

Gently, I grabbed her ponytail and pulled her head back so she was looking at me upside down as she fumbled with Anchor's hands, which were defending his zipper.

"Vena Anne Hunter, if you don't keep your hands to yourself and stop talking dirty to your man in public spaces for the next twenty-four hours, I will call your mother and tell her in very vivid detail what happened to her mummified hand last year."

Vena stopped struggling. "You wouldn't."

"Are you feeling lucky?"

She gave me sad eyes. "No. Not even a little."

"Good. Then behave, eat your dinner, and go to bed. We have enough trouble without you making more."

"Yes, ma'am," she said sullenly.

Anchor's gaze bounced between me and Vena. "What happened to the mummified hand?"

"We don't talk about the hand," she said, slapping her hand over his mouth.

I winked at him and went to serve up the food.

Once Vena and Anchor were eating on the couch, I took my plate and let myself into Cross' study. Someone had spotted Vivian near the old asylum the night of the meeting, which worried Cross. He was on the phone again, talking to one of his contacts to see if he could find any new information regarding Vivian or Orphia.

As soon as I sat in the chair across from his, he thanked whoever he was talking to and hung up.

"Any news?" I asked.

"Nothing."

"And you're more worried now than if you'd heard nothing."

He sighed and nodded.

"I'm guessing Vivian knows what happens at those meetings," I said. "If he'd wanted us himself, he would have made his move before we went inside."

"Which is even more troubling. If he wasn't there for you, then why was he there?"

"Gathering evidence that what he said in the video was true, maybe?"

Cross nodded but didn't look convinced. Neither was I. If that had been the case, he would have brought that night up in his video.

Cross' phone rang again. After checking the number, he answered on speaker.

"Shepard, Everly is listening."

"Why did you say it like that?" I asked, narrowing my eyes on Cross. "Is there something I'm not supposed to hear?"

Shepard chuckled. "I'm just calling to let you know Hugh confirmed our interview for later today. I'm on my way back and bringing company."

"What kind of company?" Cross asked.

"Hugh and some of his people. He has a plan."

CHAPTER EIGHTEEN

SHEPARD, HUGH, AND SEVERAL OTHERS ARRIVED THIRTY MINUTES later. I'd cleaned up dinner, and Vena was napping in her room, which I was grateful for when I saw who the guests were.

"Piper? Robyn? What are you doing here?" I asked.

My friends looked equally shocked to see me.

"You know each other?" Hugh asked.

"Yes," Piper said, flashing a happy yet nervous glance at Hugh. "Everly is a friend from college." She glanced back at me. "Where's Vena?"

"She broke her arm a few hours ago and is sleeping off the painkillers."

"Sleeping them off?" Shepard asked. "Doesn't she need them?"

"She's got a very high pain tolerance. I think they gave her something, hoping to shut her up. It didn't work. It made her worse."

Shepard glanced at Anchor, who was standing by the island and nodded.

"I thought you guys were in Europe," I said. "When did you get back?"

"About that…"

Hugh cleared his throat. "I believe we should sit down to have this discussion."

We sat at the table, with Cross and Shepard sitting on each side of me and Hugh, Piper, and Robyn across from us. Three other agents stood behind them like their shadows.

"Despite the footage Vena captured and public awareness, the NC meetings haven't stopped," Hugh said. "With Shepard and Curran's rings gone and Effora missing, we're assuming the worst—that Orphia has three of the four stones. If Vivian is telling the truth, which we believe he is, we need to stop Orphia as soon as possible.

"Piper and Robyn, our youngest vampire hunters, have volunteered to attend the next meeting. They've registered separately and are waiting for their meetup call."

Vampire hunters?

I glanced at Piper and Robyn, who seemed at ease with the assignment. How had Vena and I not known what they were up to? When they'd said they were going to Europe, I'd thought it was for a fun vacation. Obviously, that'd been a lie.

Did I really know them at all?

My gaze shifted from Piper to Hugh, and I noted an eerie resemblance between them. They both had the same honey blonde hair and hazel eyes that were more green than brown. Robyn was the opposite with dark hair and eyes.

I turned to Hugh. "You were watching us to keep us safe, and Vena and I still almost got hurt. What are you going to do to keep Piper and Robyn safe?"

Hugh smiled. "They might be our youngest hunters, but they're well trained. I promise you, they're more equipped to infiltrate these meetings than you or Vena were. We pulled them from the field just for this."

"The field?" I echoed.

Robyn smiled. "There's a lot we can't tell you, but trust us when we say we know what we're doing."

"Orphia and her people will likely take more precautions after last night and Vivian's video this morning," Shepard said. "Are you sure the meetings will continue?"

"Positive," Hugh said. "She's after conversions. If a few meetings go bad, she won't care about the casualties, which is why we need to get our people in there quickly. We're hoping, at this next meeting, we'll be able to capture a vampire or two to interrogate."

"If she let every vampire know where she was, Cross would already know how to find her," I said, a little impatient with Hugh.

"Everly's right," Cross said. "She wouldn't let just anyone know."

"The guy on the stage sounded like the guy on the phone when Vena got the meetup call. I think he was also the one our driver was talking to about the supposed no-shows along the route. If you capture anyone, that's the guy you need."

Hugh nodded. "Our hunters tracked the vampire who got him out of there but lost the trail after a few miles. They had a car waiting. We'll be better prepared this time.

"Now that the Night Club scheme has been exposed, we're hoping fewer people sign up for them, and we'll get Piper and Robyn in sooner," Hugh said.

As they discussed the plan's finer details, including werewolf backup, I set out cookies and water for everyone.

"I missed your cookies," Piper said with a barely suppressed moan that made Robyn roll her eyes.

"That's because you're part Cookie Monster. Don't think I didn't see that the box of cookies you bought for emergencies yesterday is now empty in your car."

Eventually, the meeting wrapped up. Hugh and his people got up to leave. Piper and Robyn stood as well but paused at the table.

Hugh paused as well. "Is there something wrong?"

"No," Piper said. "If it's okay, Robyn and I will find our own way back. We want to talk to Everly first."

He nodded and looked at Cross and Shepard. "I'll see the three of you at the studio at four-thirty. Dress professionally, and no kissing or hitting."

When Hugh left, Shepard and Cross went to the living room to give me a little space with my friends. I pointed my finger accusingly at them.

Before I could say anything, Piper said, "We saw their first interview with Denise. It was pretty funny."

"No changing topics. You both have a lot of explaining to do."

Piper laughed and sat back down at the table. Robyn followed her lead.

"What do you want to know?" Piper asked. "I swear we weren't keeping anything from you on purpose. We operate under secrecy for a reason."

"I understand that, but you're in college. What's with the hunting?"

She waved it off as if it was no big deal. "Hugh is my dad. I was born into this. Robyn, too."

Robyn nodded. "I come from a long line of vampire hunters."

I slow-blinked at both of them as I wrapped my head around the fact that my friends had a history and ties to creatures I hadn't even known were real before falling into Cross's cave. Vena and I hadn't had a clue.

"I would have never guessed in a million years," I said.

Piper shrugged. "Sounds like you've been up to a lot during summer break, too." She leaned forward then flicked her gaze to the living room. The questions in her eyes were as clear as if she'd asked them out loud.

"It's been a long summer already," I said. "Shepard is now my mate, and Cross is my..."

I didn't know what to call him. Boyfriend seemed too weak of a word when I was already committed to him. Yet, fiancé or husband wasn't right either.

"Vampire mate?" I said, unsure. "It's still new, and I'm figuring things out as I go along, but I'm really happy. Well, not about the issues with vampires. Or the Effora issue."

Piper and Robyn both grimaced at Effora's name.

"She's so horrible," Piper said. "You should see some of the people who come out of her house. Some make it to the hospital, but others aren't that lucky."

Robyn nodded. "As far as I'm concerned, she's no better than Orphia. They just go about their tyranny differently."

I spoke a little bit about my encounters with her, except for the last one. I didn't want to dwell on it.

"The bakery downstairs looks cool," Piper said, switching the topic. She was always good at sensing when someone needed a break. "Are you and Vena finally going to get your dream?"

I smiled at her. "I think Vena's dream might change after hearing about you two."

Piper and Robyn left shortly after our conversation and told me to say hello to Vena for them.

"We'll see you again soon," Piper promised, giving me a hug.

"Text us when your opening day is, and we'll be there," Robyn said.

Cross stood to show them out.

"This is weird," Piper said as she walked with Cross. "Normally, I'd be fighting a vampire, not walking civilly next to one."

"I've heard of it before," Robyn said. "But it's uncommon. Why are you different?"

"A long, lonely existence made me willing to risk everything," I heard Cross say.

Shepard wrapped his arms around me from behind.

"He's okay," he said.

"Are you a mind reader now?"

"No, I just know you worry about him. He has you, though, so he's okay. Never doubt it."

"And when he doesn't have me?" I asked. "He's very adamant that he doesn't want any children to pass down the vampire gene, and I'll eventually age and die, Shepard. What about then?"

"Is anyone meant to live forever, Everly? Even the fae, as long-lived as they are, die eventually. Death is part of life, and he knows it."

"I just don't want him to be alone."

"He won't be." Shepard turned me in his arms and kissed my forehead. "But enough of this kind of thinking. We have decades to figure that out. What we need to think about now is what suit you want me to wear. I put Cross in charge of my wardrobe, which is frightening enough, and he has two options for you to pick from."

Shepard led me to the closet and pulled out two suits that both looked nice. One was in a lighter brown that would complement Shepard's skin tone, and the other was blue, which complemented his eyes.

"He didn't want to do black suits. And I vetoed the burgundy, terra-cotta, and patterned suits. So this is what's left."

I bit my lip, trying to imagine Shepard in a patterned suit. It would need a lot of pattern to cross the breadth of his shoulders.

"Let's go with the lighter brown. It looks less serious, which is what this live show is supposed to convey...the lighter side of your relationship."

He thanked me, and I walked out of the closet to find Cross leaning against the counter.

"I preferred the lighter one as well. Thank you for convincing him."

"I trust her taste, not yours," Shepard called.

"If that were true, you wouldn't have given me your measurements," Cross said back.

"My estimation about his size was accurate, by the way," Cross told me.

Shepard stuck his head out of the closet. "Out. Not you, Everly. You can help me with my tie."

Helping involved a lot of sweet kisses and hugs, which I loved.

When he was finished, he styled his longish hair begrudgingly under Cross' watchful eye in the bathroom.

"I've done my hair on my own for most of my thirty-three years. Go away."

"Try not to look business. You're trying for sexy. Appealing. I know it's a stretch—"

Cross caught the hairbrush Shepard threw and tossed it back to him.

"Everly, are you going to allow him to treat me this way?" Cross asked with a mock pout.

"Don't pull me into your squabbling. I'm just here to spectate." I smirked. "And for the eye candy."

Shepard's ass in those suit pants was drawing my gaze every time he moved.

Cross chuckled as Shepard glanced at me with golden eyes.

"Did I mention they want you to be part of this interview, too?" Shepard asked.

That wiped the smirk right off my face.

"Heck no."

"Are you sure?" Cross asked. "You'd be a household name after today. Think of how the publicity now would help our bakery later."

I frowned. "You're playing dirty. You need to stop hanging out with Vena."

He winked at me. "I had something tailored for you, too. Go look."

Curious, I went to check the closet. Since everything was new to me, it took a while for me to find a pant-suit set in the same shade as Shepard's in my section of the closet.

I grinned, loving the idea of couple outfits. Different, yet close enough to be intentional.

"What do you think?" Cross asked, stepping behind me.

"I love it. Thank you."

Cross kissed the back of my neck. "You're welcome. I have one more surprise for you, but after you get ready."

I took a little extra time to do my makeup and hair. When I emerged from the bedroom, both men watched me hungrily. The shorter suit coat accentuated all my curves and gave me the illusion that I had longer legs than I did. The heels helped that, too.

"You look beautiful, Everly," Shepard said. "I'm glad we picked the lighter suit."

"Same," I said. Then I looked at Cross, who hadn't changed yet.

"I'll be right back," he said.

He blurred away as Shepard slowly walked around me. When he faced me again, his eyes were pure gold.

"I see that you like the view."

"Very much."

"What exactly do I need to know for this interview?" I asked.

"Nothing. Just be yourself. You're the glue that binds Cross and I together."

My eyes went wide. "We're *not* talking about our relationship on the news."

His hands closed over my shoulders, giving me a reassuring squeeze.

"We'll only reveal whatever you're comfortable with. Cross and I talked about it, and we think if you share that you woke him and worked for me that's enough. We don't need to go any deeper into what we feel for each other."

I let out a relieved breath.

"Good. I'm still not sure how to tell my parents."

"You have time. Don't rush it."

Cross blurred back into the living room, dressed in an identical suit and tie set as Shepard. They were adorable together, and it made my heart squeeze like it was being hugged by Cupid.

"Absolutely not," Shepard said to Cross. "Either you change, or I do."

I tugged on Shepard's coat and stuck out my bottom lip a little. "But I like matching with both of you. I'm fair like that. How can I be the glue between you if we don't all match?"

He groaned and darted in to suck my bottom lip into his mouth, which turned into a hot kiss that would have ended in disaster if not for Cross' quick "Don't touch her hair" warning.

I broke off the kiss and looked at Shepard's hand, which was inches from my head.

"Do you know how much product is in my hair right now to get it to look like this?"

He grinned and kissed the tip of my nose. "I do. I can smell it."

The door to Vena's room opened, and Anchor crept out, closing it behind him.

"Looking good," he said to all of us. "While you're out, I'll start dinner and keep the gremlin entertained. Put in a good word for the wolves, okay, Everly? I really need the Hunters to approve of me soon."

I snorted. "They already do." Then, my eyes went wide in understanding.

"Her arm will slow her down a few more days, but then I'm hers."

Grinning, I hurried across the room to hug Anchor.

Shepard growled, and out of the corner of my eye, I saw Cross playfully clock him in the back of his head.

"I thought you said not the hair," Shepard muttered.

"Hers, not yours."

"Time to go," Shepard said.

Cross held my hand on the way out, his thumb softly stroking my skin. My stomach was already a ball of nerves just thinking about having to be on TV. The last interview had gone horribly.

And while I knew I would keep my cool better than Shepard had, I wasn't sure I wanted Denise grilling me.

"It will be okay," Cross said, sensing my nerves, as he opened the car door for me. "If not, you have a vampire and wolf with you. What could go wrong?"

"So many things."

He chuckled and kissed my cheek before closing the door.

We arrived at the station to find out we'd have a different host this time. Craig Gloverson was a news anchor, not a talk show host like Denise. I hoped that meant their interview styles were different.

The news studio had the familiar long desk and the backdrop of the city along with several other dedicated spots for weather, sports, and even a kitchen area. Although I'd seen Craig on the news a few times, I rarely watched the entire five o'clock news program.

"How long is this segment going to be?" I asked the production assistant who had walked us in.

"It's not a segment," she said. "We're using the whole five o'clock news for a special report."

"The whole time?" I asked, the nerves getting the better of me.

She nodded with a smile. "Just be yourself, and it will be fine."

I was pretty sure I heard something along those lines for Shepard and Cross' interview as well, and it had not been fine.

I had thought we would be at the desk, but someone escorted us to an intimate interview area, kind of like the setup Denise had, but this one was branded to the news. The familiar audio guy mic'd Cross and Shepard first, then gave me instructions on how to do it so he wasn't touching me.

Just when I thought my stomach might revolt, Craig walked on set. He had an arrogant stride and a cocky smile, but when he shook our hands and told us a little about what would happen, I felt marginally better.

Craig sat on one side, and the three of us sat on the other, with me between Cross and Shepard.

"Just look at me," Craig said to us. "Don't worry about the cameras. They'll do their thing. We'll do ours."

When the floor director started the countdown, I took a breath and waited as Craig talked to the camera, telling the viewers that the news would be on after the special report. He gave a little background information about his guests, a vampire and a werewolf, and why it was such a big deal.

The giant lights hanging from a grid on the ceiling were starting to get to me. Sweat beaded on my lower back.

"So, let's introduce our guests," Craig said. "Shepard Ulv, a werewolf; Brodier Cross, a vampire; and Everly Reid, a human. Welcome."

CHAPTER NINETEEN

KNOWING THAT THE CAMERAS WERE FOLLOWING CRAIG'S GAZE, I struggled to remain outwardly calm as he looked at us in welcome.

"You've been making some headlines lately, Brodier," Craig said. "But there's more to your story that hasn't been said, yet."

"A lot more," Cross agreed. "And please call me Cross."

"Okay, Cross. Let's start with that kiss you shared with Shepard during your last interview here."

"It wasn't shared," Shepard said. I could feel him tense beside me, which only made me more nervous. Shepard inhaled deeply and immediately relaxed.

Cross chuckled. "I think everyone knows it wasn't shared. The point wasn't the kiss but the relationship between vampires and werewolves in general. Not every vampire hates every werewolf, and not every werewolf hates every vampire. Shepard and I are proof of that."

"That punch didn't look very caring."

"Would all your male friends allow you to kiss them on the mouth?" Cross asked with a knowing smirk.

"No, probably not," Craig said, laughing and shaking his head.

"So, tell us then, how did a vampire and a werewolf become friends? According to several vampire sources, it's not possible for the two races to get along."

"We met through Everly, a mutual acquaintance," Cross said.

"I guessed as much. I love the matching suits, by the way."

The camera facing me blinked red, and I realized I was on camera.

"Thank you," I said with a shaky smile.

"Were they your idea?" Craig asked.

I shook my head. "Cross'. He has a better fashion sense than I do."

"There are a lot of questions I'd like to ask about that, but first, would you be willing to tell us a little more about how you know Shepard and Cross, Everly?"

"I used to work for Shepard at Blur."

"Used to? You don't work there anymore?"

"Unfortunately, due to protesters and several vampire attacks on the business, I've had to close the door for the safety of my employees and my patrons," Shepard said.

"I did hear about that but thought it was temporary," Craig said. "A lot of people will be upset if the doors close for good. Blur has been known as one of the best spots for music and drinks in D.C. for over a decade."

"And I don't want to let down the community that has supported me over the years," Shepard said. "Right now, the best way I can give back is to focus my efforts on keeping everyone safe."

Craig nodded and focused on me again. "And how do you know Cross? Did he work at Blur, too?"

"No. I met Cross when I accidentally woke him up."

"Woke him up? That sounds interesting. How does one wake a vampire?"

"Well, I wouldn't recommend falling on him," I said with a smile.

Craig laughed and leaned forward. "I think not falling on a vampire is good advice. It sounds like there's a story there. We'd love to hear it."

I didn't want to talk about it. Looking back, I could see how ridiculous the experience was. But with what I knew now, I also understood the story needed to be told. At least, parts of it. People needed to know about a real vampire experience.

"I was hiking with my friend, and we accidentally fell into a cave. The fall was traumatic enough. Getting up and seeing what we thought was a corpse was even more terrifying."

"Describe it to us," Craig said. "What made you think he was a corpse?"

"He was lying on this stone ledge. It couldn't have been comfortable."

I glanced at Cross.

He flashed his sexy smile at me. "It wasn't. I assure you."

Holding Cross' gaze, I tried to remember what he'd looked like.

"He wore old clothes. Really old. And he was covered with dust and cobwebs."

"Was he sunken and bony?" Craig asked.

Slightly offended by the description, I looked at Craig. "No. Not at all. He looked like he does now. Handsome. A little too perfect. Aloof."

Cross chuckled next to me.

"Why did you think he was a corpse then?"

"The clothes he wore looked like he'd come over on the Mayflower. The dust. The cobwebs. His absolute stillness...it was like he was perfectly preserved. And he wasn't moving or breathing that I could tell."

"And how did you discover he was alive?" Craig asked.

"When I fell into the cave, I cut my cheek. My friend was looking at his clothes, trying to figure out what they were, and I leaned down to check to see if he was breathing because, like I said, he looked like he does now."

"Not dead," Craig supplied.

"Exactly. It didn't make sense. When I checked to see if he was breathing, I accidentally bled on him."

"Then what happened?"

"My friend realized what he was and what I'd done, and we ran before he woke up."

Craig shifted his attention to Cross. "Was that all it took? A drop of her blood to wake you?"

"It was."

"Why were you there?"

"Living as a vampire, seeing the people you care about age and then die…" Cross shook his head, and without thinking, I took his hand to comfort him. He wrapped my hand in both of his like he was capturing it. "Unlike most of my kind, it was an existence I no longer wanted. I left England and my savage brethren behind and came to the Americas, where I found a cave."

"How does a vampire go into hibernation?"

"We stop feeding. We let the hunger for blood consume us until we can no longer draw a breath."

"You died?" Craig asked.

"The only way to kill a vampire is to remove his heart or head," Shepard said.

"Or sunlight," Cross added.

Shepard nodded in agreement.

Craig turned his attention to Shepard. "You know a lot about killing vampires, it seems."

"I do. It's what my kind was created to do. Kill vampires to protect humans."

"And yet you're sitting here with Cross. Why haven't you killed him?"

"Everly convinced me he wasn't like the vampires we normally see."

"How was Cross different?" he asked, looking at me.

"He didn't kill me or my friend," I said with a little shrug. "He had plenty of opportunities and reasons to do so, but he chose a different path."

Craig's gaze darted from me to Cross. "I sense there's more to that statement."

"Everly's friend accidentally took something that was mine," Cross explained. "My kind are protective of what we consider ours. Objects and people. So I wasn't pleased when I woke to find something of mine missing.

"With the taste of Everly's blood on my lips and a hint of her life filling my mind, I tracked her to her home."

"Wait…what was it you just said? A hint of her life filled your mind? What does that mean?"

"When my kind feeds, we become intimately tied to our donor. We gain glimpses of their lives, their thoughts, and their feelings. Each drop of blood is like a puzzle piece. And with enough feedings, we eventually see the whole picture."

"Fascinating. I didn't know that about vampires."

"Not many do."

"So you tracked down Everly and her friend, and what then?"

"I tracked them to their home and found the plate of bonbons Everly had made for me, a handwritten note apologizing for the misunderstanding, and the item they'd taken."

"You stole from a vampire and left him bonbons?" Craig asked in disbelief.

"Sugar helps people feel happier, and everyone likes the sweet treats I make." I shrugged, feeling a little embarrassed in hindsight. "I think I was still in a state of denial that vampires were real and one would be coming for us."

Craig laughed and looked at Cross. "And what was your reaction to what she left for you?"

"I went to find her."

"Because you were angry and wanted revenge?"

"Because she'd bled into the bonbons she'd made. I've never met another person who had thought to atone for their mistake with that kind of gesture. It made me curious about the woman who'd woken me. The woman who I knew was kind yet courageous. Timid and stubborn. And loyal to a fault."

His words and the new understanding of how we'd started had me blushing.

"I'm guessing the second meeting went better than the first," Craig said.

Cross grinned. "I thought so, although she might not have. It's not like she wanted a vampire following her after what had happened. But seeing her for the first time was like seeing the sun after centuries of darkness."

"I feel like I should be taking notes. But seriously," he said, turning to Shepard, "that he didn't kill Everly was enough to stop you from killing him."

"No. That he protected someone I loved was what convinced me."

Craig was silent as his gaze bounced between the three of us, and I felt my panic rising.

"You love her?" Craig said. "I thought she was your employee."

Shepard winced.

"She *was* an employee," Shepard said. "From the moment Everly walked into Blur and applied for a job, I knew she was the one. I never said or did anything, though. I'm a werewolf, and she's a human. The chances of her being interested in a life with me were really low."

"Low?" Craig questioned, looking surprised. "I think there are some *The Other House* fans out there who would beg to differ. But since Everly is sitting here, I assume she beat those low odds."

"Are you two together?" Craig looked at me for confirmation.

All I could do was nod. It was the truth, and hiding it would hurt Shepard. I couldn't do that to him.

Craig looked as if my nod was the most intriguing thing he had ever seen.

"Then what about Cross? I feel there is a bit of a romance blooming there. He was pretty poetic a few moments ago."

If I couldn't hide my relationship with Shepard, then I couldn't deny Cross either. I loved them equally. They were my life. My future.

"I love Cross. And I love Shepard." I braced myself for disgust. Few people understood polygamous relationships. Even I was still trying to figure it out.

"Then do Cross and Shepard love each other? Is this the first werewolf and vampire mating?"

"No," I answered before either of them could. Shepard would probably growl his answer, and Cross would make a humorous comment that wouldn't clear the confusion. "They love me. I love them. But Cross and Shepard are friends, working together to help rid the city of vampires."

"Although I'd love to delve into your relationship a little more, I'm really curious why the two of you are working together to help rid the city of vampires." He looked to Cross. "You're a vampire. Why would you want them gone?"

"There is a lot of misinformation out there. I could say vampires are all bad, but I'm proof there are exceptions to the rule. The problem is that any vampire can tell you they are exceptions as well. They can thrall or compel you to believe whatever they want."

"I've heard about that. How would a person know if they were compelled or thralled?"

"They wouldn't," Cross said. "But the people around them might if they start acting out of character."

"I've been compelled twice," I said. "Both times, it felt like my thoughts were my own."

"Cross compelled you?" Craig asked.

"Once. To help me sleep after a different vampire compelled me."

"Would you like a demonstration?" Cross asked before Craig could ask more questions.

"Is it safe?" Craig asked.

"No," I said. "Being compelled or thralled by a vampire is never safe. That's what people need to understand."

"Yet you allowed Cross to compel you."

"Because Everly knows I would never hurt her," Cross said. "Plus, compelling is merely a suggestion that doesn't go against who you are. How long it lasts and how far it can press against the boundaries of who you are depends on the vampire's strength and the human's willpower.

"Now, thralling is different. It's more than a suggestion and requires a vampire to feed from the person. Once that connection is made, a vampire can turn you into their puppet, forcing you to act as the vampire pleases, whether you like it or not. The thrall lasts until you die, the vampire dies, or a stronger vampire takes over the thrall."

Craig's attentive expression never faltered, but I knew he was nervous when his gaze briefly shifted to the camera crew. The producer was frantically motioning to Craig, and I almost felt bad for the news anchor when he looked at Cross.

"How would you demonstrate it? Compelling, not thralling," he said quickly.

"By having you do something simple. Something that doesn't go against who you are, but something you wouldn't normally do without a nudge."

Craig looked at the camera. "I can't believe I'm about to do this." He turned to Cross. "What will you make me do?"

"If I told you beforehand, the audience wouldn't know if I compelled you or if it was an act."

"Very true." Craig let out a breath and wiped his hands on his pants. It was the first time I had seen him outwardly show his nervousness. "Please, nothing embarrassing."

"What if I told you to cluck like a chicken?" Cross asked.

"I'd say no thank y—"

"Cluck like a chicken."

Craig looked mutinous for a second and then flapped his arms and squawked like a dying chicken.

I winced, knowing this was going to go viral, and nudged Cross when Craig kept flapping and squawking.

"Make him stop."

Cross looked for the camera with the red light on. "This is why you shouldn't trust vampires. Trust is earned, not freely given."

I nudged him again. "You made your point."

"Craig, you may stop clucking and resume your duties as host."

Craig choked on his last squawk and reached for a glass of water. He took a sip and shook his head as if to clear it.

"That was strange. When you first suggested it, I thought absolutely not. But when you said to do it, I thought of every reason why what you were suggesting made sense. And that's what it felt like—a suggestion. As if I could have talked myself out of it but didn't want to.

"I knew the audience would want to see you compelling me. The producer would be happy. The network might even give me a promotion...I talked myself into it even though I'm embarrassed by what I just did."

The flush in his face and brittle smile conveyed the truth behind his admission.

He turned toward the camera. "Regretfully, or maybe thankfully, that's all the time we have. If you take away anything from this interview, please remember you are not stronger than a vampire. Let the wolves and authorities do their job. I want to thank our guests for joining us. Please stay tuned for the nightly news right after this."

As soon as the red light blinked off and the floor director yelled, "Clear," Craig ripped off his mic and stormed away.

"This better not become a fucking GIF or meme!"

I looked at Cross and Shepard as we stood. "It feels like you took turns making the hosts angry."

Cross grinned. "I didn't want Shepard to look like the bad guy alone."

Hugh came up to us with a smile on his face.

"That went better than I expected. Craig did an excellent job steering the conversation without making it look like a blatant vampire-hate interview. Explaining the different types of mind control should help people know what to look for. And understanding that a feeding enables the vampire to intimately know a person's thoughts and past should help slow down the Night Club's volunteers."

My phone started to ring, and when I looked down at the caller, I felt a little sick to my stomach, seeing it was my mom.

"Is there somewhere private I can take this call?" I asked Hugh.

He waved for a production assistant.

Shepard caught my free hand in his. "Do you think your parents watched it?"

"Yes." The word trembled a little. "I thought I was safe since they were on the cruise, but they faithfully watch the five o'clock news, and they bought the Wi-Fi package."

"Do you want us to talk to them with you?" Shepard asked.

The call went to voicemail. A second later, it started ringing again.

"No. I'd rather have this conversation without either of you."

My parents were generally accepting of everyone. That was why I was friends with the daughter of otherworld treasure hunters. However, like any parents, they'd have concerns about dating non-humans, never mind dating two at once.

"It's okay. I'll be okay. I'm just a little nervous."

Shepard nodded and kissed my forehead. When he was done, Cross turned me to do the same.

"We'll be right here when you're done."

I nodded and left with the production assistant while Hugh quietly talked to them about the next segment he thought they should do.

After leading me down a hallway off of the studio, she stopped at a door labeled Guest Dressing Room.

"You can take the call here. It's soundproofed so the mics don't pick up noise."

"Thank you."

As I opened the door, I looked down at my phone and stepped inside.

Five missed calls.

It started ringing again as I closed the door.

"It would be better if you didn't answer that."

The sound of a familiar man's voice sent a shiver of fear through me.

Swallowing hard, I looked up from my phone and met Vivian's amused gaze.

CHAPTER TWENTY

I STARED INTO THE BLACK EYES OF THE VAMPIRE WHO'D TRIED TO bite me on multiple occasions and felt my airway squeeze close in panic.

He inhaled deeply from his place on the room's single sofa, keeping his ankle balanced on his knee in a relaxed pose.

"Mmm. Your fear tempts me to play. I haven't since—"

The dark veining around his eyes spread briefly, then retreated completely, showing how smudged his dark makeup was. In fact, he looked very un-Vivian compared to the video he'd released, with his long black hair greasy and tangled.

I struggled to breathe and tried to think, but it was like trying to hold fine sand through outstretched fingers. Thoughts kept slipping away in my terror.

Run? No. It would probably just make him mad and me hurt. Keep him on the couch with that puddle of black material next to him. Distance was good. That wasn't a sack to put over my head, was it?

His hand rested on his leg, and he started tapping his thumb idly. Shepard's ring caught the overhead lights and glinted prettily, catching my attention and breaking through my chaotic thoughts.

"You want to use me to get Cross' ring, don't you?" I asked.

"You're an interesting one, Everly. I've heard a lot about Cross from Orphia over the decades. How unpredictable he was. How dangerous. Yet, for you, he's as gentle as a kitten. He even made nice with the werewolves. *Sharing* his favorite meal."

He inhaled again and stood fluidly in a way that conveyed how dangerous he was.

"After that interview and seeing you now, so full of fear but not backing away or puffing up with false bravado, I'm beginning to understand why."

His gaze swept over me from head to toe.

"That's a nice suit. Pretty. Light colors stain easily, though. That's why I go with black."

My phone continued to ring in my hand, and he flicked an annoyed glance at it.

"Power it off and leave it on the coffee table. It won't work where you're going."

Swallowing hard, I finally looked away from him and held the button to start powering down the phone. My parents were going to have a heart attack if they couldn't reach me soon.

"Where am I going?" I asked as I watched the screen go dark.

"With me."

I looked up again, meeting his gaze. "Why?"

"To spare the lives of the people you love and of those you don't even know."

He leaned in close to whisper in my ear. "Do you know how many people I can kill between here and the studio? Twelve. And someone brought their daughter to work today. She's three, Everly. Her blood smells sweet like the candy they gave her to be quiet."

My stomach churned, and my hand shook as I tossed my

phone toward the coffee table. The sweat on my back that had started to dry surged to the surface again.

"You *are* interesting. No begging. No denial. No surge of last-minute anger. Tell me what you're thinking."

"I'm wondering why you haven't compelled me yet."

He smiled, showing his teeth.

"Because I want to know the real you, Everly. Now, will you follow me out of this room, or will you scream for help the second I open this door?"

I studied him as my thoughts continued to whirl. He knew making me bleed would draw Cross' attention, but I was certain he knew a hundred ways to hurt me without making me bleed. So this wasn't about hurting me. If he'd wanted to, he would have done so already.

And if he wanted the ring, he could have held me hostage and demanded it from Cross in front of all the cameras, where he could have shown the world the real hate between vampires and werewolves. But his video message hadn't been about the hate the two races had for each other. It'd been about the power struggle.

"The clock is ticking."

"Do you really hate Orphia?"

"I do. But don't worry, like you, my hate isn't monogamous." He swept up the pile of black, which turned out to be the awful hat he'd worn the last time I'd seen him.

He didn't put it on, though. He pinned it to his side with one arm and motioned with the other.

"Shall we?" He went to the door and opened it. "To the right. And remember, how we exit is up to you."

He waited until we got close to the sunlit exit to pull on a pair of leather gloves and sweep the hat and full-body veil over his head. Then, he pushed his way out into the sunlight. I was a step behind him. We left the building and headed toward the parking lot.

I glanced at the veil, and my heart started to race harder at the thought of ripping it from his head. A second later, I was pinned against a car, and his hand was on my throat, cutting off my air and blood flow in a punishing grip.

"There are nuances to a human's pulse," he said. "Don't think I can't tell when you're planning something."

I could barely hear his words over the sound of my pulse drumming in my ears. If he didn't ease up, I was going to die.

My hands, which had automatically gone to the hand gripping me, shifted to his veil, pulling it hard enough that the hat started to slip off.

His hand left my throat. My necklace thrummed as he swung his fist toward the side of my head, but it was useless against the power of Vivian's. His necklace flashed red just before his hand connected with my skull.

Dazed and unable to breathe, my knees gave out.

"Although seeing you on your knees is tempting," Vivian said, straightening his hat and veil, "I'm no longer in the mood to play."

He gripped my arm and dragged me upright as I wheezed in a breath.

"I haven't been in the mood to play since your lovers killed mine."

He pushed me forward, propelling me toward a car with extremely tinted windows. I didn't fight him as he shoved me in the passenger seat and buckled me in. I was still trying to wheeze in air.

He blurred and was in the driver's seat as I continued to rub my throat.

"It seems I was a little rough with you," he said.

Pulling off his hat and veil, he grabbed my chin and forced me to look at him.

"You can breathe normally," he said. The pain seemed to fade, or maybe it just no longer mattered. My pulse slowed, and my next inhalation became easier.

"Good," he said. "Now sleep until I tell you to wake up."

I felt his words wrap around my mind. It wouldn't hurt to sleep. Maybe Cross would find me by the time I woke up. Sleep *did* sound good. It had been a long day. Long summer, actually. And my head was starting to hurt where Vivian hit it.

Yeah, I needed sleep. Sleep was good.

My eyes slow-blinked until they finally closed completely.

* . (* .

"WAKE UP."

The words echoed in my head, making my pulse jump and giving me a sense of urgency. My eyes opened, and I looked around, instantly remembering what had happened but not recognizing where I was.

Vivian had taken me somewhere...and I'd been with him for a while from the look of things.

The nearly full moon gave off just enough light to illuminate Vivian's face as he watched from outside the open passenger door. Behind him, I glimpsed a vaguely familiar, unlit empty parking lot surrounded by woods.

Without the gnawing fear that had consumed me in the studio, my thoughts were clearer. We were definitely outside of the city, and Vivian wanted to use me for something. What? I didn't know. My guess was Cross' ring. But he'd purposely taken me away from Cross and Shepard without confronting them. Because he knew he'd lose?

"Look at your little mind work," Vivian said. "You're trying so hard to understand what's happening, aren't you?"

I bit the inside of my cheek hard, just like I'd done the last time Vivian had taken me. The metallic taste of blood filled my mouth.

He inhaled deeply, and his eyes went black. I barely heard the click of my seatbelt before he manhandled me out of the car.

He pushed me against the closed door hard enough to bruise my back.

"Bleeding won't work this time," he said, his fangs flashing at me.

I swallowed hard and winced. My throat hurt like a bitch.

His gaze dipped to my neck, and panic started to claw its way forward.

Come on, Cross. Please be on time again. Please. Please. Please.

Chuckling, Vivian reached between us, trailing a finger over my fluttering pulse before hooking it in my necklace and tugging it upward. Only it wasn't the one that Cross had given me. I stared at the gem-encrusted cock and balls, completely confused.

"Effora's little gift to protect me against all magic. It's magnificent. Turns out, it can even block your master's connection to you."

I tried to say, "He's not my master." But the sounds that emerged were barely recognizable as words.

Vivian still understood, though.

"Only because he's never exercised that right. Perhaps by the end of tonight, he will." He dropped the necklace and patted it on my chest. "Try to touch it, and I will bite off your fingers, one at a time."

I didn't doubt his threat.

He yanked me from the side of the car. "We've waited long enough, I believe. Time to go."

"Where?" I rasped as he shoved me forward.

He pointed to a wooden sign at the edge of the parking lot. It was too far away and too dark to read it, not that I was given the chance to stay where I was.

Vivian propelled me forward with another shove.

When I got close enough to read the sign in the moonlight, I wanted to groan.

The East View parking lot of Sugarloaf Mountain.

Why there? Why the same mountain where I'd fallen into a cave and found Cross?

Vivian chose the white trail marker and shoved me forward onto the unpaved path.

"Go. And if you try to escape, just know there's a lovely wedding-vow renewal event nearby filled with aged attendees who can't run and have no idea they'll be my next meal."

Escape? I could barely walk. Even with all the right gear, I'd barely managed to reach the top of the mountain. I would never survive hiking in a pantsuit and heels.

Once we entered the trees, the moonlight only vaguely touched the trail, creating shadows and hiding obstacles. I tripped several times, almost falling. Vivian laughed softly, a predatorial sound in the darkness.

He inhaled a long breath. "You always smell delicious when you're afraid. But out here, sweating and breathing heavy through your terror, you're intoxicating. I bet when Cross fucks you, you're like a drug. He must fuck you all the time."

"How far do we have to walk?" I asked, hurting my throat in my hope to change the subject. The last thing I wanted was for someone as depraved as Vivian to get ideas.

"Enjoy the night, Everly. It will be a long one.

"Just think, if you play your cards right, you can enjoy all the nights. Who needs the sun, anyway?"

Fear spiked through me, and I tripped on something. My toe throbbed as I stumbled and fought to steady myself.

"Mmm. Even your pain is delicious. It makes me want to do things to you, Everly. With my lover gone, you could be my next toy. We did love our toys. Thoroughly used them until there was nothing left."

Distract him, my mind screamed.

I swallowed hard and tried to speak clearly. "Why here? What's on this mountain? Are there vampires hiding up here?"

"When you ask questions, I wanted to feast on your blood and flood my brain with your memories. But I have a few from the last time you bled. You love your family and friends. Baking too. You have hopes and dreams."

The way he said it made it sound like they were the worst things imaginable.

"You didn't answer my question."

"I didn't. Because I'm not sure if your little human mind can handle the answers."

"Try m—" My foot slid in something, and I went down with an awkward split. The sound of my pants ripping was loud in the quiet woods.

"Ow," I whimpered as I slowly picked myself up.

"Here, let me." Vivian yanked me to my feet by my hair and brought my hand to his mouth. Considering the way he groaned when he sucked on it, I knew there had to be blood. I hoped he choked on dirt.

He released me just as suddenly as he'd pulled me up.

"Walk, you sweet little blood cake, before I remember why I shouldn't paint this trail red with your icing."

Shivering at his words, I spun around and continued along the trail. With my focus on where to step so I wouldn't fall again, I didn't see the danger sign until Vivian told me to stop.

"Under the chain, Everly."

I glanced at the warning sign for falling rocks and risk of death, then slipped under the chained off area.

My heels didn't stand a chance of maintaining any form of stability on the narrow leaf-and-rock-covered track. In daylight, I might have found the area beautiful. In the dark, the surrounding hills and the trees suffocating the moonlight seemed as sinister as the vampire trailing me.

While I watched my feet, a sense of danger slowly grew inside. It shouted that I needed to turn around and run before something really bad happened. Knowing Vivian was behind me and he wouldn't let me go anywhere, along with the fact that there were future victims nearby, was enough to keep me going. However, the warning of danger only intensified as I continued. Soon, I was fighting with the urge to flee, even knowing Vivian wouldn't let me.

I was so focused on forcing myself to keep moving that I didn't notice we had come to the end of the path until I reached an old rusty gate stuck in the gap of a towering, split rock formation.

"Do you feel it?" Vivian said, leaning forward to whisper in my ear. "The compelling need to turn back. I felt it the first time Orphia brought me here. It works on all the races except those who put it here. Makes you want to run, doesn't it? The fae are tricky like that, aren't they? They invite who they like and shun the rest.

"Let's go inside and see what they're trying to hide, shall we?"

He pushed me toward the gate and touched a swirly etching engraved in the metal at the top corner. The lock dissolved, and the gate swung open on its own. The feeling of wrongness and the need to leave vanished as soon as Vivian shoved me through. He followed, not closing the gate behind him.

"That's better. Keep walking. You'll like what's next."

My heels clicked against a smooth stone path completely clear of any trip hazards that led through the dark, narrow passage. When I emerged on the other side, I paused to take in what I was seeing.

The space, about the size of a city block, was part grotto and part glade. Tall, thin trees grew densely and rose high along the outer stone walls, almost obscuring the moss that clung to the rock. A bluish carpet of what looked like perfectly maintained grass covered the center of the space, bisected by a small river sourced by a pretty waterfall. And millions of little crystals that trailed along the ground lit it all.

In the center of the clearing, I spotted a circle of fist-sized stones almost hidden in the low-growing grass. Someone had set up a tripod facing the circle on one side and a large, thick post jutted from the earth on the other side. The post reminded me of a telephone pole but more diminutive, only rising seven feet. A pile of rope waited at the base.

Vivian pushed me forward.

"It's not the best angle to see it from here. Keep going."

Fighting the sinking feeling of dread that Vivian was close to obtaining whatever his goal was, I walked toward the tripod and the stone circle.

As I neared, the air within the circle moved. Or rather, it changed. I paused and took a half step back, then forward again. Whatever it was, it changed like those lenticular pictures that change appearance based on the viewer's angle.

"And that, my little plasma muffin, is a fae portal. Wait until you see how it looks when you're standing in front of it."

He nudged me along, and I watched the air in the circle shift and solidify into a foggy haze that seemed to move. When I was just outside the stones, I could see a faint reflection of myself and the area around me.

"Because the portals are still closed, we can't see into the fae realm. But their world is still there, on the other side, waiting to be unlocked.

"Here." He took one of my hands and pressed something into it.

"In you go." He shoved me hard.

The toe of my stupid shoes caught on a stone, and I tripped forward into the portal.

It felt like I fell into a pool of gelatin that hadn't quite set yet. Thankfully, the thickness slowed my fall and prevented me from landing hard on my hands and knees on the other side.

Tiny yellow flowers bloomed prettily around my hands in the purple-blue grass. I pulled myself upright, looking at the mist hanging heavily in the air. It didn't feel wet like mist, but it wasn't smoke either. Whatever it was, it made it hard to see more than a few feet in front of me.

Glancing over my shoulder, I saw Vivian standing there, grinning at me. His image shimmered like I was looking at him through heat waves rising off the blacktop in summer. Only, it wasn't heat. It was a fae portal.

He'd pushed me into a fae portal!

Afraid of being trapped, I scrambled to my feet and shoved my hands through. The portal resisted then gave way. I only felt a moment of relief that I could escape before Vivian grabbed my hand and pried my fingers open, retrieving what he had given me before pushing me in.

"You make this too easy." His voice sounded distant, like it was coming through a tube.

He plucked a small round stone with some kind of engraving on it from my open palm. Then he stuck my thumb into his mouth.

The feel of his tongue flicking over my skin and the scrape of his teeth sent a spear of panic through me.

I tugged back with all my might.

Grinning at me, he watched me stumble again.

I wiped my hand against my leg and felt something on my thumb. Shepard's ring was there. Confused, I looked up at Vivian.

"Have you guessed it yet?" he asked. "You're the bait, Everly."

CHAPTER TWENTY-ONE

I RUSHED TOWARD THE PORTAL, INTENDING TO PUSH ALL THE WAY through it this time. Instead, I rebounded hard and landed on my ass.

The portal no longer had any give and was a solid sheet of fog-filled glass.

Kicking off my heels, I stood again to the sound of Vivian's distorted laughter.

He held up the rock he had taken back. "Without this, you're stuck until your lovers come to open all the portals."

I was terrified but also furious. Mostly with myself. I'd stupidly believed that Vivian hated Orphia enough not to help her open the portals, but failed to realize he'd want the same outcome on his own. What vampire wouldn't want access to an all-you-can-eat human buffet?

"They're smart enough to know that freeing me won't save me once the portals are open," I said hoarsely.

"Are you sure?"

He rolled the stone over his fingers, back and forth, teasing me with the solution to the problem he'd made. I needed that secondary key to my freedom. With it, the portals could stay safely closed. I just needed him to give it to me.

I hit the portal with the side of my fist this time, but the portal didn't even react.

"So close, Everly. Just a little more," he taunted.

We both knew that, no matter what I did, I couldn't get to the stone. Fisting my hands at my sides, I glared at him.

"The fae and their trinkets," he said as he continued to roll the flattened stone along his fingers. "Have you had enough of them yet? I heard you and Shepard played at Effora's for hours the other day."

My hate for Vivian climbed. For Effora, too, but she wasn't here, rubbing what happened into my face.

"She's desperate for Shepard to take her the way he took you. Aggressively. Deeply. From behind."

I hit the portal with the flat of my hand like I was slapping Vivian's face.

He laughed and moved closer. "That's it. Embrace the fear and anger. Show me how you really feel."

I realized that was my ticket to getting out. Vivian craved fear. It was his catnip. He'd said as much to me each time I'd encountered him. If I gave him enough of it, he wouldn't be able to stop himself from coming after me. Did I want to drive him crazy enough to pull me out of the portal? Not really. I knew what would happen next if he did. But I also knew that what would happen after the portals were unlocked would be much worse.

So I gave in to the fear and the anger just like he wanted and beat my hands on the portal while cursing at him.

Vivian laughed and turned to face the phone attached to the tripod. "Did you see the pretty ring she's wearing, Shepard?"

I froze in disbelief. He was recording me. *What had I done?*

The phone hadn't been there when he'd pushed me in. He must have set it up while I was distracted with the portal. He'd only needed a second.

"I know you won't be able to resist saving your *mate*, so I'll save you the hassle of trying to find her. Follow the GPS and claim your prize."

I wailed, "No," as he ended the video.

"Aw. That's perfect. You're a born actress," he said as he sent the video. "Take a bow. Your performance is about to get a standing ovation. Once your boy toys get this video, they'll rush in to save you. Don't worry, my hemoglobin honey cake."

"Why are you doing this?" My answer and frustration gave my voice some volume.

"Do you really have to ask? I thought you were smart, Everly."

"Pretend I'm dumb." I felt rather dumb at the moment. I was now trapped inside a portal. "Enlighten me."

"So sweet that you want to understand my desires. It's simple, my ambrosia artery. Revenge. You and your love nuggets killed the only man I loved."

"He killed himself," I said.

Vivian's face transformed between one instant and the next. The web of black veining around his eyes almost reached his twisted mouth as he snarled, "He was given no other choice. Do you think your precious wolves would have let him live?"

They wouldn't have.

Vivian calmed instantly, which was another layer of terrifying. He was *not* stable.

"I see the truth in your eyes," he said. "You know I'm right."

"Fine. You want revenge. Why the portal?"

"And ruin the surprise? Believe me, this is going to be a nightmare to remember."

He made a video call on the tripod phone and withdrew another phone from his pocket to answer the call. When he did, his face showed on the tripod's phone. He changed the view so I saw myself, milky and slightly distorted by the portal.

"It's sad that now it's your face I see when I answer his call." He gently stroked the phone. "Is this called poetic justice?

Summoning your lovers who killed my lover on his phone? I think so." He placed a kiss on it before turning to me.

"Now we can keep in touch," he said with a wicked grin. "I know you'll miss me, but I'll be back. It's a promise." He cocked his head to the side. "And I keep my promises, unlike other blood-sucking bitches."

"Where are you going?" I yelled as he blurred out of sight.

His laughter echoed from the phone on the tripod, and I saw he was still watching me as he ran away.

So, I did what any rational person trapped in a fae portal by the vampire who wanted to kill her lovers would do. I flipped him off and turned around to look for a way out of the situation I was in.

Barefoot, I walked away from the portal, watching the ground and my surroundings. There wasn't much to see. Just the indistinct purple-blue grass with small yellow flowers at my feet and the never-ending mist in the air.

Pausing, I glanced back and felt a moment of panic when I couldn't see the portal. However, the path of yellow flowers led me back to where I'd come from like a yellow brick road. And I peered out of the portal one more time.

Vivian grinned when he saw me again. Rather than flip him off a second time, I hardened my resolve to keep searching. I retraced my steps on the same flower trail and kept going this time. Not long after, I saw another portal ahead.

No fog obscured the view through the second portal. I clearly saw the soft glow emitting from the pink flowers growing on the other side. I stared, mesmerized by their beauty and by the odd butterfly that fluttered toward it. The butterfly paused and turned toward me.

I screeched and tumbled back from the portal, falling on my ass then scrambling to my feet, only to trip again and sprawl face-first on the ground.

A fairy!

Briefly choking myself when my hand caught on my necklace as I pushed myself to my feet, I blindly ran away from what had been the most messed-up fairy I'd ever seen. I didn't stop until I was winded. Unable to draw in enough air, I put my hands on my knees.

The multiple bruises on my throat made each gasping inhale burn, and bending over hurt my back where Vivian had pushed me into the car.

Why fairies, I inwardly whined.

Knowing I didn't have time to feel sorry for myself, I straightened and turned away to retrace my steps and flinched.

An older woman stood behind me, her walking stick drawn back over her head. The shock of seeing someone blinded me to her intent until she swung at me. I dodged at the last second. The stick hit the ground and she pulled back for another swing as her gaze shot to mine.

My mouth dropped open in shock.

"Grandma Hunter?"

It was as if the woman had been ripped straight from my memories and planted here. Grey hair pulled back into a low bun, brown eyes like Vena's, and a toned yet weathered and petite body. She hadn't aged a day.

She paused with her walking stick ready.

"It's me. Everly Reid, Vena's friend."

Grandma Hunter's eyes went wide.

"Barnaby! It's Everly!"

She dropped her walking stick and swept me up in a hard hug. I hugged her back just as hard, ignoring my aches in my shock that she was there.

"Is this real? Are you really here? How?" I asked, my voice still sounding hoarse.

She pulled back and cupped my face with her still strong hands, studying me as I studied her. How hadn't she aged a day since I'd last seen her?

"You've matured so much. What happened to your neck?"

"It's a long story, but I'm fine."

She nodded as she released my face and took my hands.

"How much time has passed?" she asked.

"Ten years," I said.

"Ten years." Her happy expression turned worried then sad.

"Have you been here this whole time?" I asked.

"We have." Grandpa Hunter appeared out of the mist, carrying their packs.

"You both look exactly the same," I said.

Grandma shrugged. "We're trapped in a limbo of sorts. It's between Earth and the fae realm. Time doesn't seem to exist in a space like this."

"Look at how you've grown, Everly," Grandpa said. "How is Vena? Is she still getting into trouble?"

I smiled and gently squeezed Grandma Hunter's hands. "She's well. Misses you terribly. She's going to be so happy to see you again."

The pair exchanged sad glances.

"Do you still have the rock with you?" Grandma Hunter asked. "The one they gave you to enter the portal?"

"No. A vampire tricked me and grabbed it before I understood it was the key to getting out of here. Please tell me you still have yours."

"No, sweetheart. We broke ours as soon as we realized why she'd sent us in here."

"She? What happened?"

Grandma Hunter patted my arm and looked at her husband. "Barnaby, get out the chairs. Let's sit down for a moment."

He set the packs down and dug out a pair of collapsible camp chairs. Grandma sat with me while Grandpa sat on the packs.

"It's best to start from the beginning. Ten years ago, we received a commission to find something for a private buyer."

"An artifact that will pull a race into the veil?" I asked.

Surprise lit her expression. "How do you know? Please tell me they didn't continue our search."

"Sort of. A lot has happened since you went missing. Tell me what happened to you first, and I'll catch you up with everything. But the abbreviated version, please. I don't think we have a lot of time."

They shared a worried glance.

"Well, we were hired to find a relic and were given a book that had some clues. We didn't think anything of it when the buyer contacted us a while later with another lead and asked to meet in person. We were out of leads of our own at that point.

"The meeting was at night. A vampire woman ambushed us before we even knew what happened."

Grandma reached up and touched her neck as if she could still feel the bite. And when she did it, I saw the bite marks. They were still there. Fresh like they'd only happened hours ago.

"Once she had control of us, she brought us here, gave us the rune stones so we could enter, and told us to fetch the relic hidden in the veil. However, as soon as we entered, her thrall on us vanished.

"Barnaby and I remembered everything she'd said, though. She wanted to use the relic to send all the creatures back to the fae realm so the vampires could rule over the humans without interference. We knew we couldn't allow that to happen, so we refused to get the relic she wanted.

"She left us here. But she returned later with more people. They weren't thralled but bribed, which meant they were determined to bring the relic out. We broke their runes and ours so no one could leave."

Understanding dawned.

"That's why you asked if I had one."

"You can't leave with the relic, sweetheart. No matter what Orphia promised you, you can't leave."

"She has Vena, doesn't she?" Grandpa Hunter asked sadly.

"No. Vena's fine. Well, mostly fine. I promise. Orphia didn't put me in here."

"Then why are you here? How did you know to come?"

"The abbreviated version? A lot has happened since you've been here, and most of it just this summer. The relic is only part of what Orphia needs.

"Vena and I found the book that Orphia gave you. It has four stones in the back. One for each of the major races. Vampires. Werewolves. Dwarves. Fae. They used those stones to seal the portals. And they can use them to open the portals again too."

"That's why we couldn't get into the fae realm on the other side," Grandpa said softly.

I shivered, glad they hadn't.

"Orphia has the dwarf stone, which was made into a ring. I, unfortunately, have the wolf one."

I held up my hand to show the sapphire ring.

"How did you get it?" Grandma asked.

"The vampire who pushed me in here slipped it onto my finger."

"What about the other two?" Grandpa Hunter asked. "Does she have the vampire ring?"

I shook my head. "The vampire with the ring won't give it to her, but I think that's why I've been shoved in here. I'm leverage."

"Leverage?" Grandma Hunter questioned. "How?"

"I'll leave that part for later."

"And the fae ring?" Grandpa asked.

"Effora, the fae Queen, still has it as far as I know, but she was also working with the vampire who shoved me in here."

Grandma Hunter shook her head. "This isn't good. Orphia is closer to opening the portal."

"I think so too. The people that the vampire is using me to lure here are probably already on their way."

"We can't let them open the portals. Not for you. Not for

anyone. Do you understand? The closed portals are the only thing stopping Orphia from obtaining the relic."

Grandpa stood and opened one of the packs to remove a misshaped stone covered in runes and veined with the same iridescence as Effora's belly button ring.

I couldn't believe the relic was actually here with them.

"We've been hiding it and protecting it since we've arrived. Like I said, we weren't the only ones she sent in after it, but we're the only ones who kept our sanity for this long. The mist broke the minds of everyone else."

"It's because we have each other to talk to," Grandpa said.

"And we knew what to expect when coming in here."

Grandpa nodded. "The flowers close after a while, and people lose their way and start wandering aimlessly. If you come upon anyone now, they're harmless, but they weren't when they first arrived."

"Do you understand?" Grandma asked, locking our gazes. "The portal can't be opened, and this cannot be allowed to leave, or humanity will become vampire slaves forever."

My stomach sank with the realization that I'd be stuck in the weird limbo between worlds forever. But the alternative was too horrible to contemplate.

So I nodded and stood, needing a moment to contain the overwhelming feelings of loss and fear that currently made my legs wobbly. Everything I had hoped and dreamed about was out of my reach. Forever.

"I better go back and watch for them."

"We'll guide you there," Grandma said, standing so Grandpa could pack our chairs and put away the relic.

When he finished, Grandma started off in a direction that didn't have the yellow flower path.

"How do you know where to go?" I asked.

"Look up."

Tilting my head back, I saw what looked like really faint stars among the grey mist. They flickered occasionally but were so small and faint I almost didn't notice. As I stared, I noticed the stars we headed toward were ever so slightly blue, and the ones behind us were ever so slightly pink.

"Do you see it?" Grandpa asked from behind me.

"Blue for the human realm and pink for the fae realm?"

"Precisely right. You were always as clever as our Vena and Miles. That's why we liked you so much."

"I thought it was because I kept Vena out of trouble. Sometimes."

"That too," Grandma said.

"There's no keeping a free spirit out of trouble all the time," Grandpa said. "We've missed them dearly."

My heart ached thinking of Vena and my family, who I would never get to see again.

But if staying in the portal with Grandma and Grandpa Hunter kept the rest of the world safe, I could do that.

I thought of Cross and Shepard. I didn't think either would leave once they found me. The idea of watching Shepard grow old and die while I was stuck in here and ageless almost broke me. In that moment, I truly understood Cross' burden.

He would be the only one to never leave me.

CHAPTER TWENTY-TWO

ON THE WAY TO THE PORTAL, GRANDMA AND GRANDPA EXPLAINED that the one to the human world acted more like a mirror, making it hard for people standing outside of it to see in, while the one to the fae world seemed to be completely clear.

"That means no one can see you unless you're standing right in front of the portal," Grandpa said.

"We'll stay back and let you deal with whoever arrives," Grandma said. "It's safer if no one knows we've survived."

I agreed. When we reached the portal, they stayed back as I stepped close.

Vivian smiled wickedly on the phone screen when I appeared. I ignored him and watched for Shepard and Cross, fighting to keep my tears contained as I thought of what I needed to tell them.

How long had it been since Vivian sent the video? Long enough for Shepard and Cross to get here? Were they fighting with each other because they were worried or working together? Was Shepard blaming himself because he'd lost his ring?

A tinny sound coming from outside the glade caught my

attention. Voices. They were too far away for me to hear, though, so I waited, watching the path as the voices grew louder.

Cross and Shepard came into view. Just seeing them made tears spring to my eyes, and I pressed my hands against the portal as I shook my head.

Their gazes met mine, and I saw the same fear and anger reflected in me. Outweighing both of those emotions was their determination.

They appeared in front of me a second later, each of them placing a hand over one of mine.

"Are you okay?" Shepard asked.

"You need to leave before it's too late."

"We're not leaving you, Everly," Cross said. "Ever."

"Please. I'm safe in here, but you're not if you stay. You know this is a trick."

Shepard's eyes flashed gold as he shook his head. "Trick or not, we're not leaving without you."

"Look," I said, pointing at the phone.

Cross and Shepard glanced at Vivian's malicious face on the screen.

"How does it feel to see your lover and know you'll never get her back? To hear her send you away to save you, knowing she's willing to sacrifice herself in your place. It hurts, doesn't it? Makes you want to kill someone, right?" Vivian taunted.

"Get her out of there, now," Shepard growled.

Vivian grinned. "You want to kill me. I can feel it, and it's so delicious."

"What do you want, Vivian?" Cross asked. "You know we'll give it to you. So hurry and speak your demands."

Vivian laughed again. "So much fun. I wish Master was here to enjoy this with me." He grew scarily serious. "But I only have his memory to carry with me through eternity. Are you prepared to do the same with Everly?"

"I'm ready to hunt," Shepard said, sniffing the air. "Your scent is still fresh. I know you're close by."

"My scent is fresh all over this mountain. But by all means, waste time trying to find me instead of trying to save Everly. The humans sent in by Orphia over the last ten years never came out again, even though they kept their portal runes. They have the means to leave, but they don't. I wonder what's in there that's killing them."

Shepard's eyes widened on me.

"Don't listen to him. There's nothing scary in here," I said.

His fingers moved over mine and the portal.

"Since I'm feeling generous," Vivian said, "I'll give you a hint on how to save her."

Shepard growled.

"You're cute when you're impatient, so I'll give you the answer: Open the portal. Everly already has your ring, wolf boy. Get Cross to toss his in as well."

"What about the others?" Shepard asked.

"That's the best part. I have a way to arrange for their delivery. All you need to do is play along."

"Don't," I begged. "The relic Orphia's looking for is inside the portal, and Orphia knows it. She'll get what she wants once it's open. You can't let that happen."

Shepard's gaze shifted over my face, taking in all the details. Any resistance he might have had softened in the process.

"We're not leaving you in there either," Shepard said.

"Why not? In here, I can't be kidnapped or hurt. In here, I'm safe forever."

"What use is saving a world without you in it?" Shepard asked.

Cross, who'd been watching me just as intently, looked away, his expression pained.

Vivian smiled wickedly. "Tough choice, am I right? Forsake your mate or unleash the relic and forsake yourselves and the rest of the world."

"It's an easy choice," Cross said.

He started twisting his ring free from his finger.

"Don't you dare, Cross," I said as I slapped the glass. "If you take that ring off your finger, we're done." My breath caught on a sob. "You will lose the piece of my heart that you have."

His sad smile broke me. "It was never meant to be mine in the first place, Sunshine."

He pulled the ring free and tossed it toward the portal. It didn't bounce off but sailed right through and hit my chest. I caught it and slipped it onto my other thumb as tears streamed down my cheeks.

Behind me, I heard Grandma and Grandpa whispering to each other.

"Well done!" Vivian said from the phone. "Now it's your turn to do your part, Shepard. You can still walk away and leave Everly where she is, trapped forever in the veil between the human and fae world, or you can face the camera and strip like a good little wolf."

The odd request cut through some of my pain, and I wiped my tears to look at Shepard in confusion. He looked just as dumbfounded.

"I knew you enjoyed men," Cross said. "But didn't think Shepard was your type."

"Oh, he's not. But he is Effora's type, and you need her gem to open the portal. She was more than willing to steal Shepard's for me in exchange for all the humans she could play with. But she was very reluctant to give up hers even for a century of meals. I think Shepard is a meal she won't be able to refuse."

I frantically shook my head at Shepard. He smiled at me sadly like Cross had.

"Vivian was waiting for me in the dressing room when I went to answer the call from my parents," I said. "The tripod was already here when we got here. He's been planning this for days.

Don't do this. Don't give in to him." I begged even as Shepard's hand dropped away from the portal.

"Please, Shepard. You know what's at stake. Think of your people. Their mates. Those kids."

He winced even as he retreated farther.

"You have no idea what it's like for a wolf to lose his mate, Everly," Vivian said. "He would rather damn the world than lose you. Now, make sure you remove your clothes slowly, Shepard. Effora loves to be teased."

I looked at Vivian's smiling face, wanting to scratch his eyes out. Rather than watch Shepard strip, I stepped back from the portal and looked at Grandma and Grandpa Hunter.

"Do you really think the fae queen will come?" Grandpa asked.

"Yes. She's been after Shepard for a long time. What are the chances we can destroy the relic? That's the key to all of this. If it's gone, even if the portals are opened, Orphia's plan will fail."

Grandma shook her head. "We've tried everything since coming here. Nothing has come close to even scratching it."

Frustrated, I turned back to the portal, trying to think of a way to stop them.

Shepard already had his shoes and shirt off and was reaching for his pants.

"Think, Shepard," I pleaded. "If you give Vivian what he wants, the portal will open, and Orphia will get the relic. You and every other creature will be sent to the fae realm, leaving me behind anyway. I'm safer in here, and so is the whole world."

Cross rested his other hand on the portal where Shepard's had been.

"She will send every creature but vampires back," he said. "I've fed from you, Everly. You're already mine. I won't let anyone touch you."

"That's your plan?" I asked, hitting the portal over his hand. "Sacrifice everyone, including Shepard, to protect me? What about Vena, Cross? And my parents and Vena's parents? Don't they deserve to live free?"

Behind him, Shepard tossed his pants to the side and stood fully naked in front of the camera.

"I can see the appeal, Everly," Vivian said with a slight purr to his voice. "I take back what I said. Maybe he would be to my taste. I wouldn't mind being dominated by that. Even in its very uninterested state, it's quite impressive.

"Cross, you'll find a bit of rope by that post. Tie Shepard to it, pointy side out, if you please."

Shepard glanced from me to Cross.

Cross nodded and went to do as he was told as I shook my head again, helpless to stop what was happening.

The rope shimmered when Cross lifted it.

"Do you like it?" Vivian asked. "As you can guess, it's been enhanced. It isn't actually enough to keep Shepard in place once Queen Grabby Hands gets here. He'll need to do that on his own. It's for show so Effora doesn't get suspicious."

Vivian was smart. He knew Shepard would willingly stay tied to a tree indefinitely if he had to. Anything to free me.

My heart hurt, watching the two men I love bow to someone like Vivian, who didn't care for anyone but himself and his dead master. How many lives had they ruined? How many more would be destroyed if Orphia got what she wanted?

"Stop! Please!" I begged again, but Cross and Shepard only looked at me with sorrow in their eyes. Shepard stood still while Cross bound him.

"Now we just have to wait for Effora," Vivian said. "Navigating the paths here is easy for a fae, especially one who's desperate."

Vivian cocked his head to the side as he studied Shepard. "Something isn't quite right."

"The fact that you're still alive?" Cross asked.

"Hmmm. Nope. That's not it." He tapped his finger against his lips. "I think your wilted wafer needs to perk up a bit."

"And how would I do that?" Shepard asked, pulling at the secured ropes.

"Your *other* mate," Vivian said with a grin. "Go on, Cross. Give it a stroke. Effora's going to be here soon. We need something to really get her going."

Shepard let out a warning growl.

"Are you saying you don't want her distracted so Cross can swipe the ring from her? Aw. I thought you cared about Everly."

Ignoring Vivian, Cross approached me, putting his hand on the portal as we waited. "Whatever happens, we'll fix it. I promise."

"You can't undo what will happen once otherworlders are ripped away. You can't fix everyone's lives when they're torn apart and the humans become slaves. And you can't fix my heart when people I love are no longer with me."

He looked to the ground. Even Shepard couldn't make eye contact with me.

"Try to shake some blood into it, Shepard. Effora is almost here," Vivian said.

"Already?" Cross asked.

"I arranged for her to have a little warm-up gift nearby so she was close," Vivian said with a manic glimmer in his darkened eyes.

"Your turn, Cross," Vivian said. "Once she's well and distracted with Shepard, it's just a slip of the hand, and you'll get the stone from her belly button. Toss it into the portal and you're three-quarters of the way to freeing Everly.

"Now, I suggest you move away from your pet and play a convincing sex steward, or this carefully constructed trap will spring before it's set, and you will lose your prey and condemn your lover to an eternity in the veil."

"Don't do this. Please, Cross," I pleaded.

He gave me one last look and turned toward Shepard. As he walked away, he removed his suit jacket. He set it on the ground in front of Shepard like a rug and carefully removed his tie. I watched him roll it up and set it on the jacket. Then he unbuttoned the first few buttons of his shirt and rolled up his sleeves.

One naked. One submissive. I didn't like it. No, I hated it. They're willingness to do anything for me was tearing me apart.

Shepard and Cross' gazes whipped to the side.

A moment later, Effora came into view. She paused at the edge of the clearing, her gaze hungrily devouring the site of Shepard tied to the tree.

"The ropes won't be enough to hold him," Cross said. "I'll watch for signs he's getting loose and assist when needed."

Her slow smile said just how much she liked the idea.

I hit the portal and yelled, "It's a trap!"

Effora's gaze swung to me.

"Do you like my little gift to you?" Vivian asked from the phone. "It took a bit of work to kidnap her and put her in the portal. As you can see, she's angry and will say anything to stop you from sampling her mate. The only thing keeping Shepard and Cross in line is her freedom, so I suggest using them while she's still stuck."

"They're after your ring, Effora. Don't let them take it."

Cross sighed. "We don't need your ring, but if you give us a fae rune, I can untie Shepard from the tree, and we can be on our way with Everly."

Effora's gaze swung to Vivian's digital face.

"Don't worry. They know I have one," Vivian said. "This isn't about opening the portals; this is about making them pay for what they did to Master and giving you what you want so I get what I want. They know their roles, and they *will* do anything for you.

"After you're finished, you can help me deal with Orphia like you promised."

Effora glided toward Shepard. Like usual, the wisps of clothes she wore barely concealed anything.

"Vivian, you've worked so hard, and I'm quite pleased."

Shepard snarled at her as she pressed her body against his and ran her hand over his limp, naked length.

"We need a bit more effort from you, though. Look at your lover, Shepard. She's right there, waiting for you. Imagine her naked."

I couldn't feel her power, but I saw the effects as Shepard's eyes turned gold. I yelled every truth I could at Effora, but I might as well have been talking to Vena when she was hot on the trail for treasure.

"Shepard," she purred, her body shivering as if her desire was too much to contain. "Let me help you. I feel your need for her. Look at Everly and feel her touch."

She gripped him and slowly stroked from the base to the head and back. He snarled as his body began to betray him and respond to her.

Cross swayed on his feet, his eyes turning black.

"It looks like we've found the key to tempting Shepard without using a relic," Vivian said.

Shepard turned his head to avoid her lips as she kissed him all over. "You taste divine."

"Effora," Vivian said. "You'd feel better naked. Rid yourself of what keeps you from Shepard."

He didn't have to suggest it again. The scraps she wore flew off her. I caught sight of her glitter-studded crotch just before she turned and pressed into Shepard, rubbing against his thigh. Hooking her leg around his waist, she hitched up his body like a Cirque performer.

She moaned, low and desperate, trying to sink onto Shepard's length as he attempted to buck her off while avoiding her mouth.

"Cross, help her get what she wants. Reach between them and hold him still."

Cross moved closer and slipped his hand between their two writhing bodies. Effora let out a long, "Yes," and started bucking harder. Shepard's lips pulled back in disgust, but then he dipped his head and bit her shoulder. It was a hard bite that drew blood with his human teeth, not his canines.

She screamed out her release.

As she shuddered, I watched her transformation from a seductress to a terrifying creature from the fae realm. Her ears lengthened considerably, pointing at the tips. Her nails did the same—sharp razors she held away from his skin as she threw her head back and trembled. Her needle-like teeth were terrifyingly dangerous.

A second later, Cross withdrew his wet hand, proof Shepard hadn't been the reason for her release, and threw her belly ring into the portal. I moved fast, stepping to the side so it wouldn't hit me.

"They didn't listen, did they?" Grandma Hunter asked from not far away.

I looked down at the glistening gem that I refused to touch and shook my head.

"No. They didn't."

CHAPTER TWENTY-THREE

"What have you done?"

Effora's yell drew my gaze back to the portal.

Shaking in her outrage, she stood in front of Cross. His eyes were black and filled with revulsion as he stared back at her.

She lifted her taloned hand to hit him, but Vivian's voice stopped her.

"Ah-ah-ah! That's not the vampire blood you swore to spill if I helped you feed on Shepard. It's time to fulfill your vow, Effora. The trap has set, and Orphia is coming. It's kill or be killed."

The phone went black.

Cross sighed and picked up a piece of her clothing to wipe his hand dry. "I did what needed to be done to free Everly."

I saw the moment she realized Cross was missing his ring, too.

"You fool! You haven't saved your human; you've been condemned to a life of hell. Without the fae and wolves to maintain the balance, the vampires will overrun this world and bleed every human dry."

While her back was turned, Shepard partially shifted and ripped free of his ropes.

"Which is why we need to stop her," Shepard said, returning to his human form.

Effora turned to watch Shepard pick up his pants.

"We all know she won't arrive alone," Shepard said. "She hasn't been building her numbers to fight for the food source. Her army is for now."

Her army…

My stomach churned sickeningly as I realized what he meant to do. He wanted the three of them to stand against hundreds, maybe thousands, of vampires. At night. Without the stones that enhanced their abilities.

"If Orphia wins," he continued, "and I'm thrown into the fae realm with you, I promise that I will use every breath I have left to make you pay for what you did at your house and what you attempted to do to me just now.

"If by some miracle we win, know that you have broken the treaty between our races, and I will hold you accountable."

He angrily pulled his pants on and strode over to the portal to press his hand to it. "Cross didn't let her take what's yours. I'm sorry I allowed her to touch me."

"You should be sorry that he threw her ring in here instead of finding another way," I said.

"What I'm most sorry for is letting you out of my sight. That won't ever happen again."

"I've texted the location to Doc and Hugh," Cross said, "but I have a feeling it will be too late before anyone can get here."

While Shepard turned to look at Cross, I moved away from the portal to look at Grandma and Grandpa Hunter.

"We have to find a way to destroy the relic."

"We've tried everything," Grandma Hunter said.

"Show me."

She led me to where they had their backpacks. "Barnaby, get out the climbing pick and shovel."

"We've used those before," he said. "It didn't even make a scratch."

"Take them out anyway," I said. "Everything you have. We need to stop this from going any further before Orphia and her people arrive. Once she's here, it'll only be a matter of time before she reaches this portal with the last stone."

They both began dumping things out of their bags in a hurry. A campfire pot and pan. A rubber hammer to pound in tent stakes. Climbing picks. Utensils. Sleeping bags.

Their supplies quickly covered the yellow flowers and purple-blue grass, with the relic in the center of the empty packs.

I picked up a climbing pick to try first, hoping my rage and fear would give me enough strength to do some kind of damage.

"Be careful," Grandma Hunter warned. "It has some kick to it."

I drew the pick back and slammed it down onto the relic. It deflected with a magic burst, knocking my pick away and nearly stabbing a lost human, the first I'd seen, who was muttering something about missing shoes. Where the pick had struck, the relic remained completely unblemished.

"See?" Grandpa said. "It's impossible."

"So is the chance of me giving up," I said.

I grabbed the shovel and tried that, regretting my two-handed grip when the deflection knocked me to my butt with it.

Wincing, I tossed the shovel aside and accepted Grandpa Hunter's hand up to stand. Neither tried stopping me from picking up the pot then the pan. The relic had the same reaction to both items as the previous ones. And slamming the relic to the ground and stomping out my frustrations did nothing but send me flying back and skidding on my ass.

"Sweetie, you're going to hurt yourself," Grandma Hunter said, helping me to stand. "Believe me, we've tried everything. We haven't been twiddling our thumbs in here for the last ten years."

"Everly?"

The sound of Cross' voice had me hurrying to the portal.

Cross' dark gaze swept over me. "Where were you? What happened?"

"I'm trying to destroy the relic. It's protected by magic and keeps knocking me backward."

He lifted his hand like he wanted to touch my hair but dropped it to his side again.

"When you see the portal opening, call my name. I won't let anything happen to you. I promise."

"You know how many vampires she's going to bring," I said.

He flashed his sexy smile that made my pulse race. "All fledglings. I'll knock them down like bowling pins."

"Orphia's not a fledgling. Neither is Vivian. And we both know those aren't the only two older ones that escaped the nest cleaning. Please just keep yourself safe. And if they win and get the relic, you have to promise to take care of my parents and Vena."

"I will take care of them with you."

"You know if the vampires storm in here to get the relic, I'll fight until the end." It might only be seconds, but I wasn't going to sit idly by and let them take it.

A black web of veins erupted around his eyes.

"When you leave this world, so do I, Everly."

"Stubborn vampire," I said, frustrated.

All the darkness bled out of his expression as the smile returned.

"Don't forget to call my name," he said.

"Cross," Shepard called. "I hear them."

"Go," Cross said. "Keep trying."

I nodded and hurried back to Grandma and Grandpa Hunter.

"Can we try one more thing?" I asked.

"What do you have in mind?"

"Let's all hit it at once. Maybe with three people hitting it, it will be enough."

"We can. We just have to be careful if the pick goes flying again."

We each took a 'weapon' and circled around the relic. I drew back the shovel, which Grandpa did the same with the pick and Grandma with the pan.

"On the count of three," I said. "One…Two…Three!"

We hit the relic at the same time. The magic reverberations sent us flying backward. My ass hit the ground first, followed by my back and head. The impact knocked the wind out of me, and I wheezed through my poor, abused throat.

Grandpa and Grandpa Hunter groaned nearby.

"That was a doozy," Grandma said. "Thank goodness we don't age in here and that my bones are still in good shape."

I sat up, tears flooding my eyes so much that I couldn't see Grandma kneeling in front of me until she wiped my face with her warm hands.

"We'll keep trying," she said. "We're not beat yet."

That only made me cry harder until I was hiccuping. She rubbed my back, trying to comfort me, but the only thing I could think about was what would happen once Orphia arrived.

"You do not hold the responsibility for the fate of the whole world in your hands," she said. "No one should have that power. Do not let this defeat you because, once the relic activates, we are going to need everyone. Do you understand? You have to be strong. Giving up isn't an option, right?"

I nodded, knowing she was right, and wiped away my tears.

"She's here," Grandpa Hunter said, backing even farther from the portal.

Dread filled me. Standing, I hurried toward it and saw vampires flooding the area with Orphia and Vivian in their midst.

Shepard and Cross stood together in wide stances. Effora waited just behind them.

Orphia's gaze swept over them and then me, stuck in the portal.

"Well done, Vivian," she said. "I knew as soon as I saw you that you'd be perfect for my mission. I'm so glad you survived the conversion. I'm sure I could have done this without you, but with your twisted genius, it's entertaining, too."

Orphia missed Vivian's hate-filled glare as she looked around the clearing and met my gaze.

"Be a dear and fetch the relic, Everly. I'll need it soon."

She drew back her hand and threw something. Neither Cross nor Shepard attempted to block Curran's ring from entering the portal. It landed a distance behind me, near Effora's stone in the grass.

A shuddering rumble shook the ground beneath my feet.

"We're doomed," Grandma said.

I looked at her, and she pointed at the fog near the stars. It thinned as I stared.

"Once it clears, the portal will be open."

"If these four stones had the power to open the portal, maybe they can break the relic," Grandpa suggested. "Like fighting magic with magic. Maybe both magics will cancel each other out, breaking the relic and closing the portal."

Grandma was already scooping up Effora and Curran's stones as my eyes went wide in realization, and I reached for the necklace Vivian had put on me.

It wasn't there anymore. I frantically fell to my knees at the portal and combed through the grass and flowers there.

"Everly," I heard Orphia call. "The relic is large. You won't find it in the grass. Can she even hear me? You picked a useless blood bag, Cross.

"Kill them."

I glanced back at the portal and saw a mass of vampires running for Cross, Shepard, and Effora. A second later, Shepard stood in front of the portal. I wasn't sure if it was to block me from coming out or to block the vampires from getting in.

"What are you looking for?" Grandma asked.

"A necklace with a gem-studded penis on it. It's not mine. It belonged to the vampire who shoved me in here. It cancels magic. It might work on the relic. I'm positive I was wearing it when he pushed me in, or Cross would have found me sooner. That means I lost it in here when I fell or—" I sprang to my feet. "I need to check near the fae portal."

"Here," Grandpa said, shoving a bag at Grandma. It looked like it weighed as much as she did. "Take it and the stones and go with her. I'll stay here and hold them off as long as possible. If you can't break the relic before the portal opens, go to the fae realm and hide."

She reached up, kissed his cheek, then we ran.

I watched the color of the stars above, which were growing more visible as the mist drained from the veil. It didn't take nearly as long to reach the other portal, making me wonder if the veil itself was changing.

We dropped to our hands and knees to look for the necklace.

"Found it!" Grandma called after a moment.

With an excited grin, she held up the atrocious glittering dick necklace.

"That's it!"

She shoved it into my hand and dug in the pack.

"We'll try your necklace first. If that doesn't work, then we'll try all of the stones at once. I don't want to risk breaking them unless we have to. We might be able to try closing the portal with them again if we throw them out onto the fae side once it's open."

After placing the relic on the ground, she handed me the pick.

"Give it a try."

I wrapped the necklace around my hand and the pick, braced myself for the kickback, then swung like it was Effora's nasty face. The pick hit the relic, and the tip sank into the stone.

A second later, a hum filled the air.

I tried to let go of the pick, but the necklace was still wrapped around it and my hand.

"Shi—"

The relic exploded, sending shards flying along with Grandma and me.

Stunned, I sat up and plucked a shard from my cheek and some from my arms. My bloody fingers left smears everywhere.

"Are you all right, dear?" Grandma asked.

I looked at her and saw her forehead was bleeding.

"I'll survive. You?"

"I'll live for a while longer." She got to her feet and looked at the broken remains of the relic. Then she picked up a thin piece of the stone and snapped it in two. "No more magic. It worked." She shook her head, tears filling her eyes. "All these years. It finally worked."

Standing, I looked around at the mist, which was about level with my head now.

"One problem solved and one more to go. I doubt Orphia is just going to give up and walk away once she knows the relic is gone."

"You're right. Look." Grandma pointed the way we'd come. "You can see the glow from the portal now. It's almost open. We'd better hurry."

I grabbed the bigger pieces of the relic, and we ran toward the portal to find Grandpa standing back with a worried frown and a walking stick tightly gripped in his hands.

"Where's the necklace?" he asked.

I lifted my hands, showing him the remnants of the relic and the busted bit of chain still wrapped around my wrist.

"The necklace worked," Grandma said. "It's done. Orphia will never get the relic."

Grandpa breathed a sigh of relief.

I couldn't do the same, though. I ran to the portal and looked out.

Shepard still stood partially shifted before the portal, his back blurring as he moved in front of it, fighting any vampire attempting to overwhelm him. His claws raked over them, maiming some and disemboweling others. The injured ones staggered away, and new ones took their place.

Blood covered his chest and back, but I wasn't sure it was all vampire blood.

Even without his ring, he was holding them back. Effora, who I thought was completely useless, was fighting in her fae form not far away. She wasn't taking on as many vampires as Shepard, but she was holding her own.

A vampire saw me watching.

He grinned and looked at the clear, glowing gap in the top edge of the portal. Shepard saw his attention had diverted and killed him quickly. But another one had already noticed and threw a stone at the gap. It sailed right through. He grinned at me.

"You're mine."

Shepard killed him as I quickly tugged both rings off my thumbs.

"Cross, come here," I called.

He was next to Shepard a second later, his shirt a wet red. I thrust my hand through the gap and dropped their rings into his hand.

He smiled briefly as he slipped his on.

"This ends now."

He blurred, and vampires fell like puppets with snipped strings. He closed in on Shepard, and I barely saw the handoff as he gave Shepard his ring. Shepard shoved it in his mouth and matched Cross' speed in meeting the next wave.

Orphia, who was standing off to the side with Vivian, screamed in anger as her minions died one after another.

She caught sight of me, and fury burned in her eyes.

While they were distracted, she blurred to a stop in front of me.

"Give me the relic!"

I stuck my hand through the growing opening and dropped the pieces to the ground in front of the portal.

"What did you do?" she demanded.

"Aw. Looks like all your plans went to shit." Vivian laughed from behind her. "And guess what? You're dead."

I saw the look of realization hit Orphia right before Vivian shoved a knife through her heart. He quickly yanked it out and...I squeezed my eyes closed so I wouldn't see her end.

When I opened my eyes again, she was lying lifeless at his feet. He looked at me briefly, then darted into the fray.

His target was Shepard.

"Shepard, behind you!"

Shepard killed the vampire he was fighting and turned just as Vivian thrust the knife at him. The knife sunk into Shepard's side. He let out a growl of pain and pulled the knife free, his pants shredding as his body morphed into wolf form.

Vivian laughed as if his life wasn't on the line. As if he had no care in the world.

Shepard sprang forward, and a low growl vibrated through the space. They fought, each taking hits. Without the knife, Vivian couldn't keep up. He was bloody, and I could tell each strike took more and more out of him. He'd lose, and he knew it.

Before Shepard could make the final blow, Vivian grabbed something from his pocket and tossed it into the air.

"At least I got one out of the three. I'm coming, Adriel."

The sky exploded in light that was brighter than a summer sun.

It was like the sun charm but at nuclear levels.

I winced as it felt like my retinas were on fire and slammed my eyes shut. When I blinked them open, all the vampires were dead or ash, including Vivian.

CHAPTER TWENTY-FOUR

My panicked gaze swept the area, searching for Cross as the last of the fog cleared from the portal.

He was wearing the ring. Don't panic.

But that sunburst had lit up the night so brightly I was still seeing spots. Blinking to clear my sight, I found Cross standing among the vampire remains. Tears of relief sprang to my eyes, and I opened my arms to him, desperate for a hug.

He saw, looked down at himself, then cringed.

"Ah, Sunshine, give me a moment." He blurred. Water erupted from the waterfall, then he stood in front of me, drenched but completely free of blood.

"That was a wise choice," Effora said. She was back to being the pretty fae queen. "Shepard, do you need help reaching your back?"

Shepard shot Effora a warning glare and stalked off to the waterfall as I hugged Cross.

"I can't believe he had a sun charm," I said.

"You mean one that actually worked, unlike the one you and Vena had?"

Cross chuckled when I poked his ribs.

"I'm glad it didn't work on you."

"As am I."

He glanced at the opening between the rocks that lead to the gate. "I believe our help has arrived."

"A bit late for that," Effora said, still watching Shepard like she wanted to maul him again.

Furious that she dared to still lust after him after everything that happened, I slipped from Cross' arms. Effora never saw my hand coming. It cracked across her face with a resounding snap that carried through the space.

"Get your eyes off my mate before I remove them," I threatened.

Effora's serene beauty evaporated, and she looked at me with otherworlder eyes. She flashed her pin-like teeth at me in a hiss.

Cross' hand whipped out from behind me and smacked across her face from the other side. "We've tolerated enough of your unacceptable behavior, Effora. Give Shepard the privacy his mate demands, or deal with the consequences."

She huffed but turned her back on Shepard as her beauty returned. "Hurry and clean yourself off. Blood is drying on me, and it's itchy."

I mentally boot-stomped the guilt I started to feel when I realized she'd been actually waiting for her turn to wash. She could have waited with her eyes closed.

When I glanced at Shepard, he was grinning at me from ear to ear. I shook my head at him.

"Don't begrudge him," Cross said. "He needs the ego boost to know that you don't consider him unclean after the nauseating way he was used. That's also why he's taking so long to wash."

Effora let out a soft hiss.

Cross moved to stand beside me, but not because of her. The pounding of running feet sounded from the gated path a second before people swarmed the area.

DOS agents and wolves arrived with Doc, followed by Vena, Anchor, Hugh, Piper, and Robyn.

"Are you kidding me?" Vena said as she saw the bodies and piles of ash. "Did I miss all the action?"

"Barely," I said.

"What was that bright light?" she asked.

"Sun charm," Shepard said as he walked over.

Effora walked into the river without comment...or eye contact.

"It worked that well?" Vena asked in disbelief. "I wonder what went wrong with mine."

Anchor snorted, trying to choke back his laugh, but her gaze was already fixated on the portal. Like an invisible force was pulling her, Vena shuffled closer until Hugh stepped in front of her.

"It would be better if you didn't get too close."

"It would be better if you got out of her way," I said. "Unless you want her to run you over."

Hugh looked at me in surprise but stepped aside.

Before Vena reached the portal, Grandma Hunter walked out.

"Vena? Is that really you?" she asked.

Vena's mouth dropped open. She stared as Grandpa Hunter appeared behind her. Grandma then swayed on her feet. Anchor, who was right beside her, grabbed her arm to steady her.

"Am I seeing things?" she asked. "Is that thing a mirage or something?"

"It's not," I said. "I found them in the veil. This whole time, they've been guarding the relic Orphia hired them to find."

She took a hesitant step toward her grandparents. Grandma dropped her pack and opened her arms. Vena ran into them as tears spilled over.

"It looks like you're still causing trouble," Grandpa said, joining Grandma in hugging Vena. "How fresh is that broken arm?"

"Really fresh. I can't believe you're alive. Tell me everything," she said as she wiped her eyes. "How do you look exactly the same?"

I turned away from them and watched Hugh direct his agents.

"Verify the ones on the ground are actually dead and start IDing them." He turned to us. "Where's Orphia?"

"Over there," Shepard said, pointing. "Vivian is the ash next to her. He died, along with every other still living vampire in the immediate area, due to that flash you saw before."

Hugh looked impressed and grateful.

"A job well done." He looked around the glade. "And it was only the two of you against how many?"

"Three of us," Cross said. "After Effora betrayed us and attempted to have her way with Shepard, she helped kill a few of the hundred vampires that Orphia brought with her."

We all glanced at Effora. With a glare at me, she left the waterfall and slunk toward the portal, passing by Vena and her grandparents as they continued to talk quietly under Anchor's watchful gaze.

Ignoring her, my guys and I turned to face Hugh.

"Those are impressive odds. Is there any chance you'd be willing to teach our new recruits how to fight vampires?" Hugh asked Cross.

"I think that can be arranged," Cross said.

"Only if you promise hunters won't accidentally hurt him," I said. "Hunters hunt for a reason. I don't want someone with a grudge going after Cross when he's there to help."

"I promise to ensure his safety," Hugh said. "My people can clean up here. It looks like all of you could use a real shower and some rest."

"We'd appreciate that."

Effora approached our group, and Shepard pulled me far away from her.

"You should also know that our treaty with the fae has been

broken," Shepard said to Hugh. "We will need to address this in the days to come."

Anger flitted across Effora's face before she offered Curran's ring to Hugh. Hers was already back in her belly button.

She sniffed disdainfully. "When recounting my deeds this day, don't forget my efforts to right my wrongs."

"Pretty sure your help doesn't outweigh all your scheming," I said.

She shot me a look, going full fae for a second, which reminded me of the scary fairy I saw in the veil.

"What about the portal?" I asked. "How do we close it?"

"Unless you are willing to part with your lovers, I would not suggest it," Effora said. "The cost of closing the portal is the life of each ring bearer."

"What will happen if the portal stays open?" Hugh asked.

"Not much. While anyone can enter the veil now, only fae can enter and exit the fae realm without a rune. The veil in between is harmless to humans."

"Then we'll let it be for now," Hugh said. "Go home and get some rest. All of you. I'll be in touch for your statements."

Effora left without a backward glance.

I glanced at Vena and her grandparents and saw Anchor taking their bags from them and indicating they should join us. After giving Effora enough time to get through the gate, our group followed.

"See you in a few weeks at school!" Piper called as she dragged a body to a pile.

"See you!" Vena said, waving with her good arm.

As we walked out of the gate, I said, "I want this noted right now that I'll never, ever set foot onto Sugarloaf Mountain again." I glanced around at everyone, making sure they knew I was serious. "Never. Ever."

Cross placed a kiss on my cheek. "You already got the best gift from the mountain anyway. There's no reason to ever come back."

"If you say that gift is yourself—" Shepard started.

"I was talking about a family reunion with the Hunters," Cross said, then winked at me. "Although, I come in second place at the very least."

I laughed, and it was the best feeling in the world. I carried it with me all the way to the parking lot.

Vena and Anchor stowed her grandparents' packs in their car, and I gave her a hug.

"I'll talk to you tomorrow," I said.

"You better. I want all the details. I seriously can't believe I missed everything. Stupid pain meds."

I promised her a lengthy discussion then waved as they headed to the complex on their own. When I turned to Cross, he was standing next to the SUV and held up my missing necklace.

"Found this," he said. I hurried toward him and let him put it back on me before getting into the backseat with Shepard.

"Can I borrow a phone? I need to call my parents. They have to be worried sick."

Cross pulled my phone from the center console. I saw they'd turned it on and I had over one hundred missed calls from my parents. Cringing, I called Mom. She answered after the second ring.

"Everly, we were so worried. Vena said you were missing." She started to cry.

"Mom, I'm okay. Actually, everything is okay now."

"We saw you on the news. What happened? What's going on?"

I knew she wasn't just asking about Shepard and Cross but everything.

"Well, there's a lot I didn't tell you, but basically, it's what you heard on the news. The vampire population was growing, and their leader was trying to do some really bad things. I got sucked into that riptide. The men in the interview with me have been keeping me safe. You, Dad, and Grandma too. That's why you *won* the cruise. To keep you all safe. They're really nice, Mom."

Her crying quieted after a moment.

"You're really okay?"

"I am. Tonight was a little scary, but the vampire leader is dead. And I'm safe in the car with Cross and Shepard now."

"Both of them?"

I felt my face flush.

"Yeah. Both of them."

She was quiet for a long moment.

"I'd like you to meet them when you get back. They've saved me more times than I can count."

"But aren't they why you needed saving?"

"No, Mom. The people who were trying to use me to hurt them are why I needed saving. I'll explain everything when you get home and we have more time."

"We'll be home in two days."

"Okay. Keep sending pictures. Please enjoy the rest of the trip, and don't worry about me. The danger is behind us now."

"I'll try, but I'd like a few pictures from you too."

"Deal."

I hung up and looked at Shepard and Cross. Both looked equally nervous.

"Do you think they'll be able to accept us?" Cross asked.

"I do. Eventually. Like I said, it won't be that you're a vampire or that you're a werewolf that they'll struggle with. It'll be that I'm with both of you. It will take time, but they'll come around."

When we finally arrived home, it was nearing sunrise. All I wanted was a shower and bed and to cuddle with my two guys. Thankfully, we were all on the same page.

"Go ahead and shower," Shepard said. "I'll have pajamas and a glass of water waiting for you."

Cross went ahead of me and started the shower. He helped me out of my clothes and glanced at my many bruises and cuts.

"They're fine," I said. "I'm fine."

They were both being sweet, and they both wore the same apprehensive expression. It wasn't until I was showered, dressed in soft pajamas, and snuggle-sandwiched between the two of them that I finally understood why.

I eyed both of them in the dim room. "This is because I said I wouldn't forgive either of you, isn't it? Can you blame me? You cared nothing for the world and were going to sacrifice your rings and yourselves just to save me."

"We couldn't stand by and do nothing," Shepard said.

"What about your pack? The rest of the world? You're the alpha, Shepard."

"And you're my mate. I would give up everything for you."

"Neither of us would change our minds or regret our choices if it means saving you." Cross slipped his hand into mine, bringing it to his lips for a kiss. "We also would have found a way to fix our mistakes. Be mad at us tomorrow, Everly. For what's left of tonight, get your sleep."

"You're postponing the argument."

He kissed my hand again, then my cheek. "I'm only saying the hero should rest."

"Hero?"

"You saved us all, Everly."

I hardly felt like a hero but smiled anyway because he was right. Without me and that awful dick necklace, the relic would have never been destroyed.

I WOKE with a leisurely stretch and accidentally hit Cross in the face. He laughed and caught my hand to kiss it.

"Sorry," I mumbled.

"It's all right. I was just lying here wondering how annoyed you would be if I woke you."

"Not annoyed. More like worried. Did something happen?"

"No. Shepard made you breakfast."

"Mmm," I rolled toward Cross and used him like a body pillow. He didn't mind. He wrapped his arm around me and combed his fingers through my hair.

"Does this mean you aren't hungry?"

"I'm hungry...I'm just too lazy to get out of bed when you're so snuggable."

"He made Belgian waffles. With a berry compote and fresh whipped cream."

I tilted my head to look up at Cross. "You really want me to get out of bed, don't you?"

He kissed the tip of my nose. "It's been ten hours. We're worried."

"Really? Ten?"

He nodded, and with a sigh, I untangled myself from the blankets. He watched me scoot out of bed and pad to the bathroom. All my things were neatly set out on the counter, waiting for me. Smiling, I washed up and dressed in loungewear for the day.

Cross had made the bed while I was gone and was lying on the comforter, waiting for me. His gaze raked over my silky light blue loungewear, and he gave me his slow, sexy smile.

"I chose well."

"You did. They're comfy, and today is definitely a comfy kind of day." I paused and gave him a pleading look. "Please tell me we have nothing to do today."

"Nothing that requires leaving the house. I am expecting a delivery in a bit, though." He stood smoothly and hugged me to his chest.

"What kind of delivery?"

"It's a surprise."

"I'm not really a fan of surprises. I think I've had too many of the bad kind in the last few weeks."

"This is a good one. It's more for Shepard than you, but I think you'll enjoy it as well."

"Then it's acceptable."

I walked out of the bedroom with his arm around my waist and saw Shepard setting the table for three.

He smiled at me and came to steal me from Cross for a hug and kissed the top of my head. "We were worried about you."

"I heard. Did you sleep enough?"

"Plenty. Everything is healed and back to normal. What about you? Cross noticed a bruise on your back last night."

I glanced at Cross. "What were you doing that you saw my back?"

His sexy smile contradicted the shrug he gave me. "I could say that it was when I helped you out of your clothes last night, but you like it when I touch you in your sleep. Lots of happy sounds."

Wrinkling my nose at him, I turned to Shepard and glanced at the plates. "I also heard you wanted to feed me." His eyes flashed gold, and he nodded. Cross held out my chair for me as Shepard went to the kitchen.

"Have either of you heard from Vena today?"

"Yes," Shepard said. "She called early to tell you everyone is united at home and a big thank you from their whole family is waiting for you."

"Did she say how Miles is doing?"

"He's well. Having Grandma and Grandpa Hunter back helped tremendously, as did the time he spent with Princess Indri while researching in the Mountain. He's accepted what happened and is doing his best to move forward."

I let out a relieved breath and smiled up at Shepard as he served breakfast.

"So what are our plans for the future? Are you reopening Blur now that Orphia is gone?"

"I was thinking of keeping it closed for a while," he said. "It's a good time to renovate and maybe find a new manager. Someone told me I didn't have the best work-life balance. Since I have a mate now, I need to fix that."

"But what if your mate is busy with school and running her own bakery? Won't you be bored?"

"Unlikely," Cross said. "The alphas are still—"

Something thumped under the table.

"Shepard, did you just kick Cross?"

"It was a love tap," Cross said smoothly. "He missed me while he was making you breakfast."

Shepard snorted.

"Are you going to tell me what the alphas are doing? Or do I need to go around you to find out, *mate?*"

Shepard winced at my tone. "They're still unhappy the ring was stolen and questioning if I should step down. I told them to show me a better candidate, and I'd step down without a fight. The males they're proposing are about on level with MC."

"So you'll be dealing with stupidity for a while. And what about you?" I asked Cross. "What are your plans for the future?"

"The same as Shepard's. To spend every waking second with you. That you'll allow, at least. To spoil you. Watch you smile. Shower with you. Touch you."

Shepard kicked him under the table again. "Her back is bruised."

"I didn't say this second."

I grinned, amused by their interactions. They bristled at each other sometimes, but the animosity that they'd once had for each other had vanished. Happy, I took a bite of my waffle and moaned.

"This is so good."

The doorbell rang, and Cross shot out of his seat with an excited glint in his eyes.

"It's our delivery. Stay here. Finish eating. It'll take some time to set up."

Shepard and I stayed at the table while Cross ran downstairs and returned with two people carrying a thin box that was nearly twice my height. Cross carried a smaller box and winked at me on the way through the room.

Once the bedroom door closed behind them, I looked at Shepard.

"Do you know what he's doing?"

"No. But he said it's something to commemorate our lives together."

Suspicious, since he said it was more for Shepard than me, I glanced at the door repeatedly while we finished our breakfast.

A little while after the delivery guys left with the box, Cross told us to go look.

I was the first one through the door and saw the three throw pillows he'd added to the bed—"His, Hers, and His." Laughing, I turned to tell him I loved it and caught sight of the new painting on the wall.

It was massive.

So massive.

And strategically lit by "art" lights.

"It's impressive, isn't it?" Cross said as Shepard made choked sounds.

The glorious painting of Cross, fully nude in a 'paint me like a French lady' pose, was on a canvas that was at least six feet high and twelve feet long. Cross was proportional to the size of the canvas, which meant we would be staring at Cross' spot-lit mega penis every time we went to sleep at night.

But behind Cross, on his knees to offer a bunch of grapes, was Shepard, just as nude. However, the position and the angle of Cross' top arm gave Shepard's equipment a stubby ending rather than the well-endowed length he had.

"Ass," Shepard breathed.

"We can have one of those on that wall," Cross said, completely serious and pointing to the empty space above the bed.

"I think one nude painting is enough," I said, fighting my laughter. "Vena is going to love it."

"We're covering it when company is over," Shepard said.

I shrugged, knowing she'd peek.

Taking in the sight of Cross grinning at Shepard and Shepard's return scowl, I felt happy and alive.

I never thought falling into a cave would bring so much joy to my life, but I wouldn't redo any of it if given the chance. Not even the dangerous parts. Because this ending could have only happened as it had with all the horrible, scary, and wonderful parts.

EPILOGUE

ONE YEAR LATER.

"We're here!" Vena called when she opened the door to the bakery. I peeked out of the kitchen to find Anchor and six other pack wolves. I knew Tank and Boulder from working at Blur, but the others were unfamiliar faces. "Are the cookies ready?"

"Yep! Have a seat."

Pam grinned at the men from her position at the front counter.

This was our fourth Cookie Mate event. The first three were pretty successful, considering we found mates for at least a few of the wolves. This was Pam's first time partaking in the event. She watched as guys sat at the designated tables that already had cookies plated and numbers assigned to them.

Vena quickly explained the process to them and then gave them the go-ahead to dig in.

Arms wrapped around me as I watched the wolves take their first bites.

"I say one will find their mate," Cross said, then kissed my neck.

"I say three."

"Very optimistic."

I grinned. "I'm feeling optimistic."

"You should. You're living your dream, Sunshine. Bites and Delights started out slow, but we're selling out daily and even have a line in the morning. You should be proud."

"I am. I'm proud of all of us. But I can't see how we couldn't be successful. You're too smart for your own good and keep the business running. Vena is finding books that even Miles and her parents couldn't find. And with Shepard's outreach programs letting people know our bakery is all-inclusive, we're getting more otherworlders and humans every day."

"Speaking of Shepard, he's pestering me to make sure you don't lose track of time. I'm now your keeper. It's almost time to go."

"I won't lose track of time, but you know I love the Cookie Mate event. I really hope Pam finds a match."

We watched as the wolves began to eat the cookies the single women and one man from the community had baked just a few hours before.

Pam's cookie was number four on the list, and I watched as they neared the fourth cookie. Boulder took a bite of it then stood abruptly. Pam flashed a questioning glance my way.

"I think we found a winner," I said, hurrying to Boulder. I pulled him to the side. "Number four?"

He nodded.

"You know who it is, don't you?" I asked.

Having worked together at Blur, he must have sensed something at some point.

He nodded again. "Yeah. I've known for a while. I thought I'd have more time to work up the courage to ask her on a date. Then Blur closed, and everything else happened. I had my fingers crossed when Vena said she made cookies this time."

"And now that you've tasted it?"

He smiled. "I'm going for it."

I looked back at Pam and gave her a thumbs-up. She gasped. It was a happy yet confused gasp.

"Why don't you have a seat over there," I said to Boulder, pointing to a table slightly away from everyone else.

When I walked over to Pam, she grabbed my arm and tugged me to the counter. "Are you serious?"

"Yes. He said he's known for a while but was working up the courage. Are you okay with it?"

"Are you kidding? He's like a chocolate-covered gummy bear."

I looked questioningly at her.

"The first time I saw him, I wanted to lick him all over then bounce on him."

I heard a choked cough coming from Boulder.

"Why don't you grab two coffees and have a seat with him. I'll watch the counter."

I didn't have to tell her twice. Her apron went flying, and coffee sloshed in the cups as she sprinted over to him.

"Another happy customer," Cross said. "But I'll watch the counter. You go get dressed."

I supposed I couldn't go to my own graduation dinner with my parents while dusted in flour.

Jogging up the stairs, I headed to the bedroom where Cross and Shepard were now locked in a battle of who could create the most ridiculous nude painting. Our room was covered in "art," and it made me giggle every time I saw them.

Once in the bathroom, I tossed my uniform into the laundry and quickly showered before putting on the dress Cross had laid out on the bed for me.

It was red with a gold collar, the colors of the college I graduated from.

I glanced in the mirror to make sure I looked halfway decent and that my hair wasn't frizzing. Once that was done, I opened a drawer and pulled out the surprise gift for my parents. The small box held a cut-out picture from my ultrasound last week. I still couldn't believe I was having Shepard's baby.

He and Cross were ecstatic about it. Cross had figured it out only a few days after I'd conceived, noticing a change in my scent. At first, he'd buried his nose in my neck and asked if I'd changed the detergent or worn perfume. He'd been so obsessed we'd ended up in bed for a time. But when he'd taken a little nip, something he rarely did, he'd gone crazy with his hugs and kisses and cuddles.

When Shepard had come home a few hours later, he'd taken one look at me and fallen to his knees to kiss my stomach. It'd been so sweet and so perfect.

My parents still didn't know, but I knew they'd be thrilled. Once the initial shock had worn off, they were very accepting of Shepard and Cross and even had fun getting in the middle of some of their playful squabbles.

I placed the box in my purse and headed downstairs, knowing Shepard should arrive soon so we could all drive together.

However, as soon as I stepped into the bakery, I saw it was transformed. Red and gold balloons, streamers, and dozens of familiar people were there, along with a ton of food.

Both Cross and Shepard grinned at me, wearing outfits the same color as mine.

"Did you do this?" I asked them.

"You deserve to celebrate, Everly," Shepard said.

My parents stood off to the side with big smiles. I breathed a sigh of contentment and headed over to them to receive hugs. I hadn't expected to be in this setting when I gave them the news, but I didn't want to wait.

Pulling out the small box, I handed it to them.

"What's this?" Mom asked. "We're supposed to give you a gift. Not the other way around."

"Just open it."

Shepard and Cross flanked me as we waited for my mom.

She slid off the ribbon and opened the box. A squeal burst from her, making everyone look our way. She grappled me into a hug as she thrust the box and contents to my dad. It took him a little longer to figure out why she was hug-strangling me, but he eventually smiled and clapped Shepard and Cross on their backs.

"You'll make good fathers," he said.

They both radiated their joy.

"Fathers?" Vena repeated. "Are you serious?"

She came over to me and wrapped her arms around my neck in a strangling hug.

"No matter what genders our kids are, we're getting them married so we can officially be related. How far of a head start do you have?" She didn't wait for an answer but looked at Anchor. "Operation no-raincoat is a go."

Anchor flushed scarlet.

Piper, who was standing next to him, patted his arm consolingly.

Vena's mom beamed and hugged Anchor's other arm as she excitedly began telling him about a fertility relic that promised triplets.

"It's the only way you'll be able to slow her down," I heard Mrs. Hunter say.

Miles was looking around the room for a quick escape, knowing his mom would find him next and start asking when he was going to settle down. Grandma and Grandpa Hunter were sitting at a table with my grandma, and all three were laughing and shaking their heads at Vena as she captured my face and grinned at me.

"Our babies will be smart and beautiful," she said.

I rolled my eyes at her and hugged her hard.

"Thank you for taking me hiking. I guess you're not fired."

AUTHOR'S NOTE

Thank you for reading *Magic and Muffins*! This book wouldn't have been possible without you, our readers.

While it took a lot of effort and a round of sleep deprivation to write this book, we're thrilled with its conclusion. Even though Everly's story has wrapped up, we do have ideas for spin off stories with Piper and Robyn. Whether we make that happen is up to you. Spread the word about this series! The more readers it has, the more proof we have to show our husbands we need a getaway to write another book.

If you're looking for more in The Ruin of Relics world, let us know by reviewing the books, signing up for our newsletter on our website, and joining our Facebook group. These are your "votes" to let us know to start writing in this world again.

A special thank you to the winner who named *Bites and Delights* for us, Maxine Wigley Fuqua. It was a great addition and encompassed Everly's world in a bakery name. We loved it.

And a thank you to everyone who supported us these last couple of years. We hope to add more to the Melissa Nicole pen name. You know what to do to make that happen. ;)

For all the readers curious about the bacon-wrapped watermelon and peanut butter popcorn...yes, Melissa did make the popcorn for Nicole to try. It's a messy snack that Melissa remembers from her childhood (it's really good!). Melissa is still hoping to make the bacon-wrapped watermelon.

Happy reading from your sleep deprived authors,
Melissa and Nicole

MORE BOOKS BY MELISSA NICOLE

THE SHADOW TRADE WORLD

Ruin of Relics

(Sexy shifters and a hottie vampire!)

Blood and BonBons

Fangs and Fudge

Death and Donuts

Magic and Muffins

Connect with the author

Website: melissanicoleauthor.com

Newsletter: melissanicoleauthor.com/subscribe

MORE BOOKS BY MELISSA HAAG

Did you know that Melissa Nicole is a co-authored pen name? Check out these amazing books by the "Melissa" part of Melissa Nicole!

JUDGEMENT OF THE SIX SERIES (AND COMPANION BOOKS) IN ORDER:

(more shifters to make you "grr")

Hope(less)

Clay's Hope*

(Mis)fortune

Emmitt's Treasure*

(Un)wise

Luke's Dream*

(Un)bidden

Thomas' Heart*

(Dis)content

Carlos' Peace*

(Sur)real**

*optional companion book

**written in dual point of view

Connect with the author

Website: melissahaag.com

Newsletter: melissahaag.com/subscribe

MORE BOOKS BY NICOLETTE PIERCE

Check out these amazing books by the "Nicole" part of Melissa Nicole!

Black Moon Novels

(Paranormal romance mystery series)

Whiskers & Warrants

Kittens & Kidnappers

Jade Sommer Novels

(Contemporary romance mystery series)

Mostaccioli Murder

Penne Pyro

Fettuccini Fiasco

Rigatoni Ruin

Lasagna Larceny

Bucatini Bomber

Connect with the author

Website: nicolettepierce.com

Newsletter: nicolettepierce.com/newsletter/